A MIKE BENASQUE THRILLER

WHO'LL BUY MY EVIL

CALIBER
BOOKS

Also from ALAN CAILLOU

<u>CABOT CAIN</u> Series
Assault on Kolchak
Assault on Ming
Assault on Loveless
Assault on Fellawi
Assault on Agathon
Assault on Almata

<u>MATTHEW TOBIN</u> Series
Dead Sea Submarine
Terror in Rio
Congo War Cry
Afghan Assault
Swamp War
Death Charge
The Garonsky Missile

<u>MIKE BENASQUE</u> Series
The Plotters
Marseilles
Who'll Buy My Evil
Diamonds Wild

<u>IAN QUAYLE</u> Series
A League of Hawks
The Sword of God

<u>DEKKER'S DEMONS</u> Series
Suicide Run
Blood Run

The Charge of the Light Brigade
A Journey to Orassia

Rogue's Gambit
Cairo Cabal
Bichu the Jaguar
The Walls of Jolo
The Hot Sun of Africa
The Cheetahs
Joshua's People
Mindanao Pearl
Khartoum
South from Khartoum
Rampage
The World is 6 Feet Square
The Prophetess
House on Curzon Street

MIKE BENASQUE: Who'll Buy My Evil
Book Three

For further information visit the Caliber Comics website:
www.calibercomics.com

CHAPTER 1

In between swigs from the bottle and bouts with the opium pipe, Baudelaire took time out to suggest that a love of work for its own sake is the remedy for all ills; now leave us not knock the great man's Oriental genius, but I personally choose to remember that immense harm can also be done by evil work done well.

I only once met a man whose devotion to his trade exceeded the bounds of common sense, and his name was Martin, Dr. Walter Martin. He said to me miserably, fear seeping out of the pores of his skin and his pale hands fluttering, "But what should I *do*, Mr. Benasque? This is my life's work..."

So help me, he even started to discuss the reasons for which a benevolent God had put him on the earth's surface and given him that remarkable brain; when all I could think of was a dozen good reasons why the devils of hell should hurl him down into their barbecue and feast on his ribs. But that was later, much later...

It was raining, that day in Rome.

Raining? That's the understatement of the year. The water was pouring down, and the streets were ankle deep. The tiny little Fiats that buzzed around the market stalls were sending up waves like speedboats, drenching the poor girls who hopefully stood in half-sheltered doorways. Peering out from under their bright plastic umbrellas, they laughed among themselves in spite of the discomfort. That's one of the nice things about the Roman girls—they believe that the truest philosophy lies in finding the humor that is in all things, if you only dig down deep enough to uncover it.

Though for the life of me I could find nothing to laugh at in Walter bloody Martin, once I learned what he was up to.

The rain was pouring down and washing the grime off the old red walls above the oak tree that was sprouting again, and I was eating dinner with Karen d'Arno and her young sister Simona, listening to the pounding of the rainfall on the roof and feeling glad that I was warm and comfortable. It wasn't the best apartment in Rome, nor the most expensive either. But from its fourth-floor balcony it overlooked the tiny park near the church of St. Onofrio, and the garden *trattoria* around the corner is one of the best in Rome—when it's not raining.

Karen is a professional photographer, and a good one, but my interest in her stemmed from the fact that she has the longest legs of any woman I've known. She's tall and handsome and—I suppose svelte is the word, and she's cool. You never quite know what she's thinking behind the mask of her extraordinary eyes, which seem at times quite blank, and then suddenly fill with an alert emotion which is quite startling.

They are green, those astonishing eyes, and her hair is quite properly auburn, and that's a particularly fetching combination if your weaknesses, like mine, tend toward the spectacular in a woman. Simona, the younger sister, is black-haired, white-skinned, and perhaps even better looking. She too is statuesque, and she has the damnedest way of quietly going about her sister's business without a word from anyone, seeming to know in advance what's required and getting it done before anyone has a chance even to think about it. I suppose if the truth were known she's also what might be called a rather nicer girl, because she doesn't have the strength of character that sometimes leads Karen into a kind of quiet willfulness. She has the same easy movements as Karen, and the same long legs too, though I never examined them quite so meticulously; my girl was Karen.

Simona was nearly twenty, and old for her years, with the kind of quiet competence you don't often find in a young girl. She had a peculiar knack for effacing herself as though she were just part of the furniture, much admired and very lovely, but not demanding anything on her own account. Karen, who was four years older, was just the opposite; when she was in the room you just weren't aware of anyone else.

I used to derive a great deal of amusement from the fact that when we were in company, the three of us, it was Karen for whom every man made a beeline; they would stand around her and gape foolishly, quite overcome, and hang onto every word she spoke, staring at her breathlessly and watching every movement of that wonderfully articulated body. And when you had time to wonder what Simona was doing, you would find her in a quiet corner talking earnestly with a solitary man who was usually old enough to be her father. You would realize that Karen's was the bright light that attracted the moths, while Simona's was the gentle warmth that made you want to curl up beside her with a good book.

They had come down from Florence, the two of them, to photograph the oak tree.

You may not know it, but in the park there's an ancient oak that Torquato Tasso, the great Italian poet, planted in 1595 when he came to the charming, bustling, ancient and unkempt quarter called Trastevere to die. For nearly two hundred years the gnarled old tree had been good and dead, split down the center by lightning but still standing like a macabre symbol of a dead past. And then, one day, a small green shoot appeared and began to grow, slowly but with a kind of blind determination that somehow seemed aptly Roman and particularly Trasteverian; the whole city took the tree to its heart and blessed it.

Karen, among her other talents, is an expert on time-lapse photography. And some horticultural society or other had taken up her suggestion that she spend three months photographing the tree, one single shot on a movie camera every hour, day and night, for three months. The resulting sixty feet of film would last only two and a half minutes, but would show the miraculous green shoot actually sprouting to a small branch in that short space of time, growing surely into the miraculous new tree it will one day be. I saw the film when it was finished, and it was a remarkable sight; it was easy to imagine the gentle Torquato lying in his grave and smiling.

We took turns, Karen, Simona and I, to trip that damned shutter, every hour on the hour, day and night for three months...

The film had long been finished, but Rome in the hot summer was lovely, and I was out of work again, which seems, as time goes on, to be a more and more frequent state. So, while we waited without too much alarm for the money to run out completely, we stayed on in the venerable apartment which had been there in the days when Benvenuto Cellini watched the flames of Castel St. Angelo across the S-bend of the river.

We ate and drank, and we went to the open-air opera at the Caracalla Baths, and explored the ruins of the Forum, and wandered over the pine thickets on the surrounding hills. Karen and I made love together while Simona worked discreetly in the closet under the steps to the roof that had been turned into a darkroom. Sometimes we climbed up the stairs to the old tower and watched the lights of the city across the water, feeling in love with the world, knowing the Platonic progression of love that the Greeks so revered, knowing that love of a single human being could lead, in turn, to love of all that is supreme in the universe.

We hoped all the time that something or other would turn up sooner or later to keep one or both or all of us busy. And something did turn up.

It was Dr. Walter Martin.

I should have known. Whenever I start to feel good, down comes the ax on the back of my neck. It's always the same.

Did I say it was raining that night?

It made a virulent, though pleasant, sound as it splashed on the pavement four stories below, and the windows were wide open to let in the air, for the night was stifling and not even the rain could wash the heat away.

Some people down below were shouting, but this was the usual pattern and none of us paid much attention; but then a woman screamed, and Karen looked at me and raised an elegant eyebrow that really meant: *What, in the middle of my dinner!* and walked casually over to the window and looked out to see what it was all about. And then suddenly she was moving toward the cupboard where the still cameras were, and grabbing the Minolta 35mm with the stroboscope on it, and heading back to the window again.

She said calmly, not even raising her voice, "Someone needs

help, Michael." And then the strobe was flashing, and Simona and I ran to join her and peered out, and there on the narrow ledge that ran around outside the windows was a frail and heavily bearded old man, bareheaded in the rain, his glasses askew on his nose, clutching at the soft red bricks and staring down at the street with terror on his face. He was trying to edge his way toward us, and not making a very good job of it.

I said, "How the hell did he get there?" And Simona said urgently, "Be careful, Michael, be careful."

Now I'm a bit acrophobic myself, and anything over ten feet off the ground gives me the shudders unless there's something to grab onto, but I put a leg gingerly out of the window and reached, and the old man looked at me with his eyes wide and staring, and I said to him, "Take it easy now, just one more step and I can reach you." His fingers were curled tight around an iron bar—one of those long iron bars that ran from wall to wall of the old building to keep it from busting apart; he couldn't get a grip on it properly.

Karen, close behind me, perched her pretty behind on the window ledge and thrust her long body out, ignoring the damage the rain was doing to her favorite bright-green dress, and that damned strobe kept on lighting up, and she said calmly, "A little closer to him, darling; I can't get you both in focus."

I said, "The hell with the focus, I'm about to break my bloody neck," and Simona wrapped her arms around my leg and squatted on the floor competently, holding me firmly there, and I reached a little farther for the old man and our fingers touched, but not enough to do any good. And then a police Jeep came screeching in down below, one of the flying-squad cars they call the *Celeri*, and when I looked down (not liking it a bit but hypnotized by the long drop and wondering what the audience was like), I could see all the white, excited faces staring up at us from under their umbrellas. And when I looked back, straining for the reaching hand, I almost squealed with sudden alarm.

All right, call it fright.

Right behind the old man, where the narrow ledge turned the building at the corner, there was another figure, a tall, well-built man whose fair hair was blowing in the wind, and in whose outstretched hand, pointing my way, was a revolver.

For a moment I stared at it, not really believing what I saw, knowing that it was aimed at the old man and that I was directly in the line of fire, and so was Karen. And, before I could make up my mind that I'd be best advised to get the both of us back under cover, the old man grabbed my wrist and I grabbed his. I yanked hard and we both dropped into the room in an untidy heap, falling in a wet bundle on top of poor Simona, and I reached out for Karen and pulled her away as the last strobe went off.

Her face was very white. She stared at me and said, "Did you see—was I dreaming?"

"No dream." I scrambled to my feet and leaned out quickly to pull the wooden shutters to; and the man with the gun was gone. Now, the horse having bolted, a searchlight from the Jeep below lit up the side of the building; but there was nothing there, not even a sign of disappearing gunmen. I looked at Karen and jerked my head at the Minolta. "Did you get him too?"

"Yes, I did." Her mouth was set in a thin line as though the presence of an armed man had been an affront to her own dignity; which, decidedly, it was. In the circles we moved in, guns just had no part to play at all, and it was as though our idle serenity had suddenly been shattered by a momentary brush with a kind of underworld we would rather have known nothing about. I didn't like it a bit.

I said, "Well, he's gone now. He was only a step around the corner."

"But a man with—with a *gun!*"

"He's got a nerve."

"Did he—did he fire? I didn't hear it."

"Don't think he did. Hell, all three of us in line..."

It was time to look at our alarming guest. He was still crouched on the floor on his hands and knees, patting the carpet with his hands and dripping all over the place, and I leaned down and took his arm and helped him up, and Simona found his glasses and handed them to him silently, her eyes full of accusation, and he shook himself and I saw that there was still that terrible fear in his eyes; it hurt me to look at him.

He must have been about sixty-five or seventy, much too old to be traipsing around rooftops in the middle of a dark evening, and he looked at the window and plucked at his lip, and I said, "He's gone back, wherever he came from. Who was it?"

He shook his head, trying to talk but too frightened. I said, "Take it easy. He's gone and the police will be here any minute."

He stammered, "The—the police?"

"They were down below, a Jeep full of them. What's it all about?"

Again he shook his head. "I don't—I don't know." He looked pathetically at Karen and then at Simona, as though to assure himself that he was among friends, and I said, losing a little patience, "But what in hell happened to get you up there? That ledge is less than a foot wide."

Suddenly he was talking volubly, the words rushing out as though the dam had broken. But still he stammered. "A man—tried to get into—to get into my room—"

"Where's that?"

"The Othello, the hotel around the corner, on the top—the top floor. I heard him trying to force the door open, and—and I—I lost my head and climbed out of the window and onto the roof, and—then I heard the door open and I crawled over a plank to this—to this building—"

"A plank?"

Simona said swiftly, "The plumbers were here; they left a plank across the gap."

"And then?"

"Then he came out after me, and—" The tired old eyes were wet, and so were his clothes, and he looked down at himself and said, "I'm—I'm spoiling your carpet, I'm afraid." I said, "Never mind the carpet. What was he after?" I saw that Karen, with an eye for composition, was looking at his clothes. They were good, rather Continental-looking and cut by an expensive tailor, not at all the kind of clothes that went with a dump like the Hotel Othello.

The frail old arms went out in a gesture of helplessness. "I don't—I just can't think what he wanted. I have nothing, nothing at all."

"Money?"

He shrugged. "A few thousand lire, a little English money—"

"But you're not English?"

"No." He seemed to remember his manners and pulled himself together. He said, "My name is Heinrich Muller, sir, and I am Swiss. From Frauenfeld in Thurgau." He clicked his heels and made a gallant little bow toward the girls. Karen was winding the film onto the spool of the Minolta, and I told her, "You'd better get out of that dress, you're wet through." It was sticking to her body, molding her fine breasts, and I liked the look of it fine; but I didn't want anyone else, not even a tired old man, to see her like that. It's hard not to be proprietary when the woman you love is as exquisite as an Etruscan miniature.

She nodded and headed for the bedroom, and then there was a pounding at the door and all the fear, temporarily pushed to the back of the mind, was back on Muller's face. I went into the hall and stuck my foot tight to the door and called out, "Who is it?"

The voice was polite and muffled: "*La polizia, signore.*"

I said, "Well, if you're *not* the police you may as well know that they're all around us," and opened the door.

There were three of them there, two young Roman cops with their caps flat on the tops of their heads and tilted down over the eyes, balanced on the curly black mops of hair. With them was a sergeant, who was a lot older than the others, and they were all impossibly polite. The sergeant spread his hands and said, "*Eh...scusi...*" and then he looked past me and saw the old man, and said firmly, "*Con permesso...*" He walked past me into the apartment and the others followed him, and when they saw Simona they grinned and fingered their neckties and their hairdos, and I said sourly, "It won't help you."

We had a language problem for a moment, because it seemed that our Swiss friend, whose English was good but heavily accented, knew no Italian. I started off as official translator, but when Simona said something or other they all switched their attention to her, understandably enough, beaming at her and nodding.

The sergeant was writing in a thick notebook, laboriously wetting the tip of the pencil and staining his tongue a deep purple, and when Muller said, "Someone tried to force his way into my room," he looked up sharply and asked, "The man with the fair hair?"

I said, "That's the man. He was carrying a revolver."

One of the young policemen said triumphantly, "You see? I told you so," and the sergeant gave him a withering look which shut him up promptly and said to me, "We could not see very well from down there, *signore*. If you saw him clearly, perhaps you could describe him for me?"

"Sure. He was tallish, good shoulders, a long, thin face, dark eyes, I think, wearing a sort of summer suit, dark blue or black, very fair hair brushed back. I suppose, about—oh, thirty-five, give or take a couple of years."

"And the weapon, *signore?*"

"No idea. Could have been a thirty-eight—a revolver, not an automatic. I must admit I was too—alarmed to pay much attention to anything but getting out of the line of fire as fast as possible."

"One understands, *signore*. Permit me to say, an excellent description."

"Yeah." I was wondering about the photographs Karen had taken. I knew they'd be useful to the police, and I didn't want to play games about them, but... Well, that's the way she earns her living, and I'm a damn good journalist too, but with a roll film (as opposed to plates) I knew we couldn't hand over just one or two of the shots and keep the rest; and once the police got their hands on them, the chances were we'd never see them again—or at least not until the story, if there was a story at all, was as dead as Tasso's oak had once been. There must have been some good saleable film there, and I thought the best thing to do would be to say nothing, make some quick prints, and hand over the film *afterward* with a handsome apology.

The sergeant talked with Muller for a while, examining him closely, and I went to the window and looked out across the rooftops. The rain had stopped and the air smelled fresh and clean. Listening, I wondered why the old man didn't mention the camera; he must have known about it, but I suppose he must have had other things on his mind. His fear was quite pathetic.

And then Karen came out of the bedroom with a bathrobe on, and while they all gaped at her open-mouthed (at least, the two young ones did), I said to her:

"I was trying to give a decent description of the man with the gun."

Karen said blandly, "Well, I didn't get a good look at him, really." And I knew that I'd been right in keeping quiet. We run a nice friendly household because we always seem to think alike, Karen and I.

The sergeant peered at Muller and said, "If you would like us to escort you back to your hotel, *signore*... But first you must come to the station and make a statement, if you would be so kind."

The old man began to stammer again. Something was worrying him badly, and I wondered what it was. He said hesitantly:

"Is that—really necessary?"

"If you would be so kind, *signore*."

"But—this gentleman, who saved my life—he has told you more than I can tell you—I hardly saw this man—"

The sergeant said firmly:

"*Con permesso*... I must insist, signore. It is the law."

Again there was the floundering of the frail arms. I was thinking that Muller was lost, a tourist whose guide had left him stranded in a strange and hostile place, not knowing where to turn for help. I said:

"Are you staying here long, Mr. Muller?"

He shook his head helplessly. "No—just a few days—"

"And then?"

He hesitated. "And then I will go back to Switzerland."

"Well, the police will put a man on duty in the hotel if you ask them to. For the rest of the night, at any rate. Might make you feel more secure."

"Yes, yes, of course, if they would do that."

Karen translated for him, and the two policemen looked from her to Simona and back to her, visibly simpering, and the sergeant suddenly roared at them:

"*Che razza di gente!* But what kind of people are you?"

The deflation was visible, and the sergeant turned to Karen with an apology. "Young people, *signora*," he said, "They have no manners. It is the new generation."

He went to the window and leaned out for a while, looking along the ledge, and then he and Muller began bowing all around while the young men tentatively smiled at the girls again, and then the sergeant opened the door and made a broad gesture at the Swiss.

"If you would be so kind, *signore...*"

Muller threw me an anguished glance, clicked his heels again at the girls, and went to the door. He turned around as the sergeant tried to shepherd him out and said ruefully:

"And I did not even express my thanks to you, sir. In the excitement of the moment... I ask your forgiveness. I proffer you my thanks."

And then he was gone. He was a tired old man frightened out of his wits by something I could not yet understand.

When the door had closed behind them, I put my arms around Karen and said, "I very nearly told them about the photographs."

She said calmly, "Well, that would have been the end of a happy romance, wouldn't it?"

"Yes, I suppose so."

She said sardonically, hiding something from me, "Of course, once the old man remembers to tell them about the stroboscope flashing in his eyes, that nice police sergeant is coming back without quite so much of his *gentilezza*."

"Yes, that is a point, isn't it? All the time we were talking, he never once mentioned the camera."

Karen looked at me thoughtfully for a while. She said, "I wonder if it's important? The police were trying hard to get a description. You'd think he'd at least—I wonder."

I said, "Well, at least it gives us time to get them developed before they find out."

"So we'll make the copies we need—"

"And then I'll take them over to the station—"

"And apologize to the nice man. Yes, darling. You won't mind, will you?"

"They'll probably lock me up."

"But only for a few days, darling, I'm sure."

I looked at the remains of the meal on the table and sighed. "The *osso-buco* is cold."

"I could warm it up, if you like."

"We have to be at the opera in less than an hour, and you're not even dressed."

"Not dressed? Is that a complaint?"

"Later."

Simona was perched on the arm of the overstuffed sofa, looking at her sister with a kind of amused tolerance. I looked at her over Karen's shoulder and said:

"I wish you'd change your mind and come with us—honestly."

Simona shook her head, the long black hair falling down over her breast. She wore a close-fitting cocktail dress of black silk, which suited her remarkably well and made her look a lot older than she was.

"No. I'm going to wash the dishes and remake your bed" — she flung Karen a quick glance which said nothing— "and then I'm going to develop those pictures."

Karen said briskly, "Good." She looked at me seriously and said, "What have we got, Michael? A frightened man on a ledge above a Roman street—and in one shot there's a man with a gun. It's all useless unless we know the story."

Oh, well, there it was, laid out on the line. I said, "All right, first thing in the morning I'll go talk to the sergeant. Maybe a bottle of wine—I don't know..."

Simona laughed and said, "Just find out the name of the boy with the pimples, I'll take it from there."

"Pimples? Which one is that?"

"All right, find out both their names. I'll get your story for you."

"Fine. Then I'll spend the morning in bed. You can use my typewriter."

Simona began to gather up the dishes and said to Karen, "Did you take the film out of the Minolta?"

Karen nodded. "In the coffee jar. The film in the camera is all black, just in case the police do come back for it." And when I raised my eyebrows, she kissed me quickly and said, "Well, I was just being careful. I didn't know your German friend would keep so deathly silent about it, did I"

"Swiss."

Karen said firmly, "No, darling. German."

I said, "Frauenfeld is in the canton of Thurgau, and the canton of Thurgau is in Switzerland."

"*Pattati, pattata*. His accent was German, not Swiss."

"And why the hell should—"

I was about to ask her why a German should choose to call himself Swiss, but unhappily it's a pretty frequent pattern. Sometimes it *means* something, sometimes it doesn't. Reading my thoughts, Karen shrugged.

"Yes, I know, it probably doesn't mean anything at all; there are plenty of Germans who like to hide their origins. But he *was* rather frightened, you know."

"So would you be out on that ledge. In the rain too, getting his nice suit wet."

"Ah, so you noticed those expensive clothes."

"Well, I'm not blind, darling. But you're hiding something from me. I suspect you've seen him before. A photograph somewhere..."

Karen shook her head. She said, "No, I haven't. But the fear was still there even when he was clearly quite safe. Why?"

I said, "You tell me."

Her thoughts were a long way away. She said slowly, "There's a bad smell, Michael, a smell that isn't—wholesome. I've a feeling that if we try and find out what it is, we might have a very saleable story."

"I'll make a small bet: Muller is a Swiss from Frauenfeld, Thurgau; some goddam footpad broke into his room; he took fright and bolted; and that's all there is to it. And if you don't get dressed, we'll miss the overture."

"The mutual fund is getting awfully low, darling."

"What the hell has the fund to do with the overture? I bought the tickets last week."

"If we don't sell something soon, there'll be no more opera."

"Oh."

"And since this has been dumped into our lap..."

I gave in as gracefully as I could. "Herr Muller is really Adolf Hitler, and the photographs will prove it. All right, all right. First thing in the morning, I'll go get the story."

Karen kissed me again and said lightly, "And so, I'll go get dressed: Give me fifteen minutes."

She opened the door to the bedroom, turned to look at me with a smile, and said, "And there's no overture to *Bohème*, either."

When the door had closed behind her, Simona looked at me and laughed, and began to pile dishes into my arms. She said:

"It's no use fighting her, Michael, you should know that. And we really must sell something soon."

Simona had spent all her life in Karen's shadow; she just couldn't understand why anyone should ever argue with her. But she was right on both counts. And that's why we always got along so well, the three of us; nobody ever fought *anybody*.

I carted the plates to the kitchen, and hung around Simona while she washed them.

CHAPTER 2

They were playing *Bohème* that night, and when Mimi died, Karen leaned her head on my shoulder and wept, and I patted her arm paternally, and when it was all over and the lights were on again we wandered off and walked—over to the Palatino, which has always been one of my favorite spots because it was here that the *Roma Quadrata* stood, the "strong square" of the Pelasgi which would one day give the great city its name; and there is a certain smug satisfaction, moreover, in the thought that in those faraway days the vulgar plebs were not allowed up here at all; that was in the days before I'm-as-good-as-you-are-Jack-and-don't-you-forget-it. And in the dark silence after the lights have gone out it is easy to think back a few thousand years and to remember that history goes on, while lovely women die and others take their place, and that only the land is constant.

We walked down the other side of the hill and through the little piazza they call the "Mouth of Truth," and over the Palatinate Bridge to Lungotevere, and through the narrow, twisting streets where the *disgraziati* were lying asleep in sheltered doorways; one old man had his foot in a puddle of water, and as we passed by, Karen bent down and moved it gently out of the wet; the old man did not stir.

It was three o'clock in the morning, and the silence after the noise of the day was almost uncanny; it was as though the whole quarter were resting up merely to gird itself for the outbreak of clamor and excitement that would start a little before sunup, growing in intensity until by the midday sleeping time the roar of humanity on the move to nowhere would be almost insupportable.

As we came to the old oak tree across the street from the

house, I touched its trunk for good luck, and Karen looked up at the apartment windows and said, "Simona's still up."

The lights were on. As we crossed the road, a tiny pinprick of fire glowed brightly for a minute as a uniformed chauffeur sitting at the wheel of a big Mercedes lit a cigarette; the car seemed enormous beside the little Fiats and Bianchis that were taking up every available space, and Karen looked at it and said mildly:

"How did they ever get a car like that through the streets here?"

We went on up the dark, dark stairway, so dark that I had to flick my lighter at the corner where the balustrade was a bit loose, and then Simona was waiting for us with a half-smile on her face as she opened the door, and the first thing she said was, "Visitors, Michael. How was the opera?"

I said, "It was fine."

I went ahead of Karen into the apartment, because there was a feeling of unease on me, something I couldn't quite put my finger on. But our visitors were merely a highly polished lieutenant of police and a civilian who looked faintly sinister; I imagined he was a detective of some sort, or a man from the *Questura*. He was heavily built, strong-jawed and rather handsome, a middle-aged man who had kept himself in good shape, but his hard face was unsmiling and rather unpleasant. They stood up as we came in, and the lieutenant made a little bow and introduced himself:

"*Buona sera, signori.* I am Lieutenant Rospigliosi of the Political Police." He did not introduce his companion.

I nodded affably enough and said, "I see this is a social visit."

He gestured at the glass of wine on the table beside him and said, "The *signorina* was kind enough—while we were waiting for you."

"Good. So what can we do for you?" As if I didn't know.

The lieutenant said patiently, and with a slight air of reproach, "The *signorina* suggested that she would prefer not to answer any questions in your absence, but now that you are here..." He said firmly, "It is a question of some photographs, *signore*."

"Oh, that."

It seemed important to know how long they'd been waiting for us, if Simona had had time to develop the film, and I was about to try and find out when Karen said sweetly:

"I hope you haven't been waiting long, *Tenente?*"

We always seemed to think in perfect concord.

He turned to her quickly with an elaborate gesture. "Ten minutes, *signora*, no more."

And Simona said innocently, "I'd just finished doing all the chores."

So that was all right. I said, "Of course, there's always the question of ownership. I like to help the police, and all that, but after all, I am a journalist."

"Of course." The lieutenant looked at Karen and back to me and said, "It is realized that any photographs you may have taken are your own property, but we would like to see them, and no doubt if necessary I could convince a magistrate that our need was a very real one. However, that would entail waiting till ten o'clock tomorrow morning, and I should have to leave a man in your apartment all night as a matter of police routine. I am sure that you would not wish to put me to so much trouble over such a trifling matter."

Well, that was a nice way of phrasing it. I looked at Simona, and she said to me blandly:

"I made two prints. One for us, and the other's for the police. You did say we'd better surrender them, didn't you?"

"Yes, I did, didn't I?"

The lieutenant said severely, "We could have demanded a search for them, you know. I feel I should reproach the *signorina* for not having allowed us to see them at once."

I said, "The *signorina* has to do as she's told, really. A major decision like that—I'm sure you understand."

"Of course, *signore*."

Karen was putting out some more glasses and going around with the Orvieto bottle. When she came to the taciturn stranger, he said nothing and raised a negative hand. I saw Karen's lips tighten in distaste; there was nothing she hated more than bad manners. Simona went into the darkroom and came back with half a dozen eight-by-ten prints and laid them on the table for us to see. As I moved forward to get a good look at them, the stranger pushed forward, but I did not move aside for him.

The first five showed Muller, looking frightened, on his ledge in the rain, with part of my body alarmingly in the frame in a couple of them, and the last one showed the tall fair man at the corner behind him; the revolver was quite clearly visible.

The lieutenant picked up this print, and held it out to the civilian, and the civilian took it and pursed his lips and said nothing and handed it back, and then the lieutenant gathered them all up and said:

"And now the other copies, if you would be so good."

Simona looked suitably startled and said, protesting, "But they're still wet, *Tenente*. And surely we can keep copies of them."

"I must insist, *signorina*."

I thought it was time for me to help with the act and look indignant. "But surely you're not going to take our copies too?"

"No doubt, *signore*, they will be returned to you in the course of time."

"But—" I left it trailing and waited, and the lieutenant said again:

"I am sure you would not wish the inconvenience of a magisterial order."

"No—no, I suppose not."

"Well, then..." Simona shrugged nicely, and went back into the darkroom, and I said to the lieutenant, "And in exchange for our cooperation, you might at least tell me the story, don't you think?"

He looked at me blandly. "Story? There is no story, *signore*."

"Oh, come now..."

I saw the two of them exchange glances, and something passed telepathically between them. The officer brushed a speck of dust from his nice uniform and said, as though it were something he'd learned by heart:

"The gentleman is Herr Heinrich Muller, from Thurgau, a Swiss tourist. It is my department's job to see that our foreign visitors are not annoyed by petty thieves and other inconveniences."

"And the fair-haired man?"

"We will find out in time, *signore*. Some hotel thief, no doubt, a man of no consequence. But if you would like me to keep you informed, I will be happy to do so. As you say, your ready cooperation does merit at least that much."

"A couple of good pictures like those, with a suitable story, can pay the rent for a month."

"Oh, really? Then I will do what I can. I am most grateful for your assistance."

"And Mr. Muller?"

"We have taken him back to his hotel."

"He seemed very frightened."

"Of course. It is not a pleasant experience to have your room broken into in the middle of the night."

"You see what happens when you stay in a dump like the Othello?"

I could feel the stranger's eyes moving to me, unblinking, cold, calculating. I was getting to dislike him more and more. His silence was offensive, and my not very subtle hint seemed to indicate, to him at least, a great deal more than plain journalistic curiosity. But the lieutenant smiled and said cheerfully:

"Yes, you'd think he'd find a more suitable place, wouldn't you? But I suppose—at the end of a holiday one's money begins to run short..."

"Yes, it does, doesn't it?"

Simona came back with six prints, all curled and dripping, holding them by their pegs, and we found some newspaper and tore it up and laid out the prints and rolled them up, and the lieutenant held out his hand and said:

"You have been most kind, *signore*. I will see that these are returned to you as soon as possible."

"Well, that's damn decent of you."

Again there was that calculating, hostile stare. I thought, *The hell with him.*

When they had gone, I went into the bedroom and turned out the lights, and stood on the balcony watching. I saw the lieutenant and the stranger get into the big black Mercedes; and in a moment, silently, it was gone. Karen came and joined me, and put an arm around my waist, and said:

"So, at last he told them."

I turned and looked at her. Her green eyes were enormous in the half-light. "I take it we have other copies?"

"Three more of each, safely tucked away."

"Though what good they are—"

"Who do you think that civilian was?"

I shrugged. "*Questura*, probably."

"Would they interest themselves in a harmless Swiss tourist?"

"Maybe."

"And he didn't say a word, not one word, not even good night."

"An accent? Again?"

She nodded. "He didn't look very Italian, did he? And the easiest way to hide a revealing accent is to keep quiet."

"My, aren't we suspicious tonight?" I didn't suppose it meant very much, but I added, "They drove off in that big Mercedes."

She smiled with a touch of triumph that somehow made me feel good. "Well, darling, that's not a police car, is it? Not even the *Questura*."

"No, I suppose not. But I think we're making a lot of fuss over nothing. A Swiss tourist—all right, a wealthy German industrialist, taken to a cheap hotel by a tart. Would his consulate come to his rescue?"

"Hardly, darling."

"Well, the hell with it. Let's get to bed."

"And first thing in the morning, why don't you go around to the Othello and say hello to Mr. Muller?"

"The perseverance of women!"

She twisted around to face me and put her hands up to my face, and when I kissed her she said nonchalantly:

"Of course, if you'd rather drop it, I suppose *Paris Match* might just take the pictures without an explanation of them? '*Un Moment du Drame sur les Toits de Rome.*'"

"But if we could explain them, there'd be a lot more money." I found her lips again, and when I'd finished I said: "All right, let's chase it around the block and see where it goes to ground."

She smiled, and we went back into the other room where Simona had made up her bed on the divan where she slept. She had the new prints spread out on the table and was looking them over pensively.

She said, "A frightened German, a man after him with a gun... It might add up to anything, mightn't it? To almost anything."

We didn't sleep very much that night, Karen and I. It was still hot, even after the rain, so we pulled the armchair out onto the balcony and sat squeezed in it together. We drank a bottle of wine and listened to Simona's measured childlike breathing through the open door, and we talked in whispers so as not to disturb her. When daylight came we got the *espresso* machine going, and then I went downstairs and out on the street and up the steps to the hotel next door.

The boy who looked after the parked cars, if that's the way to put it—you paid him a few lire or else he scratched the hell out of the bodywork the moment your back was turned—was just coming up out of the cellar, where he slept. I said:

"*Ciao, Francesco, hai dormito bene?*"

He was a ragged, cheerful urchin, ten or eleven years old, with handed-down shoes that were much too big for him—mine. He was wringing out the sacks he used as blankets, and he grimaced at the puddles and said, "*Eh, la pioggia—*"

"A bit of rain's good for you, Francesco, makes your hair curl."

He made an extremely crude comment that might be translated, inaccurately, as "in a pig's ear," and I went into the hotel and said to the woman behind the counter:

"A friend of mine is staying here—Mr. Heinrich Muller. Is he in? Elderly man, gray beard and glasses."

She stared at me without too much pleasure and said, "We have no one here by that name. No one."

"No?" I pulled the register across and looked at it, and pointed to the name and said, "That one. Room number thirty-seven."

She said sullenly, "He left last night, checked out."

"Oh. Forwarding address?"

"*Non lo so.*"

"Did he leave by the front door? Or the window?"

She had the grace to look embarrassed, and said, spreading her arms wide, "Eh—he left, that's all I know."

"Did he pay his bill?" I reached into my pocket for some money and said, "If he didn't, I'd better pay it for him."

She looked at the roll of bills hopefully, as though she'd like to have some of it but was afraid to say anything. I pushed a thousand lire at her, and she took it quickly and tucked it into her capacious bosom. She said, mumbling:

"Eh—the police brought him here, waited while he took his bag, and he left."

"Uh-huh."

Her wispy hair was straggling over her forehead, but the features of her face were fine; she must have been quite attractive once. She said:

"When the police come in, everything else goes out, you don't talk anymore." She looked again at the bills and said hopefully, "But I could let you know if he comes back. You live close by, don't you?"

"Number seventeen around the corner, top floor. But he won't come back." I gave her another thousand lire for good measure, thinking that my bankroll was getting small enough to start worrying about, and went outside to find Francesco.

He was surveying his domain, the tiny piazza and the three streets leading off it as far as he could see, where every parked car, by arrangement with all the other urchins and their *capo*, was fair game for him alone.

I said, "Francesco, did you see a big black car here in the early hours of the morning? When you should have been sleeping?"

He said, "Sleeping? In that *benedetto* puddle downstairs? Yes, I heard it drive up. But there was a *benedetto* chauffeur with it, nothing doing. And a cop, *disgraziato lui*—"

"I suppose you don't remember the number?"

He made a gesture that meant: *Well, there's a damn fool question, no, of course I don't, who remembers license numbers, you think I've got nothing better to do than that?* It was no more than a quick flick of the wrist, but that's what it meant. But he added, "A diplomatic plate, diplomatic corps, best not to touch cars like that. And that *benedetto* chauffeur!"

I sympathized with him. "He give you a bad time?"

"*Disgraziato arabo!*"

"An Arab?"

"Who knows? A pig." He made a few illuminating and articulate comments on the chauffeur's ancestry. He was a kid with nothing in the world except some ragged clothes, a wooden plank bed called a *tavolaccio*, and some wet sacks for blankets; but he was happy in his command of luxurious invective.

"Uh-huh. Well, Francesco, you can take a day off. Get over to the Via Veneto and look around the legations there, see if you can pick out that car—"

Francesco began to squirm uncomfortably. "But—*mio capo...*"

"I'll fix it with the *capo*."

"All right then. The Via Veneto?" I could see his sharp mind working over the angles. He said, "A Mercedes? That's a German car, isn't it?"

"Yep."

"Then the German Embassy?"

"Not necessarily. Take a look around, get a fix on the chauffeur, stay up there all day, check with me tonight."

"And you'll arrange it with the *capo*?"

"Get moving."

"*Sì, signore.*"

He threw his bundles of rags down under the stairway and ran off, a happy child moving out of his element into the fancy quarters where the tourists went, wondering how he could turn this to his advantage, not being sure how, but knowing that he'd come out of it all better off than he was before.

I thought I was wasting my time on a story we'd never write. But Karen seemed keen, if only for purely mundane reasons; and Karen was the girl I was in love with, so head over heels in love that it hurt.

I went back upstairs and found her washing her hair over the big sink in the kitchen, a towel wrapped tightly around her lovely body. Simona had gone down to the Flea Market on the Via Portuense, not far from the apartment, because we needed a new *espresso* machine and didn't feel like paying the fancy prices in the Prisunic.

I was disturbed about an indefinable air of hostility that Karen seemed to show whenever we spoke of the old Swiss, or German, or whatever he was. I said to her, worrying about it:

"But there's nothing sadder than fear on a really old man. Fear ought to be the prerogative of the very young. Somehow, a man of seventy or more—it was crippling him."

"Yes, it was."

"He needs help, Karen. I don't know what sort of help, but—"

She interrupted me scornfully. "You think only the virtuous can get scared?"

"No, I don't. But just tell me in two words what it is you have against him."

She was wrapping the long hair around her head, pinning it into place; the quick fingers stopped their movement, and she looked me straight in the eye and said:

"All right then, in two words, I will. His race."

Now I have as much cause as the next man to remember the sad days of the forties, but the sudden venom in her voice both shocked and saddened me, because I knew its origins.

Nineteen years ago, just after Simona had been born and when Karen was four, her family had been holed up in her father's farm, with a few deserting stragglers of the Italian Army, in the mountains outside Florence. Her father had been a colonel in the Alpinisti, one of those who had not sided with the Germans at the time of the abortive armistice. For three days and nights they had held out against a company of SS troops who had been sent to clean up the area, and at last a mortar attack had blown the last refuge, the cellar, sky high. The SS men had burst in then, and finding the obstinate colonel already dead, had driven their bayonets into his wife's breast, while Karen, shocked into immobility, had watched. It was not a spectacle she was ever likely to forget.

Soon after I met her—I was doing an article at the time on the Ponte Vecchio in her home town—we had stood together one night on the fine old bridge, and I said to her jokingly, "One of the great advantages of living in Florence—you can drown yourself in the most romantic river in the world."

Karen had not smiled. After a while she had said, as though she had been bruised—I could feel her shudder, "Don't talk like that, Michael, please? I've been too near it too often."

I had known then that something was haunting her, and at last she had told me. And it brought us immeasurably closer together. She had said, "Simona never knew. We had hidden her in the hayloft, and I told her—I told her Mama had died of a sickness." Karen had looked at me gravely and had added, "And she must *never* know, will you promise me?"

"I promise."

"You are the only one who knows."

"Just the two of us, I promise."

It seemed that a load had dropped from her. She was suddenly gayer than I had ever known her, and she came to me one day, waving a telegram and saying, "You want to help me photograph a tree growing?"

She spent an hour laboriously explaining the principles of time-lapse photography to me, and then we simply packed our bags and went to Rome. We had already been lovers for a while, and in Rome there was the question of laying it out on the line for the world to see. But Karen simply said, "Simona is the only world I have, and for her, everything I do is right, just because I do it."

And from Simona there had never been a moment of reproach or of discomfort; there had been only the delirium of our happiness together. Karen and I had the bedroom, and Simona, always smiling gently and never seeming put out, slept in the living room on the divan. We had a year's lease on the apartment and hoped the money might last that long. And the world had never seemed a better place to be in.

So when she said now, with brutal clarity, "His race," I knew that the old wound was still open. And the tragedy of our love was that there was nothing I could do to close it.

Then she was smiling again, and I swear that her eyes had changed color. She said gently, "Did you find out anything next door?"

"No, nothing. The police took him away in the middle of the night. I might pay a friendly call on Lieutenant Rospigliosi."

The hair was in place now, clinging to her head, and there was no makeup on her face. She put her hands on my shoulders and looked at me searchingly and said, "If you would rather drop it, Michael... You have only to say so, you know that."

"Yes, I know. But it's a story and we're both in the story business. Let's follow through."

"Are you sure?"

She was so unbelievably lovely. I said, "I'm sure. As sure as I am that I love you."

Her arms slipped around my waist and she pressed herself tight against me. I fumbled with the towel that was around her breasts, and when it fell to the floor I picked her up bodily and carried her into the bedroom.

Simona, before she had left the apartment, had made the bed up again.

Oh, well.

CHAPTER 3

We dined that night in the little *trattoria* around the corner, the three of us together. Simona wore her black cocktail outfit and I had persuaded Karen to wear the bright-blue Grecian thing that set off the glorious auburn of her hair to perfection and didn't do too badly by her figure either.

The rain puddles had dried out in the heat of the day, and the brightly covered chairs made a pretty picture against the reds and blues of the geraniums and ageratum that filled the boxes they had put out to mark the limits of the pavement dining room.

We had some fried squid and a salad and then some *cannelloni*, and washed it down with a bottle of Frascati, and while we were taking it easy over the coffee, Karen suddenly looked over my shoulder at the doorway and said mildly:

"Well, look who's here."

Simona, who had never even seen the man, understood faster than I did; it was the very fair hair, I suppose. I swung around to look, and the man from the ledge was there, the tall man who had held a gun in his hand, pointed at us, for a paralyzing moment of time. He was looking our way quite unconcerned, one long arm resting against the green-painted pole that supported the canvas awning over the geraniums. Almost as if my glance had constituted an invitation, he sauntered over to the table, put a hand on the fourth chair and said, "May I?"

I said, "Sure, if you don't mind the cops coming in any minute. They're looking for you."

"Oh?" It didn't seem to worry him. "What makes you think

that?" Before I could answer, he smiled at Karen and Simona and said, "I don't really want to intrude, but—this will only take a minute."

He sat down and looked hard at me and said:

"There's just one thing I want to know. You were taking some photographs last night. What happened to them?"

Karen was watching him closely, with just a touch of worry on her face. I said:

"Suppose you tell me why you want to know? As if it weren't obvious."

He said calmly, "Not as obvious as you'd suppose, Mr. Benasque."

"All right, you know my name, I'm impressed. Mr.—?"

"Just call me Nathan."

"Nathan what? Or what Nathan?"

"Just Nathan."

"Well, Nathan, the police got them. So you'd better start running."

He waved an elegant hand. "Oh, I'm quite used to running from the police."

"There's a marvelous picture of you about to take a shot at that man; it might just encourage them to run a little faster."

He nodded. "Yes, it will probably make them very angry. But it's the other man they're more interested in. They're anxious to keep any pictures like that out of circulation."

I wasn't sure whether or not he was trying to tell me something, but it seemed a good time to find out. I said:

"Herr Heinrich Muller?"

"Yes, Heinrich Muller." He grinned sardonically. "The gentleman from Switzerland. And when the police called on you, they took the photographs away?"

"Yes, they did."

He sighed. He would have sounded affected, except that under the pose I could sense a certain latent power. "I was afraid of that. And I could so easily have gotten them first. Do you happen to know where Muller is now?"

"How the hell should I know?"

"No, I was afraid you wouldn't." He sat back in his chair and looked at me reflectively. He said, "Would you mind telling me how Herr—Muller came to see you? Why particularly *you*?"

"My window was the closest friendly light on a dark night. There was a man after him with a gun, remember?"

"No other reason?"

"Should there be?"

"I don't know, but it's essential I find out."

"Go to hell."

He stared at me for a while, not saying a word, and then leaned forward and put his long, flat fingers on the table. "I believe you're a journalist, Mr. Benasque?"

"Everyone in the *quartiere* knows that."

"Then let me give you a word of advice. There is no story for you in this little matter, nothing at all worth reporting. The police have their reasons for wanting silence—and I have mine. Just—keep out of it."

"You're protesting a little too much, Mr. Nathan."

The look of relaxed affability had gone, and his face was as hard as nails. He said slowly, "Mr. Benasque, I am engaged in a private war of my own, a particularly dirty war, so keep out of my way or someone is going to get—no, not hurt; just put—right out of action." He made a gesture of finality and said, "Quickly and completely, right out of action."

None of the waiters understood English, but I could see that they were gathering together, looking at Nathan and whispering among themselves. Nathan was suddenly aware of it too, and he stood up abruptly and said:

"I mean what I say, Mr. Benasque. I'm not going to have any penny-ante journalist interfering in what I have to do."

It was not hard to be brave in the bright lights. I said, "A goddam hired gunman."

There was a little silence. It seemed charged with sadness rather than with menace. He said, "Yes. I suppose you could call it that with a reasonable degree of accuracy." Without even a look at the two girls, he turned and went briskly out onto the street.

Simona said, "It might just be wise to send a waiter for the police."

But Karen looked at me and asked, "Michael? You think that?"

I said, "No. I just can't see him getting caught quite so easily. There's an air of—of competence about him..."

She said slowly, "That's exactly what I was thinking. But it just might be a—a gesture."

"All right." The phone was in sight at the back of the inner room, and I went in and called the police station. It took nearly fifteen minutes to locate Lieutenant Rospigliosi, but when I did he seemed interested enough. I said, "He's probably a dozen miles away by now. He left here at—at nine-forty-seven precisely; took me all that time to reach you."

The connection was lousy and his voice was very faint. "*Mille grazie, signore.*"

"When do I get my photographs back?"

There was a pause at the other end. Then, "In a few days, *signore*, I am sure."

"Uh-huh. How's Herr Muller?"

"I—do not know, *signore*. He left for Switzerland this morning."

"Uh-huh. Are you sending a man around?"

Again there was that long pause. I had the idea the *tenente* was relaying my words and getting instructions. He said at last, "No, *signore*, it will not be necessary."

"Are you sure? I don't want to be wakened up in the middle of the night, I've got better things to do."

The lieutenant said ambiguously, "I am quite sure of it, *signore*." He put the phone down before I could think of an answer.

I went back to the table and told the girls what had happened, and then the child Francesco was out there on the pavement, and his *capo* was with him. I said to Karen:

"Dammit, I forgot to fix Francesco's leave of absence."

I paid the bill and we left, and the *capo*, a mean old man named Giulio, grinned at me and said, "Eh, *signore*, the boy told me—"

I gave him the change the waiter had given me and said shortly, "I sent him on a job, I forgot to tell you. Did you beat him?"

Giulio laughed and said, "No, not very much. But we found

your automobile, *signore*." He was fingering the loose change, and he waited. I waited too. He sighed and said, "A poor man, *signore*, with nothing but a few young friends to buy him an occasional plate of beans—"

"All right, all right, where was the car?"

Francesco began to speak excitedly, and Giulio cuffed him on the head. I said, "Cut it out! Let him speak!" And Giulio turned to the child and said angrily, "Well, tell him, tell him about the Arab."

Francesco said, "Like I told you, the chauffeur was an Arab. It's the Egyptian Embassy; we located it a few hours ago."

Surprised, I said, "Are you sure? There are hundreds of ears like that in Rome."

"But only one chauffeur like that *benedetto arabo*. And he had the same man with him, the old man who went with them last night, the old man with the gray beard and the glasses."

"Oh? What time did you see them?"

Giulio said, "At six o'clock this evening, *signore*. Once the boy had told me this was the car—"

"At six? This evening?"

"Si, *signore*."

Karen, frowning, said, "Didn't you say he'd gone back to—to Switzerland?"

"That's what Rospigliosi said, but it seems he was just telling me to mind my own damn business. I half suspected it." Looking at Karen, I saw that she was angry. I said, "So he didn't go back..." and she answered me patiently:

"One man chasing another with a gun, the police doing their best to stop us from knowing what it's about, and a German hiding out in the Egyptian Embassy, with police protection. He's no tourist, Michael."

I could see the signs in Karen's eyes. She just wasn't going to let it alone. Seeing me weaken, she drove the argument home:

"You're supposed to be a good journalist, Michael—"

"And I am, you know that—"

"Yes, I know it. So tell me why you won't start moving.

I had no answer, no answer that would make sense. But in Rome, in the summer, it's easy to say: "Tomorrow will do, tomorrow and tomorrow and tomorrow..." I knew that if it weren't for Karen, if the warmth of her bed were not all that really mattered to me, I'd be after that story with the dust spurting up from under my heels. And it was Karen who wanted me to do just that. And she was right. I gave in. I said:

"There's a gal in London, knows everybody who is anybody—English, American, Swiss or German, or goddam Malagash, come to that. She runs a political column, gal named Veronica. First thing in the morning I'll send her a copy of one of those photographs. If our Swiss-German friend is known at all, to anyone, then he's known to Veronica. I promise you, darling, if there's a story—I'll find it for you."

She smiled a dazzling smile and those damned eyes changed color again, visibly. When she leaned forward and kissed me, a policeman, who was wandering by unconcernedly, stopped and watched and then spread his hands wide and said, "Eh..."

Believe it or not, that one word meant: *What a way to behave on a public street. I ought to put the two of you in jail, to teach you both a little dignity...* Because—and believe this or not too—public kissing is against the law in Italy; it's an Offense against Morality. Heigh ho.

Giulio waited till the policeman was on his way and out of sight, and then he spat in the gutter and said loudly, *"Disgraziati loro."* Which means, more or less, "What a bunch of bastards."

At eight in the morning, Simona wandered into the bedroom, in her dressing gown, with three little cups of coffee and some figs, and said:

"How did you sleep?"

I said, "Off and on," and Karen kicked me under the blankets, and then we all sat on the edge of the bed and had breakfast, and while the girls went about their toilet, making themselves even more beautiful, I walked over to the post office and sent a copy of the photograph, the one that showed both Muller and Nathan, over to London, airmail express; I figured it wouldn't take more than a week that way. I'd written a note, saying: "If you know either of these gentlemen, honey, a quick reply might just throw a useable story my way and I can get back to the normal routine of *dolce far niente*." I'd thought about adding: "Wish you were here," but I wisely refrained; Veronica might just have caught the next plane out, she's that kind of gal.

Then I wandered back to the little park where Tasso's tree was, and scouted around till I found Giulio, sitting at a bare table outside a *bottega* and drinking a glass of wine. He stood up and gestured at the bottle and I joined him. I said:

"I want a couple of your boys, Giulio, for two or three days. *Quanto costa?*" Before he could answer, I added, "The exchequer's getting mighty low."

He raised his eyebrows right up to the hairline and nodded wisely. "We are all poor men, *signore*, but some of us are veritably miserable in our poverty."

We argued for a while, and finally came up with what might be called an equitable arrangement; I would pay the two boys five hundred lire a day each, and another five hundred to Giulio; I knew he'd finish up with most of it, but who am I to knock the capitalist system? I said:

"I want to find out if the man with the beard, whose name is Muller, is living in the Embassy or where. I want to know where he goes, and what he does. And if he leaves town, I want to know where he goes—"

"That's a very hard job, *signore*—"

"And fifteen hundred lire a day is a lot of money. Goddammit, that's nearly three dollars."

Up went the eyebrows again. I said, "And a bottle of wine each time you report to me, here. Twice a day, no more, at midday and midnight, OK?"

His wicked old eyes brightened. "OK, *signore*."

Simona came down while we were talking, dressed in tight green slacks and a brown silk shirt. Giulio sighed, thinking of his lost youth, and I said:

"And where are we off to, dressed to kill?"

She said, "The nice young policeman, the one with the pimples."

I said, "Good luck. How are you going to find him?"

"I'll find him."

"Yes, I'll bet you will too. A glass of wine with us?"

She shook her lovely head and grimaced. "A little too early in the day."

We watched her hips articulating across the square, and then I went up to find Karen. We wandered together through the crowded, noisy streets, over to the post office, and picked up the mail. By the grace of God there was a check there from one of the French magazines for an article I'd done on the lovely young Beatrice Cenci, who was horribly tortured and finally beheaded by Clement VIII for a crime of which she was quite innocent. It wasn't a great deal of money, but it would keep the pot boiling for a few more weeks.

We spent the afternoon on the island in the middle of the river, the Isola Tiberina, where in the days of ancient Rome the political prisoners were dumped to die of exposure and starvation. The view down the river from the island's point, still littered with fragmentary remains of the old temples, is one of the finest in Rome, and the island itself somehow has an air of being forgotten by the march of progress. They say the island did not exist until the Tarquins were expelled from Rome nearly twenty-six hundred years ago, and that then, the huge grain supplies the late unlamented despots had accumulated were contemptuously cast into the Tiber and the island was formed.

Karen was doing a layout on the papal poet, Camillo Querno, who was crowned here in the sixteenth century, with ivy, laurel and— so help me—cabbage leaves, and we'd been searching the cellars of St. Bartolomeo for a fresco reputed to depict this event.

And, as soon as darkness came, we walked across to the Piazza Venezia, along the lively Corso, and up to the Via Veneto, where we'd arranged to meet Simona.

The night was hot again, and all the American tourists were wearing Hawaiian shirts, which seemed oddly out of place here, as though they were interlopers from a strange and far-off country; which, come to think of it, they were. The fountains at the foot of the hill were splashing gently, and a pretty little child was cupping water into her hands and drinking, and I heard the angry mother say, "No, stupid, it's not *clean*," and she yanked the poor thing away.

Simona was waiting for us in the café where we'd arranged to meet, fending off the wolves, and when we'd sat down and ordered Punt e Mes on ice with a twist of lemon, she sighed and said:

"The boy with the pimples doesn't exist, and neither does the sergeant, and neither does Lieutenant Rospigliosi."

I said sympathetically, "The brush-off?"

"Completely. No one's ever heard of any of them."

"When I spoke on the phone to the *tenente*, I had called Police Headquarters, so that's where he is."

Karen said blithely, "So they're all from the *Questura*. Top secrecy. I told you, he's more than he seems to be."

"And I'm thirsty. The dust in those cellars—"

"And did you see Mr. Nathan?"

Startled, I stared at her. "Nathan?"

Karen smiled slowly. "You're losing your touch, darling. He was sitting in Doney's as we went past."

"Oh. Well, I had better things to think of; my mind was elsewhere."

"I'm flattered."

"He's got a nerve, for a man the police are looking for."

"If they *are* looking for him."

"If they had a picture of me climbing all over the rooftops with a gun in my hand, they'd sure as hell be looking for me."

And at that moment, the big black Mercedes came slowly around the corner. It was just like any other Mercedes, but I stared at it with an automatic reflex, and saw that the chauffeur was the same man, the man Francesco had called the Arab. And sitting in the back was the dark and silent stranger who had come to the apartment with the *tenente*, the man I had learned not to like. As it turned the corner again and headed up Via Veneto toward the Borghese gardens, I fumbled in my pocket for pencil and notebook, and ran out onto the street to get a good look at the number. And as I wrote it down, I looked up and saw that Nathan was standing there, watching me. I held his look for a moment, and then he turned sharply on his heel and walked away.

I walked back to the table, and Karen, who had seen the

encounter with Nathan, said, "My God, did you see the look on his face? He was furious!"

"The hell with him."

She fell silent, not looking very happy, and Simona said cheerfully, "Well, I'm hungry. Let's get home and make some pasta."

I had some writing to do for Karen's Querno layout, but I just didn't feel like going home. A breeze was beginning to waft down the narrow streets and I knew the apartment would still be hot and stuffy. The rich, ripe smell of cooking was coming from the kitchen, and I said:

"Let's eat here."

Karen guessed correctly that I was beginning to worry; she looked at me and said nothing. And, while we were eating, Giulio found us and came over, grinning like a banshee, his tired old face heavily lined with the years of fighting the poverty, and said cheerfully:

"Still on the job, *signore*, like you said, always on the job."

I scowled at him. "All right, where did that Mercedes go just now?"

He shrugged. "Who knows? Later tonight I will know." When I waited, he made a wide gesture that seemed to embrace all the city. "All the boys in the area, *tutti quanti*, all work for me, as many as you want, *signore*."

"I said two would be enough."

He raised his shoulders and flicked his hands around his chest for a while, meaning: *Well, at least you might allow me a little discretion to do the job properly*. He said at last:

"It probably went down the Via Appia Antica, same as this morning, maybe. One of my boys, on a bicycle—"

It's the only way to move around in Rome nowadays. Even in the tiniest Fiat you can sit for an hour on any main street, waiting for the car ahead to inch up another foot, creeping forward at a pace that would disgrace any honest, hard-working tortoise, while the kids on their bikes slip through, up on the sidewalk, down into the gutter, up on the sidewalk again, careless of the angry shouts of the pedestrians and knowing that they are the only ones moving. Giulio said:

"Tonight, a bottle of wine in the piazza?"

"Around midnight."

"I'll be there, *signore*. Ciao."

"Ciao."

He walked off down toward the thoroughfare, hobbling a little; there was nothing wrong with his legs but he liked to limp to add a little something to his general air of pathos.

A troubadour strolled by, looking hopefully at the waiters in the café and then beginning to strum an old ballad for the customers. He was a thin, undernourished, white-faced man with no chest to rest his guitar on, and an air of gentle melancholy about him. I knew he was worrying about whether he'd earn enough tonight to feed the eight or ten kids who would be littering his one-room apartment on the *periferia*, wondering if one day there'd be enough left over, maybe, to buy his pretty but slatternly wife a length of cheap cotton for a new dress. It wasn't much of a way of life for him, but I wondered if he knew, or cared, just how ancient and honorable his profession was... He would stroll from table to table, from bar to bar, singing a few old songs, and then move on, counting the small change in his pocket and worrying.

Once he would have been part of a golden tapestry, highlighted with rich velvets and brocades, and nobles would have sat with their ladies while they listened to his ballads, and they would have fed him on suckling pig and sent him on his way with a purse full of jingling coins.

As if in concord with my thoughts, a waiter came out and furtively thrust a newspaper-wrapped package into his hand; some leftovers from a tourist who couldn't stand the grease...

Watching, Karen put out her hand and touched mine and said softly, "We're almost broke, Michael, but we're very lucky people. Let's never forget it."

We took the long way home, walking slowly along the narrow street of Two Slaughterhouses to the top of the Spanish Steps, then down to the bottom, where we sat for a while on the marble lip of the boat-shaped fountain, listening to the gentle sound of the water, and then down the length of the oh-so-expensive Via Condotti, where the smart shops are, right down to the riverbank. Castel St. Angelo, a great gray bulk across the water, was a shadow against the sky in which the ghosts of Cagliostro, and of Cellini, and of the brutally savaged Beatrice Cenci wandered dismally.

And it was past eleven o'clock when we reached the long dark sweep of Lungotevere and walked through the deserted alleyway down to the tiny square; it seemed that there were just the three of us, not only in this ancient redbrick jungle of decaying buildings that was the Trastevere, but also in the whole of its violent history.

We went up quietly in the darkness, and I flung open the door and switched on the lights.

I did not know then, and I do not know now, just what it was that made me suddenly uneasy. The room was exactly as we had left it, but somehow—*something* was wrong.

I looked at Karen and saw that she felt it too; even Simona, who was not particularly aware of what went on around her unless it was clear as daylight, was suddenly staring at the two of us, wondering.

I went quickly to the kitchen and looked inside; there was nothing there, and I was about to move back into the living room when I remembered that when we had left the house, Simona had been polishing up the saucepans and had left them on the kitchen table; they were gone. I opened the cupboard door to check that she hadn't put them away, and there wasn't a single saucepan there either. Puzzled, I came back into the living room and asked Karen: "How many saucepans do we have? Five? Six?"

She nodded. "Something like that. Why?"

"Now we have none."

Simona said, "But—who would want to steal saucepans?" She went quickly to the cupboard where the cameras were kept, a thousand dollars' worth of them, and she looked back at me and said, "They're still here, the only things of value we have... It doesn't make sense."

I hate the inexplicable. If something is wrong, as far as I'm concerned it's got to make sense, at least, and then I'm not too worried. I went angrily to the bedroom to check there too, and as I opened the door it seemed the earth fell in on me. There was a loud clatter that was all the more frightening because it was the last thing in the world that I had expected, a metallic sound that seemed to go on and on and on...

I threw myself back and grabbed at Karen, and we went down

together to the floor and I yelled at Simona, "Take cover!" and saw her dive behind the divan, and we all lay still for a moment till the unaccountable jangling stopped, and then I raised my head and looked, and a stainless-steel mixing bowl was rolling slowly, gently, toward me across the floor; it stopped close by my head, and I stared at it, unbelieving.

And when I looked at Karen, I saw that the shock of it had hit her a cruelly violent blow; her face was white and her eyes were glazed, and she was back under the mortars and waiting for someone to bayonet her mother. I lifted her gently and said:

"A practical joke."

And Simona said blankly, "But who—?"

I found that I was trembling too, whether with anger or relief I don't know. I went to the bedroom, and there were all the missing utensils, scattered all over the floor—six saucepans, a few enamel bowls, a cast-iron skillet... There was an ache in my upper arm where the skillet had landed as it came down from the top of the door, and I was only now aware that it had hit me. I said, "We used to play tricks like that when we were children, only then we always used a bowl of water, propped up on top of the door."

In a hollow voice, Karen said, "This is no child's trick, Michael."

"I know."

I found a note pinned to the inside of the bedroom door with a thumbtack. I tore it off angrily and read it aloud to the girls:

Just a very friendly warning, Mr. Benasque. I told you, mine is a particularly dirty war, and this could easily have been a bomb, couldn't it?

Karen began to cry quietly, shaking uncontrollably, and I put my arms around her and held her tight to me until she had stopped shaking, and she dried her eyes on my handkerchief and said:

"Silly, isn't it? I'm sorry."

Simona had taken the note from me and was reading it over again, and she looked at Karen, faintly puzzled, and said:

"Just a warning, Karen. It could have been the real thing.

We're lucky."

She could not understand the tears, and I said, "That's just it, the shock of what it could have been. That bastard had better keep out of my way; I'll have his bloody guts for a necktie."

I'm not a violent man, and I'll run from trouble rather than face it if the odds are too strong. That's what I was taught to do in the war, and some guys, the ones who were in the Infantry, could never understand the philosophy that was laboriously drilled into me; but in my particular outfit, where we lived for months in enemy territory, we had to stay alive in order to be useful.

My old boss, Colonel Matley, used to say, in the lazy Southern drawl that I always thought was an affectation, "We've spent too much time and trouble getting you trained, and getting you where you can do some real damage, so don't go off half-cocked and get yourselves killed. You hit and run, and then you can hit again, and again and again—but only as long as you've sense enough to know when to run. Leave the heroics to the poor bastards in the front line, to the cannon fodder. They're paid to die and you're not—you're paid to stay alive."

Matley could afford to be cynical; his own three sons had been with the U.S. Seventh Corps in their magnificent but suicidal assault on Cherbourg, and all three of them had been killed on the same filthy afternoon.

And now, quite clearly, was the time to run; or at least, to heed the warning. Simona said:

"Just a story, Michael; it's not worth it, not for a story in the papers. A moment of interest over the breakfast table—that's all it will ever be."

But I could not shake off the image, momentary but horrifying, of my Karen in tears because of a stupid and brutal threat. The past had been callously thrown in her face, and it was a past she was trying to forget.

I carried her into the bedroom and put her on the bed, and she lay there for a while, staring up at the ceiling, and then she said:

"For just a moment, at the first sound, I was thinking—"

"I know. Try and forget it."

"It's such a long time ago."

"A cruel and silly gesture."

"Take us back to Florence, Michael. Please."

"Of course. There's nothing to keep us here. Nothing at all."

There was a little silence, and then she said, "Have we got enough to finish the Querno story?"

"Plenty. We'll put it together on the banks of the Arno."

She smiled hesitantly. "The most romantic river in the world."

"And the most beautiful city. We'll leave first thing in the morning."

She nodded. For a while we did not speak, and only the night sounds of the piazza came to us through the open window. And then she suddenly sat up straight and said emphatically:

"The hell with it! The bloody *hell* with it!"

"And what's that supposed to mean?"

Karen said wrathfully, "It means we don't run for our lives, that's what it means. Just because some two-bit gangster—"

I began to laugh. Karen's English is immaculate, except when she uses phrases that don't really fit her. The "two-bit" sounded ludicrously out of place. Knowing what I was laughing at, she switched to Italian and said:

"*Un benedetto fannullone, un malvivente, un—*"

She gestured hopelessly, There are some things you just can't say in Italian. I said seriously:

"Make up your mind, darling. We go, we stay, whichever you like. Only—if we stay, I'm liable to tear the arse off that bastard."

She looked at me somberly and took a deep breath. "We'd never forgive ourselves if we ran away." When I did not answer she said, "Well, would we?"

"No, of course we wouldn't. We'll stay."

The hell with Colonel Matley and his wisdom. I left Karen and Simona getting ready for bed, and went downstairs to find Giulio.

CHAPTER 4

Giulio, I suppose could properly be classed as a rogue.

He was one of the vast army of Roman unemployed, or, more correctly, unemployable, who have been left in the mud by the onrush of sudden prosperity which the new industrial revolution has brought to modern Italy.

He was shrewd, and cunning, and callous, and in his torn, bedraggled clothes he cut a pathetic figure. But he had a finger in every muddy pie that was opened on the streets of the slums, and you could never be sure that under all that obvious distress there wasn't a money belt, well packed, tied around his skinny waist. Somewhere, he kept a wife and family; but I never heard him speak about them much.

As I walked across the little darkened square, I could see him sitting there on his favorite bench where the lamplight cast dappled shadow across the table under the trees, and his bottle of wine was in front of him. As an exercise of the imagination I tried to guess how much wine there would be in it, knowing that he would have told the short-sleeved bar boy to bring him just a glass or so in the bottom of the bottle, that I would pay for a full one, and that they'd split the profit. A third? A quarter? A few drops only?

There was just one glass in it, which Giulio poured for me with elaborate ceremony. I said, "You finished your bottle quickly, Giulio," and his face dropped, then lit up again when he saw I was pulling his leg. I signaled to the bar boy who came out and carefully removed the crumbs of a meal from the table now that a *gentiluomo* was sitting there, and Giulio pulled out a dirty scrap of paper and said:

"Number eighty-four, Viale Sanderino, an old house, *signore,* nobody lives there."

"So?"

"That is where the big car went, three times today, always in a hurry. And once the old man came out, the bearded man you said was named Muller. There was something he forgot, and the other man in the car was very angry and told him, I think, to go back in again, though I could not understand the language."

"German?"

"Si, *signore*."

"But if nobody lives there—"

"In the cellars, *signore*. After dark, there was a light there, and I could see inside. I do not think the old man is accustomed to hiding, or being hidden. He is very careless."

While I digested this piece of information, Giulio screwed up his eyes and said pathetically, "I am trying to please you, *signore*... It is the old man you are really interested in, isn't it? Not just the car?" The lamplight etched the outline of his sharp features.

I nodded. "Where's Viale Sanderino? I never heard of it."

"Not really much of a street, signore, just a few old ruins out beyond the *periferia*. Off the Via Tiburtina."

That was a hell of a way out of town. I had a vision of Francesco bicycling madly to keep up. But a distinctive car like the Mercedes would not be hard to trace out there. I said:

"Francesco had his work cut out."

Giulio nodded gravely. "It was not easy, *signore*. When he lost the car, he asked by the roadside, and at last he found it again. It was not easy, not for five hundred lire a day."

"Somebody sweetened the pot, Giulio; we don't have to worry so much about a few lire now."

"That is good, *signore*, I am very happy for you. Though I am a poor man myself, I do not like to see a man of quality suffering the misery that ought to be reserved for people like me."

It's the damnedest thing about the Romans: people like Giulio are close to illiteracy and it's a major effort to write a word of more than two syllables, but when it comes to talking... They love their language and they use it well. I said:

"You're a sad case, Giulio, but hang onto my belt and you'll be all right. Can I get into this house and take a look at it?"

His face lit up with genuine pleasure. I wondered how long it had been since he'd done a little burglary. He said happily:

"Of course, *signore*, it is not precisely legal, but under the circumstances... If you wish me to help you?"

"So let's go now."

Giulio hesitated. "Of course, *signore*, whatever you say. I would not presume—"

"But what?"

He said promptly, "Four o'clock in the morning is considered, by those who know, to be the best time. It is then that a man is sleeping most soundly. But if you say now—"

"No, no, you are the expert. But maybe I'd better do this on my own. Your bad leg—"

"My bad leg, *signore*, is miraculously cured whenever I have the sudden occasion to run. Perhaps because I pray so devoutly to the saintly Virgin."

"I'll bet. All right then, meet me here at about three." I looked at my watch. "That's three hours from now."

I left him with a fresh bottle of red wine, and went upstairs to find Karen.

Simona was already asleep on the divan, sleeping like a child, sweet and innocent, her hand under her cheek; there was even a slight smile on her face, as though Nathan's cruel joke had already been forgotten. I wondered if it was a sign of danger; I've always learned to take good note of warnings, wherever they came from. The old reflexes die hard, but it's surprising how fast they spring to life when danger threatens.

I tiptoed past her into the bedroom, and Karen was lying there awake, naked under the white sheet, waiting for me. I undressed quickly and snuggled in beside her, feeling the luxurious warmth of her body tight and close against me, and she put her arms around my neck and pulled me even tighter; it seemed that there was almost a desperation on her.

She said, "Love me, Michael, love me, I love you so much..."

And when the bell in the old church of St. Onofrio chimed three, I awoke and slipped quietly out of the bed, and left her sleeping there in the darkness.

So help me, Giulio had produced a bicycle for me. I had thought of calling for a cab to take us within walking distance of Viale Sanderino, but Giulio said, horrified:

"*Ma costa troppo, signore*, it costs too much, and besides, a bicycle is quieter."

I said, "I hope you didn't steal the damn thing. All I want is a year in the clink for stealing a goddam bicycle."

He grinned his assurance. "Honestly bought and paid for, *signore*. It belongs to one of my boys."

It was a ramshackle old bike, even worse than the one he was riding, but I noticed that it was nicely oiled and easy to ride.

God knows when I last rode a bike. I almost enjoyed it, and I only fell off once. We cycled slowly over the bridge, around the Palatinate, past the great ghostly, silent bulk of the Colosseum and up to the Domus Aurea, the "golden house" where Nero had such a gay old time, and out along the Via Labicana, till we came to the railway line, and then on along the main road that leads out to the lovely hills of the Ciociaria. I was surprised to see so many other cyclists around; there were porters from the markets coming in with their early produce, and waiters from the nightclubs that were just closing down, and peasant girls coming in with baskets of figs precariously balanced on their handlebars...

I began to get a little stiff from the unaccustomed use of my leg muscles, but soon the town dropped behind us and the road was flanked with tall trees through which the moon shone brightly, lighting up the countryside with its pallid gleam. Somewhere close by some charcoal was burning, and the scent of it was ripe in the air.

It only took us half an hour to get there. Giulio put a finger to his lips and pointed, and we glided silently past a tumbledown row of two-story houses that were stuck there, incongruously, in the middle of a wide thicket of trees and tangled brushwood that stood up among the grape-planted fields, as though not only the houses here but the land itself had been abandoned. A low hedge separated them from the road, and when we were well past, Giulio said quietly, "The middle one, *signore.*"

We wheeled our bikes expertly around—I was beginning to enjoy it now—and cycled past it once more, and then we stopped and thrust the machines into the bushes and went forward on foot.

It was impossibly clear in that damned moonlight. I've always liked the dark, and I looked up at the clear sky, wishing some clouds would take over, but the stars were bright and there was not a wisp of cloud in sight. Only the houses under the trees were in chameleon shadow.

Giulio moved like a wary ghost, his feet moving in absolute silence, his body erect and alert, and when we came to a short flight of stone steps that led down into a sort of cellar, he pointed silently at the closed door at the bottom. I nodded, looked for a while at the steps, signaled to Giulio to stay where he was, and went down them slowly; and with infinite patience I tried the door. As I expected, it was locked, and I came back up the stairs and withdrew a little and Giulio whispered reproachfully, "I heard you moving, *signore*; you must be more silent." The damned nerve of him.

I signaled him to go around the house one way while I went the other, and we separated. I tripped over a strand of barbed wire in the bushes and fell, but soundlessly, onto grass, and then there was a sort of open space at the back where a car had recently been standing. I could see the tire marks clearly in the moonlight and there was a black drop of oil there too. I went clear around the house, finding no window, no other door, not even Giulio...

I stood there in the darkness between the ruined buildings for a moment, wondering what the hell had happened to him, and then I nearly jumped out of my skin as a tiny pebble hit me on the shoulder. I looked up, and there was Giulio on the skyline, perched up on a broken piece of wall that once had been part of the second story. He was pointing, and when I looked I saw how he had clambered up. An old water barrel, empty and dry now, was the first step, and then there was a projection where a collapsed floor joist was sticking out grotesquely. And then Giulio was there to help me up, and we stood together for a moment, looking around and seeing nothing through the trees but sleeping countryside, gently washed with moonlight, with wisps of smoke slowly spiraling up where distant fires were burning. There was a strong smell of eucalyptus and honeysuckle somewhere. Oh, the scents of the night in the Roman countryside!

Below us, ten feet down, was a tiny square, an inner courtyard of the house, littered now with refuse and covered with rampaging weeds. On one side, where the shadow cut diagonally across the whitewashed wall, there was a window, sloppily covered with planking, boarded up carelessly as though it didn't really matter very much. The window was on the side of the house where the cellar door was, and was low in the wall, close to the ground. I nodded at Giulio and was about to drop down when he restrained me with a gesture.

While I waited, he jumped down in silence, landing like a fox on padded feet, and then he looked up, grinning, and reached out to help me down. I thought, *There was a time, buster, when I could have done that just as quietly*. I lay down on the edge of the wall, reached for his surprisingly strong hand and used it as a fulcrum to swing myself down beside him. He grinned again in the moonlight, and I went over and looked at the boards over the window.

They had been nailed on long ago, and the nails were rusted, and I put my lips close to Giulio's ear and whispered, "Can we get a couple boards off without any noise?"

That damned grin didn't leave his face. He reached down inside his trousers and brought out a short steel bar with a notch at one end, and very slowly he began to lever a board off. A nail squeaked a protest, and he stopped and listened for a long while, and then went silently on with his work. It took him ten minutes or so to clear a big enough aperture, and I was about to start climbing in when once again he restrained me, pulling me back into a shaded corner and squatting down in the tall weeds, squirming himself into the angle till he was no more than part of the garbage there. I crouched down beside him, and he whispered, "A few minutes, *signore*, to make sure no one heard."

I knew all these tricks myself once. I waited for fifteen minutes by the luminous dial of my watch, listening to the night noises: the cry of a bird, the distant, muted whine of a small car, the bark of a dog in a nearby farm... And then I got to my feet, flexed my muscles and touched Giulio on the shoulder.

I whispered, "Wait for me here." He looked at me in the darkness and raised his eyebrows, but I shook my head, meaning: *I want to do this myself now*. I didn't like the idea of two of us crawling around inside in the cellars, neither of us knowing what he was looking for.

The thought raised a point: What the hell was I looking for? I just didn't know. I knew that if the old man was in there somewhere, hiding, I was going to find out what he was up to; if he was alone.

And if he wasn't? I could only shrug it off and hope for the best. Take a step forward and see where it leads you. Take another step and move on from there. Or back. Something might happen that might lead you—somewhere.

It did.

I clambered through the window and dropped to the floor inside, surprised how far down the floor was, but my rubber soles made no noise, and I crouched where I had landed for a long time, listening and trying to get my eyes used to the utter darkness after the bright moonlight outside, wondering if I was in a room or a corridor or on a goddam flight of stairs; I just didn't know that either.

Cautiously I felt the stone wall behind me, edging my way along it till I came to a corner, and then along that too. For a while I was worried because there seemed to be no furniture of any sort, but then my groping hands found a cupboard and I knew that I had arrived—somewhere.

Groping some more, I found it was a kind of sideboard, and my fingers crawled along its smooth top surface till I found—a glass? No, it was a bottle, a short squat empty bottle with foil around its top. I lifted it carefully and smelled it: beer—there were still a few dregs in it.

I placed it back on the dresser, feeling for the wood with my little finger under its bottom till it was safely and silently in place again, and then I found a glass that moved with an imperceptible sound as my exploring fingers got a little clumsy. I swore under my breath and moved around the dresser.

Now something was at my shins, touching me gently. A chair? I moved back to the wall and waited. For a long time I stood still and silent, listening, listening for any kind of sound that might tell me—anything.

But there was nothing.

It was time to risk a light. I took the slim pencil flashlight from my breast pocket and switched it on, letting the small beam play over the empty room. I had walked, it seemed, down a narrow corridor between two stone walls, and had come into a small room that once had been a wine cellar. On the other side there were still the slatted cases that once had held the bottles, and besides the chair I had found with my shin there was a narrow sofa bed neatly covered with a bright-red blanket, a small desk, and a floor lamp next to a wooden chair. I tried the switch, but there was no current. The dresser had an oil lamp on it, but before I lit it I thought I'd better make quite sure I was alone.

I explored the cellar and found another small room with a flight of stone steps leading up to another part of the house, but the door at the top was locked. There were some rickety bits of furniture here too: a table, a few wine barrels, a couple of chairs, an empty cupboard, a small iron grate where the charcoal was still warm. But there was no sign of life anywhere in the building.

I went to the window I had clambered through and called out softly:

"Giulio? *Non ce nessuno.*"

There was no reply. I shone the light into the courtyard for a moment, but he wasn't there. I wondered where the hell he'd gone.

And then there was the slightest sound behind me. Sound? It was so slight that there's probably no word for the kind of noise it was, and I knew that whatever had caused it was the same thing that had scared Giulio away and sent him, with the decisive instincts of the constantly hunted, scurrying for safety.

It was like a sudden intake of breath. The alarm speeded up my instincts, and in a moment of panic I swung around and threw up my arm, and a heavy blow came down that knocked me sprawling off my feet, and then I was suddenly fighting for my life in the darkness, rolling over and over with someone who was stronger and more agile than I. The body was tight against me, pressing hard, and I drove my knee into a stomach and heard the painful grunt, and something clattered noisily to the ground and I knew it was a gun.

I was on my feet again, and so was my adversary, and there he was, for a fraction of time, framed in the light of the window, and it was Nathan.

As he moved toward me I reached back and belted him so hard in the mouth that my knuckles cracked, and down he went, slithering across the stone floor, and then the gun went off and I knew that he'd found it again and I stood still and waited; there's nothing like the sound of a bullet whizzing past your ear to make you think twice about diving for a weapon that a trained man is holding. And I knew from the way he had moved up on me, in silence from an empty room, that this man was no amateur. A real pro, I thought, a professional gunman who's been long enough in the business to know which side is up.

Strangely, I wasn't scared. Not of being shot, at least. It seemed quite clear that if he'd wanted that, he wouldn't have tried to put me out of action with a blow over the head, so I stood still and waited; and in the light from the window he was suddenly, lithely on his feet in front of me, reaching out and patting me expertly all over. His face was white and drawn and there was a ghastly cut across his mouth where I'd hit him, and at the sight of the venom there all the fear came back again and I thought for a moment that I'd been foolish to think that a sudden death was so far away.

I said sullenly, "I don't have a gun, I'm not a bloody hood."

He was breathing fast, dangerous with excitement, his pale eyes on fire, and he whispered, "I told you—I told you—"

He was trying to catch his breath, and he suddenly drew back his arm and hit me savagely across the face with the gun, and when I went down, feeling the explosion inside my head, he said savagely, "Don't you *understand*? Can't you *learn*?"

I lay still, looking up at him and waiting, watching the anger on his face; the moonlight back-lit his thin features, and he raised the revolver up in front of his face and waved it and demanded, more calmly now:

"This—is this what you need before you learn? This is—this is the last time, *the last time*; can you understand *that*, at least?"

The blood from his mouth was dripping down onto his shirt, but he paid it no attention. Panting hard, he said:

"I told you—keep out of my way, you're crowding me. As God is my witness, the next time I see you—even *see* you—I'll kill you."

He stared at me for a moment, and then looked quickly at his watch. Somehow it seemed a very strange thing for him to do, as though he were going to be late for his breakfast. And while I was wondering about it, he put the gun under his arm and disappeared. I heard a door open somewhere and when I clambered to my feet and painfully staggered off the way he'd gone, I found open the door that had been locked on the inside when I'd first tried it.

In the silence, I could hear him running, crashing through the undergrowth, making a lot of noise, and then in the distance there was the sound of a car door, a motor starting up, and the sudden roar as a high-powered car took off, fast. I could even hear the splurt of the tires on the gravel road.

I went around the house slowly, feeling the aches all over my body, but there was no sign of Giulio. And when I looked for the bicycles in the bushes, there was only one there—mine.

Well, he'd at least told me he could run when he had to, I cycled slowly back to town, and when I reached the piazza in Trastevere the sun was already up and the square was beginning to come to early life.

One or two passersby looked at me curiously, wondering about the great bloody gash on my cheekbone, and a woman stared and snorted, and said something about drunken hooligans under her breath; but when I went upstairs Karen put her arms around me and kissed me, and Simona quickly broke out the first-aid kit and said unhappily:

"And I went out to get some chicken livers for breakfast, I thought you'd like that."

Karen's face was white and alarmed and she was close to tears for me. I said:

"I had a tussle with friend Nathan. He won, but only just. And I found out nothing, not a goddam thing."

She touched my face with the tips of her fingers and began to cry softly, and I said, lying bravely:

"Don't worry, it's not half as bad as it looks."

I went and took a shower, and when I came back in a bathrobe the kitchen was ripe with the smell of the oil in the skillet.

Doing the practical thing, as always, Simona was cooking those chicken livers.

CHAPTER 5

I slept right through the morning, into the siesta time, and when I awoke the bruises on my face had gone down somewhat, but still hurt like hell.

Simona came in cheerfully with the coffee the moment she heard me stirring, and while I sat on the edge of the bed and sipped it with her, Karen came in and tried to take my mind off the night's events by showing me the developed photographs she'd taken for the Querno story. They were pretty good; as I said, Karen is a highly competent young woman.

And then a message came from Harry. Through the extraordinary vicissitudes of the Italian post office, my query had reached London a lot faster than I expected. But it wasn't Veronica who answered it; that came later. It was a smart-aleck of a man who used to be my boss, an eager, boyish, charming powerhouse named Harry Slewsey.

You should know about Harry.

He is the owner and publisher of a fascinating little newsletter called *The Outspeak*, which I would call a political rag if it weren't so full of good sense and erudite journalism.

Harry, a rare, rich man through the intricate maneuverings of his devious talents, likes to think he steers the course of the world's history-makers, not by telling them what to do but by simply laying out the facts for them to read, and he probably does; he has a wonderful clarity of mind that permits him to expose those facts, picked to the bone and stripped of all their fuzzy trappings. And while he does this, he contrives to profit financially (in order, he says, to make the vast amount of money he needs to keep the paper going) from the same realities he lays out for the world to chew on.

He's neither Right, nor Left, nor even in the middle. He just watches what goes on in the world, peels off the grime or the chromium plate, and says, "Look, fellows, this is what's really behind all the noise." And his paper is most carefully read in the most important places.

Does this sound complicated? It isn't really.

Like the business in the Congo... That one was covered over with both the grime of commercial greed and the chromium plate of phony piety, and it needed a man like Harry to put the whole disgusting mess into its proper focus; and that's just what he did. He wrote, in the very early days of the fighting:

The British-French-Belgian Union Minière, located in Katanga, is one of America's most serious competitors in the world copper market. Although Katanga is the only province of the Congo which has shown any signs of stability and order, it is a fair assumption that one competitor will do its damnedest to drive another out of that market; the opportunity to turn chaos to commercial profit is just too strong. Look, therefore, for a prompt and sustained attack on Katanga, and its reduction to that same state of disorder which pertains in the rest of the Territory. Under the flag of the United Nations, of course, since the prosaic, and ruthless, demands of commerce must not seem to interfere with the pious will for tolerant self-determination...

Well, that was all very fine and true. A lot of people, no doubt, felt a mite uncomfortable under Harry's spotlight, but the voices of reason were drowned out, if you remember, by the hysteria of sophistry. That was a battle which, politically, Harry lost. But at the same time he was doing just what the manipulators were doing—buying and selling copper shares; and, like them, making a killing.

I told him then, very angrily, "You're making a million, Harry, out of rampaging murder."

He had answered harshly, "Point one, I need it to continue telling them what goes on. Point two, I did tell them, they chose to ignore me, and now there are other problems I must clarify if my work is to mean anything at all. If I get bogged down in one crisis—No, Mike, we move on to the next."

"You can move on without me, Harry."

He had raised an amused eyebrow. "You're going to fight the United Nations all alone? You're just one more cry in the darkness. They will destroy Katanga's economy, there will be chaos, and there's nothing you or I can do about it. We told them in time, and the barons were too strong for us, and now—we'd be flogging a dead horse."

I'd said, "How much did you make on your copper deals, Harry?"

And he had answered smoothly, "A very great deal, Mike, and I need it to finance my next project."

Harry used to be an evangelist, so help me, and you could never tell where the sincerity stopped and the cynicism began.

That was the beginning of the little tiff that sent me off in a sulk, telling him I didn't want his lousy money; he had shrugged it off, and the next day he had sent me a bottle of Courvoisier Cognac, 1909, no less, with a little note saying, "No hard feelings, Mike. Come back to work when you feel like it."

I hate people who call me Mike. And Harry knows it.

And the answer to my London query came from Harry.

Someone knocked on the door when I was in the shower, and I called to Karen, "Are you decent? Will you get it?"

But it was Simona who answered the door. An elderly woman gave her a packet addressed to me and went mumbling on her way, and Simona tossed it to me as I came out of the bathroom.

It was addressed to "Michael Benasque, Esq." Not "Mr.," mark you; "Esq." yet. And the package was the size of those huge Italian thousand-lire notes that feel like hunks of wrapping paper. Somehow I just knew it was a large bundle of currency, and that could mean only one thing: Harry was around someplace. "Spread it around like fertilizer," he used to say, "so that it can do some good."

I sighed and opened the package. It contained five hundred of the big bills, which amounted to well over a thousand dollars in

American money, and a cheerful hail-fellow-well-met note as well.

Karen, dressed in a big yellow towel, came over and looked at the cash I threw on the table, and opened her lovely eyes at me and said, "I was worrying about the exchequer, but I see I don't have to."

For a moment I had a vague hope it might be a nice assignment to go to Paris, or Cannes, or Lago di Como, or some other peaceful spot where the world goes slowly by and a man can dream. I should have known better. I read the note to the girls:

"I knew you'd come back sooner or later, Michael"—if he'd said "Mike" I swear I would have torn it up there and then—"and let me say at once how pleased I am. We need men like you, Michael"—damn his blandiloquent soul to hell!—"or more correctly, the paper needs you. That photograph you sent to Veronica is exciting. We don't know the blond boy, but the elderly gentleman, under all that fuzz, might just be someone we've been wondering about, a man who's supposed to be in Bonn and perhaps isn't. If it's the man we think it is, we're on to something really worth our attention. Meet me at the Nerone for dinner tonight. And if I gauge your reactions correctly, you are about to tell me to go to hell; I urge you, Michael, don't. On this one, you can name your own price and I don't care how high it comes."

There was no mention of the money, but that's the way Harry operates; he wanted me to think he'd already forgotten such a trivial matter, which, no doubt, he had. And he was right about my reactions too. There was nothing in the world I wanted more than to tell him where to get off, but— The fertilizer was already working its way into the mire of my brain.

I said to Karen, "Well, at least we get a good meal. It's the most expensive bloody restaurant in Rome."

In spite of all the harsh things I sometimes thought about him, it was good to see Harry again.

He was on his breeziest behavior, a tight-knit, wiry man with an easy manner that didn't try very hard to mask a kind of animal alertness. His suit was silk and immaculate, and the whiteness of his shirt fairly shone; I'd dressed myself up like a dog's dinner too, not wanting to appear anything but prosperous, but Harry made me feel like a down-at-heel bum. He even carried a briefcase and a cane, which at nine in the evening is carrying things a bit far, if you ask me—a malacca cane with a gold knob on it just large enough to look expensive and small enough to be unpretentious, he hoped.

He grabbed my hand and pumped it vigorously, holding on tight with an earnest, jolly-good-fellow grip, and the teeth in his handsome face were sparkling bright as his shirt; you'd think I was a long lost brother come back from the grave.

I said, "Harry, come off it, it's only been a few months."

"Too long, Michael, far too long," he said, and looked at Karen with that evangelist smile. I made the introductions and he held her hands in both of his and said:

"I knew your uncle, the Count of St. Cristoran, the finest Renaissance archivist the world has ever known." I knew he'd done some hasty homework somewhere, but I wondered how he knew about Karen in the first place; and then I stopped wondering, because Harry always knew. He said, "But your charming sister—isn't she dining with us too?"

Karen was already delighted with Harry. She shook her head and said:

"She's cropping photographs; she thought she'd leave it to the two of us. I felt—I felt it was an imposition even my coming, but Michael insisted—"

"I'm glad he did," Harry said emphatically. "Your uncle told me that you would one day grow up to be the loveliest woman in Florence. That was nearly fifteen years ago, my dear, and if he were alive today—"

I wanted to say, "I bet you never even met him," but after all, Harry had elected himself as my boss again, so diplomacy prevailed and I merely put on a fatuous smile and waited.

He snapped his fingers, click, just like that, and the maître d'hôtel came hurrying forward as though people snapped their fingers at his august personage every hour of the day; I wondered if I'd dare try it myself one day. Harry said, in tolerably good Italian (something else I hadn't known about him!):

"The table I ordered, the waiter I ordered and the dinner I

ordered. We are ready."

He had the damnedest way of talking. He said:

"Rome is not exactly the culinary capital of the world, but here, at least, you can eat well."

I said, "It's not bad. I usually have my lunches here."

When we were seated and some wine had been poured to start things rolling, Harry said, "I won't talk shop till we've eaten. I thought we might go for a drive around the city; it's a long time since I was here."

It's the damnedest thing. Harry is an American, from San Francisco, but his origins are as mixed up as mine are, and I swear he was beginning to talk English with the touch of an Italian accent; it was just an inflection, a kind of unconscious mimicry. He still carried the briefcase, which he would never part with for anybody, and the cane as well, which was resting against the table; I wondered if he'd hurt a leg or something, but then he reached for it and handed it to me and said:

"You've always liked the good things, Michael. What do you think of it?"

The malacca was as smooth as silk, with that delicate sheen that can only be brought out by patient weeks and weeks of hand-rubbing; it must have cost him a fortune. I said, meaning it:

"It's a work of art, but I'm glad it isn't mine." For a moment he looked surprised, and I said, "I'd be terrified of losing it; it's much too beautiful to carry."

Then he was beaming again, and he said, throwing a quick glance at Karen:

"Take a look at the knob."

I turned it over carefully, and there, on the underside, in the minutest possible script, so small and finely done that I had to squint to read it, was the name *Michael Benasque.*

I suppose I must have stared; Harry patted me on the shoulder and said, "Just a memento, dear boy, a token of my esteem."

"Well, Harry—"

What can you possibly say to a thing like that? And then, Santa Claus in person, he reached into his briefcase and brought out a pair of slim packages. He handed them to Karen and said, "I took the liberty—since I was a friend of your uncle's—there's one for Simona too."

I could see the pleasure shining on Karen's face. It turned out they were two beautifully worked filigree cigarette cases, one in silver and one in gold, each big enough to hold no more than five cigarettes. She almost squealed with pleasure, and I must admit they were pretty marvelous to look at. I did some quick calculating: even if my letter had reached Veronica in record time, Harry had had just twenty-four hours, and here he was, bearing gifts. I fear the Greeks, especially when they move so fast.

I knew Harry too well to get carried away. But I looked at Karen's happiness and thought, *She's Harry's for life, and all it takes is a thousand-dollar cigarette case*. It was unfair, I know, and I'm not a jealous man. But somehow, I knew I'd never be able to give her things like that; at least, not quite so casually. I'd been broke too often, and however little you care, it leaves a mark.

But Harry was smiling and joking and enjoying himself immensely, and I just didn't want to spoil things by saying:

"All right, you stinker, what have you got up your sleeve for me this time?"

We had a fabulous dinner, with far too much Valpolicella, and when we went outside into the hot Roman air, a *carrozza* was there already waiting for us. The maître d'hôtel himself saw us safely off the premises, and Harry said grandly to the driver:

"Show us your beautiful city."

He'd already been told, the driver; they're a nice bunch of old men, and they're proud of Rome, and once you get within sight of anything more than a hundred years old, out comes the whole history, word for word from the guidebook. But not this one. He just sat up front and drove his horse clop-clop-clop over the cobbled streets in the dark and narrow alleys until we reached the stately, somber trees by the Caracalla, and then Harry said:

"Well, are we ready for a course in recent history?"

I said, "After a dinner like that, I'm ready for anything. Even for whatever chapter of horrors you have up your sleeve. So tell me who Heinrich Muller really is—the man on the ledge."

It wasn't only my knowledge of Harry that made me think there might be some nasty business ahead; I suppose I'm as naive as the next man, but it's pretty obvious that the kind of story which changes history is usually pretty important to a lot of ruthless people. If someone had tried to get, too early, the story of Caesar's invasion of Britain, he'd probably have finished up dead too. Harry smirked at me and said:

"Good."

He leaned back in his seat and when I glanced at the driver, knowing that some of them have a fair command of English, and knowing too that Harry was nuts about security, he looked at me and said smoothly:

"Not to worry, Michael; he's one of my own boys."

The driver looked around at me and raised his cap and grinned and said, "I hear nothing, *signore*, not even the sound of my horse's hoofs."

I sighed. I should have known. Harry patted his overfull stomach (I wished I knew how he kept that waistline!) and said:

"What do you know about Abu Simbel?"

I saw a spark of heightened interest in Karen's eyes. I waited for the color to change, and when it did, by God, I said:

"No more than any schoolboy. The ruined temples, thirty-three hundred years old and about to be inundated by the Aswân Dam, unless they manage to shift them, twenty or thirty million dollars' worth of high-class engineering by the Germans, the Swedes, the French, and the Italians; and I wish them luck."

Karen said mildly, "There'll be so many photographers there, an army of them, and I'd give my soul—"

I said, "If I thought Harry was really interested in anything as innocent as Abu Simbel—but I know him too well."

And Harry knew me too well to show any annoyance. He simply sighed and said:

"Michael, dear boy, you know I'm as free from guile as a baby lamb. But you might like to know that your Heinrich Muller is an engineer from Bonn, en route to Egypt to work at Abu Simbel. He's supposed to be a bit of an antiquarian on the side, and his firm is closely tied in with the German government, apparently, because they put up part of the cash for the three million dollars Bonn is lending Nasser. All very complicated, because it was on the strength of this that Muller's outfit got one of the subsidiary contracts involved. I won't bore you with the details, but some of the more complicated engineering feats involved will bring not only a certain monetary reward, but also an enormous prestige to the people who carry them out—the kind of prestige that can be turned to good political common sense when the whole of Africa is coming into what is blithely called, by the ill-informed, an awakening."

He recited the facts as though he'd learned them by heart; and as though he didn't believe one word of what he was saying and was waiting for me to tell him it was nonsense.

I said, "And so the esteemed German engineer calls himself a Swiss, hides out in the cellar of an abandoned building, is moved around silently in the night by the secret police, and is on occasion the target for a prowling gunman."

Harry said carefully, "I've already made certain detailed inquiries, and I know that he is incognito, and I know that the Italian police—no secret police here, dear boy—are keeping a discreet eye on him, after a hotel thief tried to shoot him. But what's this about an abandoned cellar?"

"Ha! So there's something you don't know."

"I gather it has something to do with that abominable bruise on your face, or otherwise you might have mentioned it before."

"You gather right. In the early hours of this morning, I went to look at Herr Muller's hideout—"

Harry said quickly, "How did you know where that was?"

With as much modesty as I could summon, which wasn't much because it was nice to crow over Harry, I said:

"I also have my sources of information."

"I see."

"And the German engineer on his way to good works in Abu Simbel had been hiding out there but had gone. And while I was idly examining his empty beer bottles, your hotel thief came in and belted me one across the face with his gun, just as a friendly warning to mind my own goddam business. And in the light of that little tidbit of information, perhaps you'd like to re-examine this fairy tale you are spinning so expertly?"

Harry leaned back in the *carrozza* with a smile on his face and listened to the soporific sound of the wheels. He said:

"After all, I did suggest in my note that he might be someone else."

"Who?"

Harry shook his head. "If I tell you what *I* think... It's what *you* think, what you can find out—that's what I want to know. It might, or might not, agree with my own deductions, and if it does, we're right in the middle of a really important piece of news. But I'm not going to head you in what might turn out to be the wrong direction. You know how I operate, Michael; I want you to find your own direction."

"So tell me one thing. There really is a Heinrich Muller, engineer and archaeologist? I suppose you've made some inquiries there too—"

"Yes, there is. His history goes back for two years, no more, that's where it comes to a dead stop. In other words, Herr Muller is a carefully contrived: cover, and that's all he is. The government here insists that he is what he seems to be, and I think that some of them really believe that. But higher up, in the secret circles, his true identity is known and being kept secret. Someone in government is up to something or other that he doesn't want exposed, something that might lead to awkward questions in the wrong places. High-grade diplomacy, dear boy. The fairy tale I have been spinning is the story we're all supposed to believe, and I want you to set me straight; either to confirm what I think—or show me where I'm wrong."

"Then you'd better tell me what it is you think."

"No. I want you to find out for yourself why Herr Muller, the oh-so-eminent and highly respected engineer, should be hiding out in dark cellars in fear of his life. If what you learn confirms what I think—then we're in business. If not—"

He shrugged elegantly. "If not, then you've had a good time and made a lot of money, and I will have to find something else for you to do." There was that smile again. "It's pretty simple, isn't it?"

"Too damn simple. I'm walking blind into something that stinks."

"If I open your eyes to the wrong things—I could so easily be quite wrong."

"I'll bet."

Well, we'd all of us wanted, *needed* to get some work. Here it was being offered on a silver plate. He was right about one thing: so elaborate a cover story as the Abu Simbel nonsense could only mean that some high-powered brains were at work, and that often means high-powered muscle as well. But that's what all the money was about.

Harry raised a polite eyebrow and said, "Well, Michael, what do you think? Are we working together again?"

"Find Herr Muller, find out what he's up to, and who he really is. That's the assignment?"

"That's it precisely."

"It might take a while."

Harry shrugged. "Why should you worry; you're on the payroll as of now. But you know what I want. Facts, not guesswork. And solidly supported facts too."

I said sourly, "All right, I've heard the story before."

Harry insisted, "What's *really* happening. If anyone can find out what Muller is up to, I know you can."

"All right then. I don't like it, but—"

"Good! That's just splendid, Michael!"

I'd never heard him so cheerful. I said, "That shows what a good dinner will do to a man's reasoning. As if you didn't know."

Ignoring the jibe, he said eagerly, "There's a man in the *Giornale d'Italia* here, his name's Gardo Santini, just a junior editor, but his father is a Deputy and he has a brother in the *Questura*, and he's useful if you want any strings pulled in your behalf."

"Then you'd better give him my name first thing in the morning. I'll be around to see him, get the government-interest angle sorted out—"

Harry said smoothly, "I already told him about you, Michael. And he's ready to pull all the strings you want."

"I see. Can I trust him?"

"Implicitly. He's already given me one piece of top- secret information about Muller, and he's looking for more. Muller is leaving Rome by charter plane tomorrow afternoon, for Egypt."

He was already reaching into Pandora's briefcase, and he came out with another bulky envelope and handed it to me. "Your first month's salary, Michael. I think you'll find it sufficient." He added modestly, "I might even say generous. But I have always known that a good man is worth his hire." He also gave me, with a grin, a note from Veronica in London. Like the dear girl herself, it was uncomplicated and to the point:

Tell those two Italian Jezebels of yours that if I come out there I'll scratch their big black eyes out, both of them. But since I want you to be happy, darling, and know how terribly expensive a ménage â trois can be (isn't it?), I've passed your billet-doux on to Harry; he has the most marvelous plans for you.

VERONICA

I shoved it in my pocket and turned to the more important things. The envelope was comfortably heavy. I passed it over to Karen and said, "Into the communal pot, darling; we're back in business."

She smiled, and the pressure on my hand increased. I knew that she was glad I was working again. Not just for the money; because whatever the smart boys say, there's a hell of a lot of dignity in doing your job and doing it well.

And just recently, it seemed I'd been living off her earnings, which is not exactly the most dignified thing in the world.

If only I'd known the price I'd have to pay for my new respectability!

When we finally got back to the apartment that night, I sat up till daylight writing the text for the Querno story, and then I sealed up the photographs and my twelve pages in a manila envelope, addressed it, left it on the dresser for Simona to post, and then climbed wearily into bed beside Karen to sleep, I hoped, till noon.

The decks had been cleared for action.

CHAPTER 6

It seemed that once this caper started I was never to get a decent six hours' sleep.

At ten o'clock I dimly heard the phone ring, and turned over on my stomach, thinking about Karen and knowing she would take care of it, whatever it was. But a moment later I felt her hand on my shoulder, and as I turned sleepily over she leaned down and kissed me and said:

"It's Santini, darling, that man from the *Giornale* Harry spoke about."

Simona was right behind her with the coffee—oh, the service in our ménage! —and I put a towel around my naked waist and wandered over to the phone and said:

"Michael Benasque."

Santini's voice was thin, careful, precise. He said guardedly:

"Signor Harry Slewsey, for whom I have the privilege of working occasionally, gave me your name, Mr. Benasque."

I said, "I know all about that, when can we get together, a few questions I'd like to ask you—"

He said, "First of all, the plane you were told of, the charter flight out of the country?"

"Yes, I know the one you mean."

He said pompously, "In view of what might be described as unforeseen exigencies, both the place and estimated time of departure have been changed, and it is a private plane belonging to a certain government."

"Harry said something about this afternoon—"

"Now it is tonight, but from the landing strip at—" The voice went silent for a moment and then resumed. "Perhaps if we could meet, Mr. Benasque? Fairly soon?"

"Well, for God's sake, that's what I suggested."

"Then, if you could perhaps permit me to come to your apartment? Say, within the hour?"

"OK, I'll put a pair of pants on."

"I beg your pardon?"

"I said I'll be expecting you. You know where it is?"

"Mr. Slewsey told me. In one hour then?"

"You bet."

"Thank you, Mr. Benasque, you are most kind."

The phone went dead, and there was Simona trailing me with the coffee, and I took it from her and stood on the little veranda in my towel, looking down on the street below.

It was crowded and noisy, and an elderly woman was walking slowly across the piazza, carrying a huge basket of flowers; as I watched, she passed the oak tree, Tasso's oak that had brought us here, and she put out a hand and touched it for good luck, then went slowly and sadly on her way.

Karen was suddenly and silently beside me, taking my arm in hers, and she said, "You're not sorry, Michael?"

Surprised, I said, "About what?"

"That I talked you into taking this job with Harry?"

I said, "Take a look at that bundle of money and ask me again."

She squeezed my arm and I kissed her, and then I took a shower and we waited for Santini.

He came precisely on time, just as the clock in the church struck eleven. He was a small, slight man, with a big, aristocratic nose and very sharp, watchful eyes. I had the impression that he could do better than junior editor even on a first-rate paper, but then it occurred to me that with a father in the House, a son in the *Questura*, and another son on the staff of the country's leading newspaper, the family wasn't doing too badly, come election time.

I made the necessary introductions, and for once I saw a man quite unmoved by Karen's or her sister's startling good looks. He said smoothly:

"May I talk here, or should we find somewhere more discreet?"

I said, "No secrets from the girls, let's talk. Who is this Heinrich Muller?"

He started to give me the same Abu Simbel story that Harry had told me, and when I protested, he spread his arms wide and said:

"Of course, nobody believes it, but for want of a better story... What can we believe?"

I said, "Harry had to be a little secretive to make sure I'd go to work in the way he likes, but what's your personal view?"

He said, "My brother is one of the officers who have been ordered to keep an eye out for Herr Muller. Top government priority."

"And yet he stays in a sleazy little dump like the hotel next door."

"The Othello? Yes, some of us wondered about that. My brother—" He thought for a while, and then said slowly, "When Muller first arrived here, someone fired two quick shots at him as he got off the plane. The stewardess standing beside him was hit, though fortunately it was only a flesh wound. The sniper was on the road, in a small car, and he used a high-powered rifle, presumably with a telescopic sight—"

"How long ago, Santini?"

"Ten days, ten days exactly."

"I don't remember reading about it in the papers."

"No, you couldn't have." There was a slight smile on that over-nosed face. "We had a little note from the proper authority, telling us to kill the story. All the newspapers. So—we did."

"And is that why he was put up in the Othello, instead of one of the big hotels?"

"Perhaps. It would be a good reason. My brother merely said that the Othello had been selected by his superiors."

"And was there a police guard on it?"

"Yes, there was. In the kitchen, stuffing himself with *pasta asciutta* at the time of the incident."

"We tried to get Tenente Rospigliosi after that nonsense with the photographs. No one had ever heard of him."

Santini shrugged. "Rospigliosi is a member of the *Questura*, They do not like too much publicity. The nearest thing we have to a secret police is their Political Branch, where my brother is also employed. Rospigliosi is in the same department, but he knows even less than we do."

"And they never found the sniper?"

"No, I'm afraid not. And, of course, you will never get those photographs back, but I assume that you already realized this."

"Uh-huh. What's this about the government plane?"

"Ah, yes. The plane that is to take Herr Muller to Egypt was due out this afternoon from Ciampino Airport. But my brother called me this morning, knowing of my interest in this matter, on Mr. Slewsey's behalf, you understand, and he tells me the plans have been changed, though he does not know why. Now a private plane will take Muller to Egypt from a small airstrip on the road to Ostia."

"And the police will see him off, I suppose?"

Santini smiled thinly. "I thought you might ask that. No, Mr. Benasque, they will not. Apparently Muller's—is 'sponsor' the right word? His sponsor insists on a remarkable degree of secrecy, perhaps because of the second attempt on Muller's life, which you so fortunately inhibited."

"The same gunman, presumably. The sniper?"

"Perhaps. I do not like to jump to conclusions, but it is possible that they know who that man is, as a result of your photographs, and are aware that he may have his friends in the police department."

"Do you believe that?"

Santini said smoothly, "I am a journalist, Mr. Benasque. I do not believe anything that is not patently indisputable. All I know is that as far as the government is concerned, this party is going from Bonn to Abu Simbel, secretly, and is using Rome as a staging area."

"For ten days?"

"Perhaps they were waiting for something."

"Such as?"

"Your guess is as good as mine. Except that I do not make guesses."

"You and Harry too. Raises a problem, doesn't it?"

"I beg your pardon?"

"Since they're not what they seem, they might not even be heading for Cairo, and the only way I could find out where they're really going would be to get aboard the same plane, wouldn't it?"

"Quite impossible."

"That's what I was afraid of. Of course, I could waylay Muller at the airstrip, but that wouldn't do much good, would it?"

"None at all." Santini shrugged, a gesture that meant: *I'm afraid the problem is yours, not mine. I'm merely here to tell you all I know, which isn't much.* Just a shrug, but that's what it meant.

I said, "And the sponsor?"

"A man from the Egyptian Embassy. Unfortunately, I do not know whether the name I have been given is correct, but it seems to be Malafir, if that means anything. He came from Egypt to meet Muller when he arrived in Rome, and will escort him to Cairo. Another Egyptian, incidentally, escorted him here from Bonn and then turned back when Malafir had taken over."

"And I suppose you've no idea what the secrecy's all about? If it stems from the government—"

Santini's impossibly elegant shoulders moved a trifle. He said:

"As in any other government, one party works against the interest of another, of all the others. Behind all the secrecy, there could be the Communists, the neo-Fascists, the Liberals, or any one of our two-and-seventy jarring sects. Muller might be the villain in our story; he could equally well be its hero."

I said, "Well, that's a lot of help. I wish you could tell me how to find out where that plane's going. I can't just hop on a charter and say, 'Follow that aircraft.'"

Santini said with relish, "And it just might be true, mightn't it? The whole Abu Simbel story."

I answered him with the phrase Francesco had used, the one that meant, when it was cleaned up, "in a pig's ear." He looked suitably shocked.

I really had no plan of action, because there just wasn't a feasible move to make. The intriguing Herr Muller was quietly slipping away under my nose and there was no way I could possibly stop him or even find out where he was going.

It was one of those situations in which there really ought to be a Giulio or a Francesco around who would know the right answer at once and part with it for a few thousand lire; but there wasn't, and the bloody man was just—slipping away.

I decided to play it off the cuff.

Because of the previous night's hassle, I wanted to leave Karen behind, but perhaps for the same reason she flatly refused. I said, "Hell, I'm just going to take a run out to the airstrip and see what there is to be seen, that's all."

But she said firmly, "I'm going with you, Michael."

I began to protest some more, but when she started fitting the miniature strobe to the little Tessina camera that was so small it would strap to her wrist like a watch, I knew that there'd be no use in arguing, and so I gave in.

I tried again at dinner, but it was useless, and Simona took her side and said to me imploringly:

"Let her go with you, Michael; you know how much she worries about you. And I do too..."

I said wrathfully, "Good God, do you expect her to hold my hand and see I don't get into trouble again?"

Karen said sweetly, "Something like that, Michael. I'm coming with you." She held up the tiny camera. "Fast film; we might find something to photograph."

Whatever arguments you may have against one lovely woman are quite negated when there are two of them. We arranged for Simona to sit by the phone, in case something turned up, and we rented a car and drove out on the Ostia road soon after dark; I had a vague feeling that it would be better to be there ahead of time.

We drove the small Abarth, a hotted-up Fiat that went like hell, fast along the Via Ostiense, where the tall trees cast their moon-shadows over the road, and we stopped for a drink at a pretty little roadside café that was heavily decorated with climbing blue wisteria and little pots of bright-red flowers. We looked over the map that Santini had given us and located a roundabout route that would bring us to the wrong side, so to speak, of the airstrip, the side away from the road where any traffic would be.

I had no idea of what the hell I was going to do once I got there. "Wait and see," Mr. Asquith had said, and if that was good enough for him it ought to be good enough for me. So we decided to drive the little Abarth right up close to the airstrip, park it under the trees, and then sneak around in the pitch-black night and see if there was anything there that might give birth to an idea.

It's always nice to know that you're ready for anything that might turn up; but sometimes this philosophy turns out to be nothing more than unmitigated gall.

We found the airstrip with no trouble at all. Although it had been more or less abandoned as a going concern, it was still in partial use as a private landing ground. There were three or four small Pipers and other oddments there, and there were lights in the small control tower and in the squat, whitewashed building that served as offices. A big truck was running gas out to an old twin-engine plane that was on the runway, and it seemed that an aircraft was circling overhead too, coming in, perhaps, for a landing.

We parked the car under some trees by the side of the road, and wandered off in the direction of the office building, I was looking, specifically, for a big black Mercedes; and wondering what I could do about it if I found it.

But in the darkness I could find no cars other than an old Bianchi with its hood up as though a mechanic had been working at the motor, and there was a strange silence, in spite of the truck's motor. We were close to the ruins of the old town, and even here I could sense the peculiar melancholy the archaeologists spoke of whenever they talked about Ostia Antica; it was something to do with the soft, sad murmur of the wind in the pines and cypresses, and the whispered sibilance of the words as I spoke them to Karen seemed to accentuate the rustle of the leaves high over our heads.

The moon was dark that night, and the turf under our feet was silent, and the rumble of the distant truck, bright under the lamps, was muted and somehow hostile, as though all the sound in our world came to us only from that sphere of light in the black that was all around us.

I like the night. I have always loved the silence and the darkness, when, if you are alert, you can see and not be seen, when all the life around you goes on unwatched and only the night things move.

Sometimes, in Paris (which is the closest thing I've ever had to a home town), I would sit on a dark bench under dark trees in a dark square while the clocks chimed out the early-morning hours, while lovers and bums and market porters were the only people on the streets; I would sit there, in silence, until the first light of dawn came, and in that time I would learn to know my city better and to love it more, because its life went on while only I was awake to watch it. It sometimes made for an eerie feeling of detachment, as though I had long since died and were watching the progress of life after my death...

It was like this now, only Karen was beside me, holding tight to my arm and trembling slightly in the clutch of the lonely silence; there was not even the cry of an owl to break the mood; just the sibilance of the leaves and the ghosts of an age long dead.

An old ruin of high brick, an aqueduct that had carried swirling water two thousand years ago, was gaunt against the sky, a reminder that once this turf we walked on had teemed with the life of a bustling Roman town.

But now all was deserted. The nobles and the Caesars were dead, and all that was left was a group of white-overalled men clambering over a winged machine that might have come from another planet.

We walked clear around the field that was the airstrip, and a great depression settled over me. I said to Karen, whispering:

"What the hell are we doing here? He'll come and go and there's nothing I can do about it. And even if I could stop him, or even *should*—what then?"

She did not answer, but there was comfort in her closeness.

We came back to where the car was parked, and by some instinct, I suppose, I drove it a few yards deeper into the shrubbery that was hiding it until it was completely concealed; a useless gesture! We sat inside it and lit cigarettes and smoked in silence for a while, and I put my arm around her and felt better when I touched the cup of her breast, and when I looked at my watch it was close to eleven.

We got out then, put our cigarettes out, and walked across the field toward the office building, and I found a patch of intense shadow where none of the lights could reach and we stood there and waited, listening for the night sounds; listening too to the voices of the service mechanics as they came to us clearly across the open space. They were Italians and their voices were oddly detached in the silent, empty darkness.

"The old lady's pregnant again."

"Tighten it up a little, Pepe."

"My finger's bleeding. Kids, nothing but kids all the time, I hang my pants on the bed she's pregnant again."

"Me, I like to knock on the door, find the nearest knock shop you can't go wrong, no kids and it's better too, much better."

"But it costs..."

There was a Roman phrase if ever there was one! *Ma costa*—it costs... The voices broke into giggles.

"They've got a new girl at Anna's, from Bologna."

"Ah, the Bolognese... A bit more on the wrench, Pepe, whatsa matter with you?"

"I'm gonna strip the threads I tighten it anymore. Where's this crate going?"

"Cairo. That's in Egypt."

"I know that, stupid, it'll never get there, the wings'll fall off. You ever go up in one of these things, Gianni?"

"Nope. Only jets."

"It'll never make it, the wings'll fall off."

Someone grunted, and then said, "What time is it?"

A voice answered, "*Porco Dio*, it's eleven, we'd better get out of here."

"All right, all right, is it ready?"

"As ready as it ever will be."

"*Allora—andiamo—*"

As we watched, they gathered up their tools and threw them noisily into the back of the truck, and then the truck door opened and a man climbed out slowly. His gait was vaguely familiar, and I felt Karen's grip on my arm tighten, and then, as the mechanics clambered aboard, he turned toward us and I saw that it was the dark and taciturn man who had been with Tenente Rospigliosi that night when all this had begun, the man Santini had tentatively called Malafir.

He was still not talking; he stood there silent as the other men climbed on the truck, one hand thrust deep into his overcoat pocket and the other holding a small attaché case. One of the men spoke to him. "It is all ready, *signore*." The dark man only nodded. His face was set, and he looked tired.

The truck slowly pulled away, leaving the plane in the circle of light cast by the solitary work light that stood on its tripod close by, and the dark man stood and watched it go, and then undid his attaché case and took out the two parts of a rifle-stock Luger, snapped them together, dropped the magazine into his left hand to check that it was loaded, thrust it back again, pulled up the breech to put a round up the spout, then tucked it under his arm and began to prowl up and down beside the plane. In a moment, he halted by the lamp standard, peered at it for a moment, and then reached up and switched it off.

The field was in darkness again. We waited.

The moon came out and shone briefly, and then disappeared behind the clouds, and there was no noise except that damned eerie rustle of the pines and cypresses. And it must have been half an hour before anything happened.

We heard the car approaching first, driving quite fast along the route we had taken from the Via Ostiense, and then we saw its lights, and as it turned onto the field the lamp by the aircraft came on in answer, and the prowling dark man was standing there, his gun ready to fire now, waiting.

The car slowed down—it was the big Mercedes—as it began to lumber over the rough surface of the field, and then it was on the runway and approaching the aircraft, and when it was close it stopped and three men got out.

One of them was Heinrich Muller. He clutched a briefcase and he moved hesitantly, and at every step he looked around him as though scared of his own shadow, and again I could not help but feel sorry for him. The fear in the very old—it didn't seem right.

The two other men were much younger, more agile, and both were dressed in civilian clothes, though from the way one of them went up to the starboard propeller and patted it affectionately I guessed he was a pilot. They were both very dark, with neat and well-groomed mustaches, not dark like the southern Italians but more swarthy, and I knew that they were probably Egyptian. And then one of them, the man I guessed was the pilot, said in Arabic, "She's old, but they don't make planes like this anymore, there's nothing to beat them."

His Arabic, which I speak quite well as a result of many years' residence in North Africa with the French and British armies, was the hard, guttural Arabic of the Egyptians.

The other young man began piling suitcases on the runway near the aircraft's door, and then—

Suddenly, and without a word of warning, a single shot was fired from the bushes not far behind us. It was so close that I was certain someone was taking a shot at us, and I threw myself on Karen and pushed her down and lay on top of her and got a crick in my neck trying to see what was going on.

The dark man with the Luger was staring out into the black night wondering whether to reach for the lamp and switch it off, and as he made a move in that direction another shot sounded and the bullet smacked neatly into the plane by the side of his head; I saw him wince. I'll say this for him; he knew that the miss was intentional, and he didn't waste time in foolish argument, because the field was suddenly alive with lights and the sound of racing engines. He dropped his gun like a nice sensible fellow and put up his hands.

Four small Italian cars were suddenly hurtling toward the plane, their throttles wide open and their headlights bouncing up and down in all directions until they were on the runway, and two more came out of the darkness behind us and their lights went on as they drove past us and headed for the plane, bathing the scene with their headlights.

Karen was already clambering to her feet and pulling back the sleeve of her arm where the miniature camera was strapped, and I said urgently, "No, don't, they'll see that damned strobe—"

She shook her head and was aiming the camera at the plane, and I heard the shutter click and knew she'd decided there was enough available light from the car's headlights for the ultra-fast film she was using. And then one of the cars swung in our direction and came racing back toward us, and there was no time to duck anymore, and as we began to run the car jerked to a stop beside me and someone leaped out and grabbed me by the lapel of my jacket. I jammed the heel of my hand into his thumb joint and heard his yell. Then I took a wild swing, but missed, at a second man who had almost fallen out of the car and was grabbing at Karen; his arm was around her waist and he was swinging her off the ground. And as she struggled, his hand went roughly across her breast and tore her blouse, and so help me, he said, in heavily accented Italian, "I'm so sorry, *signorina*, please forgive me."

But he had her in a good grip again, holding her tightly by the shoulders, and now there were two men holding my arms, and one of them yelled out something in a language I did not understand, nor, indeed, could remember ever having heard before.

Now, I can speak French, and Italian, and Spanish, and German, and Arabic, and even a little Greek and Turkish, because with a French mother—she was Yvette Rossini, one of France's truly great dancers—and a father who was part American, part Maltese, part Spanish and part anything else you can think of, you really get to realize pretty young that if you can't communicate you may as well stay home in Scranton, Pennsylvania, which is where my father, for his sins, eventually settled. Now, with six or seven languages, besides what I like to think of as a tolerable working knowledge of English, there's nothing more maddening than when some bum comes out with a language you've never heard of, particularly when your arm is twisted up behind your back and almost out of its nesting place.

I saw that Karen was more angry than hurt; it even seemed that the man holding her was holding her gently, and there was a kind of pain on his face at the thought of the unkind thing he was doing. This was the man who had yelled out, and now he called out again, loudly, the hell with shattering the silence, something that sounded like *shlosh-shlosh-shlosh-shiosh*.

As soon as it dawned on me that I was breaking my own arm by struggling, I looked from Karen over to the aircraft, and there everything seemed fine, all completely under control: the two young Egyptians, and Heinrich Muller, and the dark, taciturn man were all standing with their hands up in the light of the headlights which ringed them like tiny bright-eyed monsters.

I could make out the silhouettes of a dozen armed men milling about with an air of urgency and efficiency, and then I was pushed firmly toward the aircraft, and I heard the man who held Karen say apologetically, "Please, I'm sorry, but—"

We stumbled across the field onto the runway, and I said to Karen morosely, "Well, after all, we were hoping rather that something would happen. Are you all right?"

Nobody seemed to mind our speaking. She said, "Yes, I'm all right, did they hurt you?"

"Only my dignity. That bastard tore your dress."

"Yes, I know, it's nothing." The white of her brassiere was almost luminous against the ivory of her skin; it was the kind of skin that seems lighter in the darkness but quite dark in the sun.

We hit the round circle of light, and there was Heinrich Muller staring at us with a kind of hope on his face, and I shook my head at him, meaning, "Don't expect me to do anything this time, brother." And one of the men holding me began his *shlosh-shlosh-shlosh* gibberish again and let me stand there listening and not understanding a goddam thing and it made me furious; I began to realize how the monolinguals must feel when they want to order a steak, rare, with little button mushrooms and fresh asparagus, and finish up instead with a hot dog, just because that revolting culinary affront to man's palate is the same in any language.

I was dimly aware that there were ten or twelve men gathered around us, and they all carried pistols pointed in our direction. The dark man began to speak, in English, but he only got as far as, "Do you realize that this is Italian—" when someone said abruptly, "Keep quiet, please. It might be necessary to kill you even as it is." He fell into a surly, watchful silence. And in spite of the threat, he was quite unafraid. I felt this wasn't the first time his life had been threatened.

It's a funny thing; it's never the man who says he's going to kill you who does.

One of the men was running toward the office building, and a moment or two after he disappeared inside, the lights went on and I could see him vaguely through the big glass window; he seemed to be looking for something, and in a moment he found it and the runway lights went on, lighting up the flare path. And then one of the men pulled a small black box from the car and took out a transistor air-to-ground phone and began talking into it, in his gibberish, very urgently. He kept saying *"B'seder, b'seder,"* and I wondered what the hell that ought to mean and in what language.

There was some quiet whispering behind me, and then I was aware of another sound, a drone that grew to a harsh roar as a small plane came hurtling over our heads, no more than a hundred feet up. He banked tightly, so close to the ground that it seemed his wingtips were digging trenches, and the next minute he had landed and was braking to a stop. I'm no airman, but it was one of those things the layman knows just can't be done, and it's frightening to watch.

Now they started shoving us toward the new plane, all of us, and someone yelled, "Quickly, aboard, all of you, hurry!" The young Egyptian pilot, who was still staring at the plane as though he'd never seen a landing like that in his life and never wanted to see one again, began to protest, but he was lifted bodily off his feet by three of the men and literally thrown aboard. Muller was shaking, and the tears were forming in his eyes, but they shoved him aboard too, and when someone pushed me toward the door I put my foot up against it and shoved back hard and said, "You go to hell!"

It was hardly the right thing to say, and for a moment I worried that someone might lose his temper, and there was a moment of back-and-forth gibberish again, and at last one of them said in English, "There's no *time*—"

Karen, taking her cue from me, was holding back too, making it as difficult for them as possible, and one of the men jumped up onto the plane and through the tiny portholes I saw him hurry to the forward cabin and open the door and another man came back with him and stood in the doorway, looking down on us. The surprise on his face must have outmatched mine, because this was my night for anything to happen...

It was Nathan.

He was dressed in a flying jacket and helmet, and for just a moment he stared down at us and then he said bitterly, "Don't say I didn't warn you." He said something else, in gibberish again, to the others, and then went back without another word.

And there was no more arguing. I was lifted up and flung inside, and I scrambled to my feet in time to see that Karen was following me, more gently, and then Heinrich Muller and the taciturn Malafir, and in a moment Nathan poked his head out and counted us quickly to make sure we were all there, and then the door was slammed shut. Only one of the newcomers, of the opposing forces so to speak, had come aboard with us; but he carried an Italian Beretta submachine gun, and from the look on his face he intended to keep us all in respectful order with it.

And, almost immediately, the plane was racing down the runway again. When we were airborne, I reckoned that the whole job of kidnapping all six of us had taken less than three minutes. It was a tight, efficient operation, and in the old days when I used to play games like this, I would have been very proud of it indeed. But this time, I was a lot older and more sedate, and I really couldn't approve of goings on like this; besides, this time I was one of the victims.

The man with the Beretta gestured, and we sorted ourselves out. I sat next to Karen on one side up front, and with Muller beside us, and the two young Egyptians sat with Malafir on the long bench opposite us. We looked at each other hopelessly and wondered where the hell we were going.

It wasn't the first time I'd wondered. I looked at Karen and made a hopeless gesture. But all she said was:

"I hope Simona doesn't worry too much."

CHAPTER 7

I never had a chance to find out what sort of plane we were traveling in. It was a twin-engine job, with seating accommodation for about sixteen passengers, on two long benches that faced each other across a narrow aisle. The furnishings were Spartan, to say the least, and there was an indefinable military air about it, although in the few brief moments it had been on the ground I'd seen no markings of any sort—not even a number.

We were flying perilously low, it seemed to me, and I supposed that this was to avoid radar; but the knowledge was small comfort when I looked out of the portholes and saw the lights of towns and villages flashing past us at what seemed a couple of feet under our fuselage.

We skimmed over mountains, the aircraft bucking like a mad thing, and once or twice some searchlights went on, rather futilely, I thought. And then there was darkness below us that must have been water, and the time went by in silence and neither of us spoke because there seemed nothing worthwhile saying. I dozed a little, because sleep's a mighty panacea, and when at last daylight came and there was something to see, all that was below us was the bright-red sand, sunrise-colored, of a vast and empty desert.

I wondered what desert it was.

The shadows of the dunes were pretty obviously lying more or less on the west at that time of the day, and I judged we were flying approximately southeast. Karen was asleep with her head on my shoulder, and I looked at her with regret, not knowing what I had dragged her into. Her torn blouse had slipped down over her shoulder, and I pulled the blanket up to cover her a little; it was cold in the aircraft.

It was a funny thing about that blanket. Our guard, a somber young man with wide-awake, passionate eyes, had only moved once from his position at the far end of the aisle, and that had been to reach under the seat and pull out a blanket to throw to me—just when he had seen Karen shudder and wrap her arms tighter around herself. And all that time the barrel of his gun had stayed menacingly pointed in our general direction. He had not talked, or smoked, or apart from that one gesture, even moved.

I had said to him once, "Do you speak English?" and he had looked at me for a moment without a word and then looked away again. When Karen and I talked quietly, he did not try to stop us, but when Muller had looked at me and had said helplessly, "They will kill me," the guard had said abruptly, "No talking, keep quiet."

Karen stirred and opened her eyes and looked at me almost in shock for a moment, and then she recovered and looked out the window at the sand and said, "But—where are we?" She looked beautiful even just coming out of sleep. She fingered her torn blouse and seemed to remember, and again she said, "Simona—she'll be worried."

I said, "She knows we're together."

"Yes."

Just then the door to the cockpit opened and Nathan came out. He was carrying a Thermos bottle, unscrewing the top. He crouched down in front of us, poured some into a cup, and handed it to Karen, then poured some for me too, and then he screwed the top back home and placed the bottle on the seat beside us. He said:

"It's laced with brandy, I hope it's all right."

Trying to be as patient as possible, I said, "And if you would be kind enough to tell me what the hell this is all about, what the bloody hell you're up to?"

He stood up then and held onto the rack over our heads, a tall, gaunt figure with an animal tenseness about him in spite of the tired lines on his face and the red-rimmed eyes. He rubbed a hand over his head in a peculiar gesture, reaching into his scalp like a monkey and said:

"From one point of view, you've a right to know. But from another—I warned you twice, when once should have been ample. And now, Mr. Benasque, *you* are my major problem. You and—Signorina d'Arno. A major problem." He gestured at the others and said, "I know what to do with *them*—but the pair of *you*—"

From behind him, Muller said pathetically, "Perhaps, if I could have just a little of that coffee—please?"

Without turning his head, Nathan said coldly, "No."

I leaned forward and handed the old man my cup, and for a moment I thought Nathan was going to knock it out of my hand, but he checked himself and said:

"There is a great deal you are not aware of that you will have to be told. And what happens to you then—well, I suppose that in the last event that depends on—on someone else. All I can tell you now is that I am very unhappy about your presence here."

I said sarcastically, "We didn't even have our tickets; you should have left us behind."

He said sharply, "That was quite out of the question. You were an interested spectator in something that was not your business and which no one must know about, no one. You've only yourself to blame, whatever happens now." He threw up his hands in a gesture that was furiously, desperately hopeless. "Of all the damned—"

I said, "That was a pretty smooth operation back there."

"And you completely fouled it up."

Remembering what Muller had said, remembering the gun, I said shortly, "And so, you're going to knock us off, all of us, just like that."

His eyes went briefly to Karen and there was a peculiar expression in them that I could not clearly read, and he said quietly, "Perhaps. If it should appear necessary." He looked quickly at Karen again and said, "Mine is a brutal business, I know that, I've lived with it for a long time. Don't think I don't hate it sometimes too."

He turned away sharply and went back into the cabin, and Muller said eagerly:

"You see, he's going to kill all of us, I told you—"

The guard leaned forward and said angrily, "*Schweigen!* Be quiet!"

And then no one spoke until we landed.

Again there was that quick, effortless landing. At one minute we were flying at naught feet above racing red sand that was flat as a pancake below us, and then the next minute we hit with a thump and pulled up in a swirl of dust. Accustomed to the big jet liners, I had never seen a plane land in so small a space. With hardly a pause we taxied into a narrow, smoothed-out space close to a tall sandstone bluff, and then the door was flung open and some khaki-uniformed men were ready to help us down.

The wind was blowing a gale, beating the sand up into gigantic eddies around us, and one of the men called out in German:

"Out, everyone out, over there by the hut."

Some soldiers with their rifles at the port were standing close by, and I said to Karen as I turned to help her:

"Thank God for the uniforms; at least, it's an army of some sort, wherever it is... They don't look a bit like Egyptians to me."

One of the men, in a colonel's uniform that closely resembled the British, stared at me in surprise and then looked even more surprised when he saw Karen. He said something angrily to Nathan as he descended from the cabin, and Nathan took his arm and drew him to one side; while we stood there waiting, they talked quietly in whispers, still in that goddam gobbledygook, and there were some angry gesticulations, and then the officer came over and saluted politely to Karen and said:

"Allow me to present myself. I am Colonel Vicek. Mr. Benasque and—Miss d'Arno?"

I nodded. The colonel gestured at a long hut that stood under the lee of the bluff and said:

"This way, please."

He shepherded us into a room that looked like a mess hall, made of prefabricated asbestos sheets, and politely pulled out chairs for us to sit in. He stood looking at us for a moment, wondering and worrying. I could see that our unexpected presence had shaken him considerably, and he didn't like it a bit. He pulled at his ear, and then, as if just remembering his manners, offered us both cigarettes. I saw no reason to be over courteous with him.

I said, "If you'd tell me at least where the hell we are?"

The colonel nodded. "Yes, of course. You are in Israel, Mr. Benasque, in the Negev. On behalf of my government, let me say at once that we deeply regret this unfortunate occurrence, and we will make every effort toward your comfort until"—there was the slightest pause— "until we can send you back to Italy."

I said, "You *are* going to send us back?"

This time there was no hesitation. "Yes, of course, as soon as possible."

I said, "This doesn't look to me much like a military post, in spite of your soldiers."

Outside, through the blinding dust, I had seen half a dozen trucks, mostly four-wheeled vehicles of an army type; but none of them carried any insignia at all. There were no white-painted barracks, no divisional signs, not even a flag; nothing to show precisely what this place was apart from a dozen uniformed soldiers; I began to wonder if they really were soldiers.

I said, "The language you were talking—I suppose it was Hebrew?"

"Yes, it was." His English was impeccable, with no trace of an accent, and he was courteous, apologetic—and a little reserved. Most of all, he was—visibly upset. It's always the reservations that worry me, because behind them there are always reasons, and I don't like things I don't understand. Perhaps that's an arrogance, because there's a hell of a lot going on around us that is quite beyond our comprehension, and while I was wondering about this, the colonel said carefully:

"I shall have to ask you both to stay here, in this building, until the proper arrangements can be made. We are a long way from anywhere here, Mr. Benasque, surrounded by particularly uninviting desert. We are surrounded by sand dunes, and if you were to wander around outside you might easily get lost, and we just don't have the men to search for you. The only water, the only food, the only—safety, within several thousand square miles is right here, at this spot. So if you would consent to stay here where we know you are all right..."

In a nice, friendly way, he was saying, "You're my prisoners and you can't escape."

I nodded. He looked at the bruise on my face and at Karen's

torn blouse and said anxiously, "I was told that there had been—a scuffle at the airstrip in Rome. I feel I should apologize. If there's anything I can do...we have no facilities here for women, but perhaps I could find a shirt or something." He seemed more worried about that damned dress than anything else. "And I'll have some breakfast sent in to you at once." He got up to leave, and when he reached the door he said, "I suppose you do not happen to be carrying your passports?"

"No. We hadn't really planned any long trips just now."

"No, I suppose not." He indicated a door on the other side of the room and said, "You will find some bathroom accommodation over there. I will reserve one of the rooms for Miss d'Arno."

When he had gone, we took stock of our surroundings. We were in a prefab hut, not too inelegant, with interior walls painted in the light shade of blue they use in the Middle East to discourage flies. The windows were screened but had no glass in them, and on one side they were covered with army blankets—to keep out the dust, I imagined. The furnishings were Spartan, though adequately comfortable—some Windsor chairs, a few card tables, a long dresser on which there were glasses and some assorted magazines in German, French and Hebrew, and an electric fan that was not working on a big tripod in a corner of the room.

I went to the door and tried it, and was surprised, somehow, to find that it had not been locked, but there was nothing much outside to be seen except a huge expanse of brilliant desert, reaching right to the horizon, broken here and there by gaunt pinnacles of red rock and clusters of giant boulders. It was quite spectacular, and under other circumstances I would have rather enjoyed it. I'm susceptible to beautiful things, whether they be landscapes or women or ancient Greek statues. But I wasn't in the mood to appreciate it at all, and I wondered what the hell was going to happen next.

There was no sign of Muller and the others, but the aircraft we had come in was being refueled. I wondered where Nathan had gone. I closed the door again to shut out the dust that was blowing in, and Karen said, "Anything?"

"No shortage of sand is all."

I looked for any trace of anxiousness on her face, but there was none. She seemed to be taking the contretemps very well, and not wanting to worry her, I let it rest, not saying a word about my suspicions. But she seemed to read my thoughts. She said, "There's something worrying you, Michael."

"Of course. We've been kidnapped, just like that; of course I'm worried, I don't like it a bit."

"But they're going to send us back—"

"Sure." I didn't say, "After all this trouble, it doesn't seem very likely," but again she knew what I was thinking. She said slowly, puzzled more than anxious:

"This is an Israeli Army post, isn't it?"

"I think so. Can't think what else it can be."

"Then there's nothing to worry about. Nathan made a mistake in picking us up, and the colonel is going to rectify it. That's more or less what he intimated, isn't it?"

"Yep. I could do with some breakfast."

The entry was right on cue. The inner door opened and a cheerful young soldier came in with a tray full of dishes and a khaki shirt under his arm, and he said cheerfully, "Good morning! Breakfast in ten minutes." He handed the shirt to Karen and jerked his head back to the door. He said, "The one marked 'Ladies.' Not very much like the Strand Palace, but I think you'll be able to manage. I put some clean towels there."

He began to set out the dishes and Karen sighed and went to the improvised ladies' room. I said to the young soldier:

"You're an Israeli?"

"Yes, sir."

"And this is an Army post?"

"Yes."

"You speak pretty good English."

He began to laugh again. He said, "Of course, most of us do. A little easier for me, perhaps; I was born in London and spent the first fifteen years of my life there. Came out here six years ago."

"And you like it?"

There was a note of emphasis in his voice. "The only mistake I made was in not coming here to get born. It's the only place for a Jew to be."

"The dreariest piece of desert I ever saw, and I've seen some beauties."

He said, "Don't you believe it, sir. You get to know it, you'll find it's the most exciting place in the world."

"I never will get to know it like that. And you won't mind if I put that down to an excess of nationalist zeal, will you?"

He grinned cheerfully. "Of course, it's not much like Green Park, is it?"

Just then the sound of running water came through the thin walls from the bathroom, and the soldier grinned and said:

"You hear that? Two years ago the nearest water was forty miles away, but there was an old aqueduct, buried under the sand. We cleaned it out, and we found the source, and we reinforced the dam. Ask me about the dam."

"All right, what about the dam?"

Polishing the forks on a cloth, he said happily, "Precisely eighteen hundred and sixty years ago the Roman Emperor Trajan demolished the dam, which had been built by my ancestors the Nabataeans, and precisely two years ago I helped to rebuild it. The aqueduct had already been built by the peaceful king—"

"Solomon?"

"Solomon, the man of peace. Yes, he built it when he was sending the Tyrian ships to the land of Ophir, and it was built so well it survived not only the Roman armies, but the desert sand and wind as well, for more than two thousand years." He said with satisfaction, "I helped to rebuild that too, to complete a work that had been started by my people when in Britain the men were savages who still lapped up water like animals. The time passes, but the work of my people continues."

He looked at me and grinned, a cheerful young expatriate pleased with his way of life. "Yes, I like it. One day this dreary desert will be covered with fields and cities, just like it was in Solomon's time." He pointed to the west and said, "Water, always water, and out there somewhere, not far from here, Ishmael the son of Abraham must have discovered the miraculous well in the desert that saved his life and that of the Egyptian concubine Hagar. If he had not found that water, none of my people would have been born; and if I had not helped to rebuild those waterworks, perhaps none of my people would have survived. You see? There is a God in this desert who always comes to our rescue in times of peril."

I said, "What's the peril now?"

For a moment the cheerful grin left his face and he looked at me sharply. Then he smiled again and said lightly:

"The peril? I'd say the breakfast, sir. Tea and biscuits and goat's cheese; not much like bacon and eggs, is it? But we're all terribly kosher here, and I'm afraid that will have to include you."

"Well, it won't be for long."

The smile did not leave his face, but he said nothing.

Karen came back wearing her oversize shirt, rolling up the sleeves and looking somehow quite different in it. She'd redone all her makeup, and her skin was soft and delicate, and then the soldier went out and brought in the biscuits and cheese and the tea made with the water that Solomon had arranged to be brought to us. I was surprised how hungry I was, and we both ate ravenously.

The wind had died down by the time we finished, and I said, "Let's go for a stroll."

Karen, not looking a bit as though she'd been awake most of the night, said, "You think they'll let us?"

"Only one way to find out, isn't there?"

We went outside into the hot sun, already beating fiercely on the red sand, and I took off my jacket and tie and rolled up my sleeves too, and we wandered off toward the high, copper-colored bluff that stood out sharply etched against the bright blue of the sky; I had not seen a sky as blue as that for a long time, not since the old days in the Sahara.

It's strange how the desert air, once the sandstorms have gone, regains its miraculous clarity, devoid of any mist or fume to take away the cutting edge of vision.

Up on the top of the peak there was a small sandbagged enclosure with a machine gun mounted on it, and as we watched a soldier stood up, silhouetted against the sky, and a Jeep was laboriously making its way up there along a narrow trail, its nose incredibly in the air. It looked as though it was standing on its tail, but it still kept moving, inching its way up while little dry rivulets of granite came dropping down the steep slope from under its wheels.

We went through a narrow chasm, a hundred yards or so from the hut, and the shadows on the eastern side were a dark purple, quite unreal, and as we came out of the confining gap we stopped and looked out at the huge expanse of rock-scarred desert. I heard Karen catch her breath. She said:

"It's beautiful, Michael."

The harsh redness that had been there when we landed had gone, and now the sand was a glorious golden yellow, and in the distance there were dark-blue shadows where the dunes, crescent-shaped, overlaid their moon points on the harder, orange-colored stone. Huge broken bluffs stood up sharply, some of them needle-pointed, on the distant horizon, and half a mile or so away I could see some broken remnants of small round buildings that looked like Stone Age huts. There was a sound behind us, and Colonel Vicek was there.

He said, "The old Nitsanah of the Bible, where our archaeologists have found some most excellently fashioned flint implements. Shards of crude pottery, and some well-polished stone bowls as well; some of the oldest Neolithic remnants in the world."

I said politely, "And is that what you do here, dig up the past?" He smiled. "Sometimes. Unhappily, it's dangerously near the Egyptian border."

I looked at the machine gun on the bluff. "Is that what the guns are for?"

"Oh, yes, indeed. Border raids, you know. They sent two armored cars over last week to show us how strong they are, but they didn't get back, so I suppose one could say they really failed to make their point."

"Is that what you came to tell us, Colonel? Or are we straying out of bounds?"

"No, no, of course not. As long as you remember that your only protection is from our guns."

"Protection? Against what?"

He pointed with his cane to the edge of the bluff where the Jeep had gone and said, "Why don't we sit over there in the shade and have a little talk?"

"I think it's about time we did."

We walked over to the base of the sheer sandstone cliff that was like a solid wall of red marble, streaked with green and seeming to shine, and the colonel ran his hand over the astonishingly smooth surface of it, feeling it delicately, as though admiring the texture of it. He said:

"Have you ever seen this before?"

"The marbling, you mean? No, I haven't."

"The whole of this rock," he said, "is porous, a finely honeycombed mass of hard sandstone, heavily impregnated with mineral salts."

"Copper?"

He nodded. "It must have been something like this that guided the Nabataeans and showed them where to dig for copper, yes. But, over the centuries, the occasional rain, the flash floods that usually seep away into the sand and are wasted, have filled up the honeycomb. The water trickles out at the sides until the minerals close up the tiny holes with a hard and brittle deposit, first here, then there, till at last the whole rock is a gigantic sponge, with the water still sealed inside it. And all you have to do is break off the deposit. Watch this." He dug his cane into the surface, using it like a pick for a few moments, and soon a flake of brittle rock, looking something like green mica, was chipped off; and from the tiny cavity a gentle trickle of water began to flow down the side of the rock. The colonel held his cupped hand under it, and when his palm was full he tasted it and said:

"The sour taste of gypsum, but quite drinkable. Not too bad at all, really, if you're thirsty. Try it."

The trickle was still coming, and while Karen watched with amusement I caught some in my hand and gave it to her to drink, and the colonel smiled and said:

"When Moses did that, they called it a miracle. To a people dying of thirst, of course, it was, though today we know better. The growth of knowledge, from faith to the logic of understanding..."

It brought back a lot of schoolboy memories. I said, "The White Hand of Moses on the Bough puts out..."

The colonel smiled. It seemed as though some, but not all, of the worry had gone from him. He said:

"You have to know where the honeycombed rock is, but you can usually tell if you know what to look for. The Bedouin can always find it, even today, and after all, that's exactly what Moses was."

Well, that was mighty interesting, but there was something else I badly wanted to know. I said:

"Let's forget our ancient history for a moment; it's beginning to come out of my ears. Tell me who Heinrich Muller is."

"That's what I brought you here for. To tell you that and to help me decide what's to be done with you."

"I can tell you that right now. Put us on that plane and send us back to Rome. Now."

He sighed. "The simple solution. But I'm afraid it won't do, Mr. Benasque." The agitation was coming back, ominously.

I said, "There was talk on the plane that someone was going to get killed."

He looked uncomfortable, but he said, "I am a soldier, Mr. Benasque. I will be perfectly frank with you because I lack the—the devious intelligence that my present work might force upon me."

"Nathan suggested he was a soldier too, something like that, but it didn't show very much."

"No, I suppose not. He is—a different kind of soldier. But even he—" He seemed confused, hesitant, embarrassed. He said slowly, "Israel is engaged in a vicious and undeclared war, Mr. Benasque, and in wartime many people are hurt who should not be. Sometimes death, which is part of a soldier's destiny, unavoidably embraces others as well. Sometimes the question arises: Are a thousand lives worth the price of one? and when that question has to be answered there can be no hesitation even from so simple a man as myself. I must tell you that had you been alone—" He spread his arms wide in a helpless gesture, and went on, "I do not know. I only know that if you had been alone, some of the arguments concerning you would not have been entertained. But an innocent young girl... Am I wrong in thinking that a man engaged in a dangerous occupation ought to expect danger? But that—"

Again that helpless gesture. He just didn't know how to go on. He said at last, speaking very clearly, as though he would not try to hide his purport in looseness of speech:

"I must tell you frankly. You saw Nathan doing something— you saw us commit a gross breach of international law, the kind of breach that is committed quite frequently but which must, at any cost, be kept secret. At *any* cost, Mr. Benasque, however—terrible that cost might be. I have discussed your case with Nathan, and he has said, albeit with reluctance, that you must both be killed to prevent disclosure of what we have done."

The skin was beginning to tingle at the back of my neck, I said harshly:

"You're talking about murder, Colonel."

"Yes, I know. But it takes a fine intelligence to justify the killing that takes place in war and to condemn it outside that vicious area. War is not a circle on the ground that you can step into, and out again, and kill inside but not outside it, and still maintain the morality that our God gave to us."

I said, "Good God, but this is not my war! I know about your troubles with the Egyptians, but—" There was only a stubborn silence. I said desperately, trying to rationalize, "It would help if you told us just who this goddamned old man Muller is."

"He is an enemy," the colonel said, "a man whom we must, at whatever cost to us or to anyone else, prevent from reaching his objective. You saw what we did, we kidnapped him, and because you were a witness—we brought you here, hoping that—" He sighed. "I do not know what we were hoping for. Nathan did the only thing possible under the circumstances. It was a flagrant breach of international law, and we must do everything we can to—to hide it. To an outsider, it may well be impossible to justify, but I can at least try to explain it. I think we—owe you that. You may recall that a few years ago we had a considerable difficulty with the Argentine government, one which we are anxious not to repeat with the Italians. Or with anyone else, for that matter."

He hesitated, and then said firmly, "In this dark world of espionage and sabotage, of clandestine killing and—and terror, we must not get caught. This specialized world is part of our existence whether we like it or not, and, frankly, I do not like it. But I am a soldier, and I must admit its necessity. I'm afraid your inquisitive nose has led you into our corner of that world. It is a dark and dangerous corner. I will not insult your intelligence by letting you think that it is otherwise."

He began to pace up and down, groping for the right words, determined not to pull his punches. He said, "There was a time when, as a soldier, I could pretend that men like Nathan did not exist; or at least, that they did not exist in the—the idealistic state I serve. But I have been posted here in charge of the men who keep watch on this vitally important post—"

"An Army post with no divisional signs, no markings, not even a flag."

He hated every minute of it. He said, "An interrogation center, where the military control is protective, and nothing more. Its essential function is the concern of—another department, a department which deals with our enemies, like the man you saw being abducted."

"If you tell me that Heinrich Muller is Martin Bormann, I just won't believe you."

"No, not Martin Bormann, though one day, no doubt, we will find him too. Muller is Dr. Walter Martin. Perhaps you've heard of him?"

I said politely, "No, I haven't. Do tell."

The colonel gestured at a pile of boulders at the foot of the cliff. He pulled out a handkerchief and dusted one of the rocks for Karen, and I tried hard not to look at her white, tight-lipped face.

He said, "Why don't we all sit down? And then—I will."

CHAPTER 8

"Dr. Walter Martin," the colonel repeated, "and the man who was with him during the—" He hesitated, and I prompted him.

"During the kidnapping."

"Yes, exactly. The man who was with him is Aboud Malafir of the Egyptian Political Police, lately attached to the Special Military Projects Department of the Army. The other two men are pilots of the Egyptian Air Force who have been receiving training in Bonn—in heavy bombers primarily, although very concentrated efforts were made to have them attached also to the NATO Missile Development Laboratory. Unsuccessful efforts, I am happy to say. Dr. Martin himself, the real object of our efforts, is one of Germany's foremost missile engineers, at present on the payroll of General Nasser. He has been working nearly a year in Factory Number 333 in Heliopolis, a factory that is heavily guarded by former Nazi SS troopers, if you please, and has proved to our intelligence men to be quite impenetrable.

"Dr. Martin's career is an interesting one. He was at Peenemunde, where he worked on the V-2 rockets that did so much damage in London, and then the Russians nearly got him, but he was enticed away in the nick of time by the Americans, together with a few other rocket specialists who have since become, may I suggest, the subject of a rather hysterical hero worship in the United States. The Americans wouldn't give him quite the freedom of movement that he seemed to want, and one day he just disappeared; but he turned up a little later in France, where he worked for a while on the French Veronique rocket. For some reason or other, probably his outspoken impenitence concerning his role in the war, he fell into disgrace there and was shipped back to Germany, and that is when we began to take a more serious interest in him. He was receiving a good number of Egyptian visitors, and one day he just disappeared again and turned up in Cairo.

"There are four hundred and fifty German scientists and technicians in Egypt, Mr. Benasque, most of them working on missiles. One of them, a man named Otto Joklik, was on trial in Switzerland last June, and he stated publicly that President Nasser's intention was, and I quote, 'the de facto extermination of the Jews.' Because this had become so obvious to him, Joklik gave up his work there and attempted to persuade some of his fellow scientists to do the same. He went so far as to threaten them with physical violence, which is what his trial was about, and although we must admire this belated twinge of conscience, we must also worry about the other four hundred and forty-nine, who were not, apparently, so affected."

It was an old story. The details of Joklik's trial had been published in all the European papers for anyone to read. And so had a lot of other interesting details.

I said, "And I also read that one of the secretaries those scientists employed had half her face blown off when she opened a parcel that was sent to her boss."

The colonel nodded gravely. "As distasteful to me as it is to you." He stared unhappily at the sand under his feet and said, "I understand the package was intended for a certain Wolfgang Pilz, another of the deadly brethren. The academic question again, Mr. Benasque: Is the life of one man worth the lives of a thousand others? Of course it is. The rockets are meant to be armed—and the news has even been made public—with atomic, biological and chemical warheads, intended for the destruction of Israel."

I had read the trial report, and he was quoting it accurately. I said:

"And the attack on—What was his name? Professor Kleinwaechter? Was that your friends too? I suppose it was."

The colonel shrugged. "Our people tried to kill him too, but they failed. Perhaps next time... Our worst enemies among those scientists can be reduced to four men—Goercke, Pilz, Kleinwaechter and Martin—and of these four, the first three have been working on the ABC missiles—"

"ABC?"

He said, "Atomic, biological, chemical. So far, the work of these German gentlemen has produced nothing more powerful than President Nasser's Zafir missile, with a range of just over two hundred miles, and the Kahir, whose range is nearly twice as long. But Nasser has boasted publicly that these rockets will reach every inch of Israeli soil with no trouble at all. And perhaps you remember the damage the V-1 and V-2 rockets did to London, over twenty years ago and before the destructive capacity of German genius had reached the proportions that modern science has given it."

I had to remind him again that these things were known outside Israel as well, though perhaps no one had ever bothered to do very much about it. As Harry would say, the Arabs control a lot of the world's oil, so let's not be beastly to them, even if they are threatening genocide.

I said, "I'm a journalist, Colonel; I know this background; it's been there for a long time, ever since nineteen fifty-eight. And no one has ever doubted that the Israeli Army can whip the hide off the Egyptians any time they choose. They did it once and they can do it again; any thinking man knows that."

It seemed it was a good thing to say, even if it happened to be true. The colonel said:

"Yes, we can. Just as long as it remains a conflict on the ground—and no longer. Israel is a tiny country, at no place more than seventy miles across and only twelve miles at its narrowest. Twelve miles across, Mr. Benasque, less than a good-size city! We have only eight thousand square miles, and more than half of that is the barely populated Negev you see all around us. If the missiles begin to fall... Nine-tenths of our population is crowded into a narrow corridor, averaging some twenty miles wide, and only a hundred miles long. If they start firing missiles at us... Well, half of them would fall in Jordan or the Mediterranean, no doubt, but if only a small percentage get home... You see what I mean by one man's life against a thousand?"

"Yes, I do. And there's only one answer to the academic question, I know that. But I still want to know when we're leaving for

Rome."

Ignoring the question, the colonel said, frowning, "So far, perhaps we've only been playing at stopping them, and perhaps they'll only be playing with their missiles too. After all, their vaunted jet fighters were built in Spain and are flown mostly by Spanish pilots, but now—"

The journalist urge was coming to the forefront again, in spite of the fear. I said, "Now?"

"Now Dr. Walter Martin. He has his own research laboratory in Germany, and his specialty is—the gamma ray and cobalt." I didn't like the sound of that one. I said, "Cobalt is supposed to do something for cancer. Among other things."

"It's the other things that worry us. It's the base for the radiation bomb."

"Which is still in the theoretical stage."

The colonel said impatiently, "So, before Peenemunde, was the jet-propelled missile! Yet you must know that it was your own intelligence men who killed, in Peenemunde, the men who were working on them! And if they had not done that, the V-2 rocket would have come nearly two years earlier, and London would have been wiped off the face of the map! It's in the theoretical stage that we must begin to worry. If we wait for the embryo to grow—we'll just be too late."

"Well, no one's going to deny that."

"And this is why we will take any steps, any steps at all, that might stop the chosen four of Nasser's top Germans. And of those four, none is more deadly than Martin. Pilz is the propulsion expert, Goercke is the guidance specialist, and between them they built Nasser's two rockets in a little under eighteen months. They haven't got a reactor yet for a nuclear warhead, but if Martin's cobalt plans lead anywhere... How good is your imagination, Mr. Benasque?"

I said, "Hiroshima a hundred times over."

"In an area the size of Connecticut."

Not believing a word of it, I said, "The United Nations might just step in if they ever got as far as that. The word itself—'cobalt bomb'—it's enough to scare the pants off anyone, even those nearsighted gentlemen."

"Oh, yes, I'm sure they would," he said sarcastically, "once the damage had been done. It is our job to see that the damage is not done."

"And that means cutting Martin's throat?"

"It means—stopping him. And as many of the others as we can get to."

"And stopping any—interested spectator as well. You've made a good job of justifying Martin's murder, all tight; I'll go along with it because I know that you're right, much as I disapprove of murder." I tried to keep the anger from my voice and said, "Now go ahead and justify killing us."

"He looked at Karen as though determined not to hide his eyes from her, and then he stared out into the desert and waited a long time before speaking. He said at last:

"I can't. I have put the matter in someone else's hands. Whatever he says—"

I never saw a man so desperately miserable.

I said, "There's another way out, surely, without recourse to savagery! You people are mighty friendly with Germany these days; they're even training your Army, aren't they?" I saw him wince. "So why don't you bring pressure on the German government?"

He said, "Oh, we do that all the time. Their official view is that it is unconstitutional for them to keep their citizens from working where they choose." He said bitterly, "The Germans paid Israel eight hundred and twenty million dollars compensation, remember? For the lives of the six million Jews they slaughtered. So now they owe us nothing, not even their consciences." He looked at me angrily and said, "At a hundred and thirty-six dollars and sixty cents a head, they bought back their right to prove once more their genius for carnage."

I could not help thinking of the anxiety I had felt on behalf of what I had thought of as a poor, frightened old man. I could not refute the colonel's arguments, even if I wanted to; I knew he was so damned right.

I looked at Karen and saw that she was looking out at the horizon, her eyes dulled and glassy, her thoughts a long way away. In the silence, she said suddenly:

"There is no yardstick for tragedy. My own was a much

smaller one. But it hurt just as much."

The colonel looked at me and raised his eyebrows, and I said roughly:

"No one's going to stand up and defend the German talent for war; it's part of their nature. Go back into your precious history as long as you like, the sharpest sword has always been Germanic and probably always will be, even if it takes the Marshall Plan to keep it sharp."

The colonel looked at Karen again and said, "Sometimes I despair of finding anyone who hasn't suffered at their hands. And now a whole new generation is growing up and being taught to forget."

I said, "I'm damn sure none of my kids ever will, if I ever have any. What are you going to do with Muller? Or Martin?"

The colonel said briefly, "If you can face the question, I can face the answer. We will kill him, Mr. Benasque. There is nothing else we can do."

"Eichmann all over again. Only this time he hasn't broken any laws. So this time it's in secret."

"Yes, it has to be. In Eichmann's case, the outcry was on pure grounds of reason, of logic, of law. This time we do not even have that justification. Eichmann was charged with murdering Jews, as though this were somehow worse than murdering Christians, or Frenchmen, or redheaded men, or men with false teeth. And shall we now charge Martin with *plotting* to murder Jews? I'm afraid we wouldn't have much of a case. That is why some of us, in that dark corner of the world I spoke of, must work in secret, must do the immoral things we *must* do in the name of a greater peace—without the knowledge of the rest of the world."

I almost guessed the next thing he was going to say. He looked me squarely in the eye and said:

"Can you suggest any other way we can assure your silence, Mr. Benasque?"

Now, I'm not the bravest man in the world, and that damned tingle at the back of my neck was there again. But the colonel was so damned polite and reasonable and cards-on-the-table that it was hard not to agree with his arguments. I said:

"Academically speaking, if I gave you my word—and I'm not

doing that yet, by any means—would you take it?"

He hesitated. "Personally, yes, I would. Unfortunately, it is not entirely up to me. I have to obey orders like any other soldier." He said quietly, "And I will obey them whatever they are."

"At least you're frank about it."

"I will not attempt to deceive you, Mr. Benasque."

"And Miss d'Arno?"

"As I said before, a potent argument in your favor. Though if we were to rationalize, why should it be harder to kill an innocent woman than an innocent man? Is that a comment on the stupidity of our culture? I suppose it is."

He looked at her again, searching for any trace of fear; there was none. He said, "'Academically' was the term you chose. Academically, would you both give your word? And could we really rely on it? I am well aware that you are both journalists, and a promise given—under duress like this—it could hardly be binding."

It was an argument for which there wasn't really an answer. I said unhappily, "You'd be surprised what a man will do when his life is at stake."

"And also what he will do when the danger is past."

"Yes, I suppose that's true too. Meanwhile—are we under arrest?"

The colonel sighed. "I would advise you to stay within sight of the barracks. With us you have at least a chance. Out in the desert you would have none at all. For nearly five thousand years the desert has been the enemy of my people, and we are only just beginning to tame it."

He sort of half-saluted, and went off, and I said to Karen, "I can't believe a man can think he is so right when he's so wrong."

Surprising me, she said calmly, "We've put ourselves on the wrong side, Michael, just by being found with Martin. But we can promise not to talk about what we've seen."

"Right. But can we convince them? As he said, under duress, they might think a promise wasn't worth a goddam thing."

She looked at me curiously and said, "You're still sorry for that Martin man."

"No, I'm not. I think what they're doing is right, and I can't justify it any more than the colonel can. But I know one thing. They won't believe we can keep quiet about this. Hell, I don't even believe it myself. And there's only one answer to that."

She saw me looking out at the desert and said, "We could never cross it, Michael, never, even if they let us get out of their sight."

"I've crossed impassable deserts before."

"And if we failed, if they caught us—our last hope would be gone. They just wouldn't argue anymore."

"You've got a point there. But, dammit, these are civilized people, an army; what the hell are we afraid of?"

She said somberly, "We're in that dark corner he spoke of, and that's not a very civilized place in any language."

I couldn't help thinking of a woman I met, twenty years ago when I was with the Maquis in France. I'd holed up for the night in a tiny cottage in the Ardennes, with half the German Army looking for me, and one night, out of the blue, a crew-cut man dressed as a *Feldwebel* of the SS dropped in by parachute, a cheerful ruddy-cheeked man who chewed gum incessantly and said—and I'll remember his words as long as I live—"Take it easy, folks, I'm an American, OSS, the pilot kind of lost his way a bit, they told me the peasants around here were pretty helpful..." He was such a caricature of an American that I couldn't possibly take him at face value. And the woman who was hiding me, a charming, elderly housewife who had that quiet, unpretentious courage that was born of tragedy, said, "If he is OSS, they would have told us he was coming."

I cross-examined him for half an hour and couldn't shake his story; he *appeared* not to speak very good German, and to know America well, but the *Sicherheitsdienst* weren't all fools, and we'd lost our radio in the last fight and couldn't check... Anyway, when the Germans finally burst into the cottage, we fought them off and ran, and in the brief, chaotic shooting the parachutist was suddenly dead. And the charming, elderly, cultivated woman looked at me across the rubble of the bombed-out bridge we were hiding under and said, her voice hollow with pain:

"I shot him myself; I couldn't let you take the risk..."

She was an elderly, kindhearted, cultivated woman, far less inured to violence than the colonel, and yet she had shot him because she believed it was necessary...

The memory lived with me for a long time, because I just didn't know who he was; until I found out. It took me two weeks, but finally I got a radio message from Colonel Matley: "HIS NAME IS STANNEMAN, PFC, AND WE'VE LOST CONTACT WITH HIM. WHERE IS HE?"

Just how do you answer a question like that?

Karen's voice tore me away from the indelible remembrance. She said quietly:

"We'll just have to wait, Michael, and hope."

"Sure."

But I'm not the waiting and hoping type. And that damned desert was only seventy or eighty miles across at its widest point. A piddling little desert.

I thought, *Three days on foot, or three nights under the stars... But how to get clear? And to leave no tracks? How about water? And once clear of the camp? And where to then?*

Beyond the Negev lay the Sinai on one side and the Arabian desert on the other, where nothing moved for a million miles—no water, no food, no life and no hope.

Karen said again, urgently, "We must wait and see, Michael."

I said again, "Sure." Only this time, I believed it.

CHAPTER 9

But I was not the only one worrying.

It was obvious what had happened. A strange plane hovering over an almost disused airstrip, a scheduled aircraft mysteriously left abandoned on the turfed field... No matter how quickly the little army of fast cars disappeared back into the Roman night with their armed men aboard, someone must have known about it pretty quickly, and I had the highest regard for the Political Section of the Italian Police.

They wouldn't be wasting any time, and I could imagine the frantic fury in certain circles when it was learned that the special guest, Herr Muller, and his taciturn bodyguard had been abducted.

There would have been urgent phone calls and meetings, and angry protests and angrier demands, and meanwhile, the Egyptians themselves would have been swinging into action with that wild abandon that is peculiarly theirs.

I should have known where the next move was coming from, but I didn't; I was too concerned with our own predicament to realize that behind Muller, or Martin, and his friends there was a huge and potent military machine, and that this was backed, too, with a long established and highly trained intelligence network. In Cairo too they knew just what was going on and didn't waste much time doing something about it.

We were both in the mess hall, sheltering from the afternoon sun and trying to digest a particularly nauseating lunch of sausage, and red cabbage, and sour pickle, and more of that damned tea; though I must admit that when I sighed rather obviously, the young soldier who was looking after us found me some beer.

Karen was sitting quite calm and unperturbed in a Windsor chair, and I was studying a wall map of the Negev, although there was no indication of just whereabouts on it this interrogation center was. Even the place names marked were the ancient ones: Bir Mithnan, Gadesh Barnea, Ezyon Gever, Elusa, Bir Birein... The last name meant, in Arabic, "The Well of Two Wells," and I wondered if that could be where we were; there was water here somewhere, although the young soldier had said our water was piped for forty miles. The colonel had mentioned a border raid, and he had pointed to the west, so we were close to the Egyptian frontier, but that was all we knew.

I looked at the names along the nebulous dividing line that ran through nothing but empty sand, and looked for wells and cisterns: Bir Birein, Bir Reseisiyeah, Bir Hafir, Bir Mithnan, Ain Quadeis, Ain Netifim—six wells over a stretch of a hundred and twenty miles, and most of them, I knew, either mythical or dry. A long thin pencil line marked the Way of Shur, and under it, in parentheses, were some words in Hebrew that I could not understand.

I found a name that interested me—Kirbet Wadi Nahas, which means "The Ruins of the Valley of Copper"—and I wondered about the green sheen on the honeycomb rock; we were certainly in a sort of valley, and the rock was ripe with copper, and a little way off there were some ruins... But it seemed a hell of a long way from the border, too far for a rapid hit-and-run raid with armored cars. Nitsanah, which the colonel had called the ruins, was not marked.

Karen was nonchalantly turning the pages of an old copy of the *Weltwoch* as though she didn't have a care in the world, when we heard a shout outside, coming from a long way off. The shout was repeated and I heard a vehicle start up and take off with a roar, and I looked at Karen and said:

"Come on, the sound of alarm—" And then a siren sounded, not for more than twenty seconds or so, and by that time we were both standing just outside the hut and looking toward the top of the bluff; the men up there were running, diving into a sort of gun emplacement, and I saw an antiaircraft gun swing around and start firing, and only then did I hear the plane.

It came in fast, very low, and although my plane recognition is not what it used to be, I thought perhaps it might be one of the HA300 jets of the Egyptian Air Force that look so much like the French Mirage.

With what seemed incredible speed to my World War Two sensibilities, a burst of rockets left the underside of its wings, and two of them smashed into the aircraft we had come in, and then the fighter was wheeling high into the sky above the flaming wreckage; we could feel the heat of it, and I grabbed Karen's arm and we ran toward the relative shelter of the high bluff.

A second fighter roared in, and the sand was torn up all around us with machine-gun bullets, and then I heard the colonel's angry voice yelling at me from somewhere behind us:

"Benasque! To your right, the shelter!"

I stumbled and looked around and saw him standing by the door of the hut, and then the young soldier who had brought the meals came racing across the sand toward us, holding a rifle and racing fast, pointing to one side, and we reached the bluff and waited for him and he came up breathlessly and said, still grinning:

"Over here, sir—look sharp about it."

We followed him quickly to a wide overhang of the tall mountain, which had been reinforced with concrete, and he said:

"Not much of a shelter, but it's better than nothing."

I shoved Karen into its farthest corner, which wasn't very far, and she didn't seem to want to stay there anyway, and the soldier and I stood at the door and watched the circling fighter, surrounded now with little puffs of dark smoke. He looked at me cheerfully and said:

"Don't worry, it happens all the time."

I said, "Who's worrying?" As the fighter swept past us, firing its machine gun at the hill above us, he raised his rifle and fired once and said:

"Those damn things are armored, but it does a man good to get a round off, doesn't it?"

"I know how you feel."

The fighter came back and roared in low again, and deep behind the hut we had left there was a tremendous explosion, and then the hut itself caught fire and the anti-aircraft gun was pooping away and not doing very well, if you ask me. The clamor of the firing was awful, and it reminded me of the occasional wartime days in London.

And now a great burst of fire spread over the sand, rolling along in a yellow mass of billowing smoke and flame, and I said:

"We didn't have napalm in my time."

The soldier started firing again, and then he was suddenly staring at the sky to the west, and he said:

"Oh-oh."

There were two bigger planes coming in, some eight hundred feet up, quite a long way off and moving much slower, and I said:

"Bombers. They've got a nerve at that height."

He said, "No, they can't be bombers, not at a thousand feet."

We watched them for a moment or two, and then they swung around to the south as though they didn't want to get too close, and I said:

"Don't you have fighters here?"

He shook his head. "No. Just antiaircraft, but they're a bit out of range by the look of it."

"How far's the nearest Air Force field?"

He looked at me and grinned quickly and said, "You're not supposed to know that, sir. But it's a hell of a long way off, and they got the radio tower in the first salvo."

Then a tiny black object fell from the first far-off plane and the white of the parachute spread out above it, and then another and another, and soon the two sticks were in the air, floating down gently, more than three miles away, and the soldier said:

"So that's it... We'd better expect trouble, hadn't we?"

I tried to count the parachutes; esters were more than fifty or sixty of them, and I said:

"How many men do you have here?"

"Thirty. That makes the odds about even, doesn't it?"

"Slightly in your favor."

He grinned again and said, "That's the spirit!"

The sound of the gunfire was increasing and was bringing back memories. Karen had found her Tessina 35mm in her handbag and was standing close against the entrance to the cave where we were, clicking the tiny shutter as fast as she could, and the soldier said mildly:

"Better watch out, miss, there's a lot of lead flying around."

The planes swept out of her field of vision and she smiled at him and said:

"Are you going to try and stop me? Funny how nobody likes a camera in a military installation."

"No, nobody's going to mind very much." He didn't add that they could easily take her equipment away from her if they wanted to. I supposed they most certainly would.

Then the colonel came running over to us, worried as all hell. He looked at Karen, snapping her shutter again, but he didn't object. Instead he said:

"This is the kind of story we like to see documented. Are you both all right?"

I said, "No damage so far. Just a little winded is all; I haven't run like that since I was ten years old. Anybody been hurt?"

"Yes." He didn't elaborate and I didn't ask him for details. He was watching the, parachutists coming down, and he pulled a compass from the case at his belt and took a bearing on them, and then he turned to me and said:

"I'm afraid I'm going to be a little busy from now on. I think you'd better stay right here."

He spoke to the soldier in Hebrew, and the soldier nodded and went running back to the mess, and the colonel said:

"I've sent him to get some water bottles. If we have to move out you'll be taken care of, but stay here until you hear from me or from one of my men. Stay right here, is that understood?"

"It's understood. Where are the other prisoners?"

He said, correcting me carefully, "The prisoners. We've got them safely tucked away in a mine shaft, and it's probably a lot safer there than it is here. If you'd like to join them... I just assumed that perhaps you wouldn't."

Karen said, "It's fine here."

"Good. I don't think there's too much to worry about."

He spoke with a great deal of confidence; too much. It was the easy confidence which is put on for show, as a matter of pure dignity and nothing else. Underneath it I could sense both a feeling of desperation and relief that he could now turn his attention to military matters, in which he was more competent and a great deal happier.

I said, "There are fifty or sixty parachutists out there. How many men have you lost?"

"Too many, but we're well armed and we've had troubles like these before."

"Parachutists too?"

"No. But there's a first time for everything, isn't there?"

The two jet fighters had gone, and the colonel moved away from the sheltering cave and looked up at the sky, still dotted with nebulous puffs of smoke, drifting grayly now in the hot blue sky. When we walked over to join him, he said:

"Keep close by the shelter; they're almost certain to send some more planes in as soon as we move out for a ground attack."

I said, astonished, "But surely you're not going out there to attack them?"

"We must."

"But—why in hell don't you wait for them to come in here? You're all set up for it. If you go out there in the open—"

I knew that military tactics had changed since my day, but even so, it was suicidal to move away from the defenses. But the colonel said patiently:

"Under normal circumstances, of course, you'd be right. But they've come here for only one thing—to rescue those prisoners. If we leave them out there they will wait for darkness and then move in. And we won't have a chance. Our main generator's gone, and our radio's out too, so all we can do is go out there and blast the hell out of them before nightfall."

I said, "It's suicidal!"

He answered quietly, "Any form of warfare is, really, isn't it? Believe me, Mr. Benasque, I know what we have to do. Once the sun goes down, our only hope of keeping those prisoners goes with it. And I'm going to keep them."

The young soldier came running back with four canteens over his shoulder and carrying an S-phone—a short-wave walkie-talkie affair. The colonel took it and spoke into it in Hebrew, and listened and spoke again, and his face was grave.

We saw now that five Jeeps were moving into the open space in front of the hut; they were all mounted with, machine guns and the men aboard were armed with rifles and with grenades that were slung around their belts; a young lieutenant was shouting orders, *shlosh-shlosh-shiosh*, at everyone.

I said, "What do you make it—about three miles out?"

"A little more. There's a deep wadi that runs past the old copper workings; they'll be sheltering there and waiting for us to come out. They should have come in later and they'd have had a better chance."

The colonel was peering up at the sky again. I asked:

"A second wave?"

"I expect so. Unless they think sixty men will be enough. They really ought to know better."

The Jeeps were waiting for him. He said:

"There are a few men left in the camp, and this man will stay with you at all times." He spoke to the soldier and then repeated, "At all times."

He spoke into his little box and listened, and then switched it off almost angrily and stood for a moment staring down at the sand and worrying. He said at last, and his voice was very tired:

"Our casualties—they're rather heavy." Then he straightened up and said quietly, "It might go badly for us, Mr. Benasque. Would you rather I put you in with the prisoners?"

Karen said, unexpectedly, "No, we'll wait for you here."

He looked at her with a peculiar expression on his face and said:

"A while ago, I was discussing your disposition in this matter rather—dispassionately, wasn't I? It might be taken out of my hands now, and I strongly recommend that you join the prisoners. Then, if anything should go wrong, you can more easily claim the protection of any rescue party that should manage to force its way in."

I said, "You think it will come to that?"

He was looking out at the Jeeps, waiting for them and counting the weapons; so was I. He said:

"I hope not. But I think—"

I said, "We'll stay here."

I don't know to this day why I said that. I didn't feel in the least happy with the decision. He nodded, unsmiling, and said:

"If by chance I should not get back, good luck to you both."

He saluted, made a little inclination of the head toward Karen, and walked quickly over to the waiting Jeeps. Three of them, with him in the leading one, moved off south, and the other two swung around to the northwest. I shouted, "Good luck!" and he waved an acknowledgment. The dust swirled up under their wheels as sixteen men went out to do battle with sixty. They were singing.

I said to the young Israeli, "What's your name, soldier?"

"Marks, sir, Benjamin Marks."

"They call you Benny?"

He grimaced. "They'd better not."

Karen took some shots of the retreating Jeeps and then said, "The colonel said you'd lost some men. If there are any wounded—I'm not much of a nurse, but..."

Marks hesitated. He said finally, "No, I think we'd better stay here. The colonel doesn't like his orders being twisted around, even for a good cause."

She said, insisting, "I could be a lot of help to them, wherever they are."

He shook his head and said firmly, "Thank you, miss, but they'll be all right. We've got a couple of medical orderlies." I could see he wasn't going to let us out of his sight. To change the subject, he said, "Just like the Westerns, cowboys and Indians, only these Indians will drive their Jeeps around and around that wadi till there's not a cowboy left." He said, with what I thought was rather forced cheerfulness, "They'll get into range with their guns blazing, and they won't stop firing till they've wiped them out."

I didn't think it would be quite so easy, and I said so.

A strange sort of silence fell around us. There had never been much noise all the morning, but now it seemed that there were just the three of us on the whole of the scorched desert, sheltered from a hostile world by the great bluff that towered up high above us. Marks sat on a boulder and nestled his rifle in his arms, trying not to look worried, and I walked out into the hot sunlight and tried to see what was going on, if anything, at the top of the cliff. All I could see was one man, gaunt against the skyline. I said to Marks:

"Just the one man?"

"Two."

"Not much, is it?"

He shrugged. "It's enough. If we had any sense we'd get up there; it's the safest place to be. One man can hold this little spot against an army. In daylight."

I wondered if he was worried about the darkness too, and when he looked at his watch he seemed to indicate that he was.

I said, "Four hours or more until nightfall."

"Yep. They timed it badly too, didn't they? They just won't learn."

"How far to the border?"

For a long time he didn't answer, but then he said shortly, "Ten miles to the barbed wire."

"For a place like this, that's mighty close, isn't it?"

"No, not really. Our main protection is the sand dunes; there's not much can get over them, you know."

"And the planes would have come from Suez? Or Port Said?"

He didn't answer for a while, and then he grinned and said, "I expect so. It doesn't really matter, does it?"

We hung around and waited for a while, and then at last the sound of gunfire came across the desert. Marks said morosely:

"They've made contact, anyway."

The machine-gun fire was interspersed with the heavy thump of bazookas or recoilless rifles, and I could visualize the Jeeps speeding past the gully while sixty determined men, well dug in, opened up on them with all the weapons of a modern parachute battalion.

It was somehow symptomatic of the way these people were striving for existence in their tiny state, hemmed in on all sides by Arabs sworn to destroy them, outnumbered more than ten thousand to one, and still holding their own.

Marks had come out from his shaded seat on the boulder and was watching the sky, and I knew that he was worried about more planes. He said slowly:

"The old man's taking a gamble that the planes won't back them up in time, but if he waits till dark... The only benefit we have here is that we're impregnable in daylight. In the darkness, even with our searchlights, we're too vulnerable. Too bloody vulnerable."

I said, "That's the history of Israel in a nutshell."

Just then there was an explosion out across the dunes, and a column of black smoke rose heavily in the air, and Marks frowned and said:

"They've got one of the Jeeps."

The firing was heavy and continuous, and it was strange to be sitting here, in relative safety, knowing that a vicious battle was being fought, out of our sight, little more than three miles out in the desert. It began to worry me, and I said to Marks:

"I think we'd better get up to the top; at least we'll see what's going on."

"No, sir, we'll have to stay here. The colonel's orders."

I said angrily, "The colonel's not coming back, don't you know that? He knew that himself before he left."

He was about to protest again, but suddenly the firing stopped out there; it was only a momentary interruption, but when it was resumed it seemed that something was missing, and it was the sound of the Jeeps' motors; none of them was moving now. I could see that Marks was worried, and I said:

"Have your people taken cover?"

He shook his head. "There's no cover out there a Jeep can get into; just a long gully, an old riverbed that dried up a million years ago. If they've stopped moving it's because they've had it. The only hope they have is in moving fast, on the move all the time."

"And now they've all stopped moving."

He did not answer.

Now a faint sound came to us that could have been almost anything; it sounded like the muted roar of a distant, angry crowd, and over it the shooting started, then stopped again, and was then resumed in half a dozen short bursts, and Marks looked at both of us and said:

"There was a note of triumph in that shout—"

He was about to say more, but the machine gun in the emplacement above our heads started to chatter, and suddenly Marks said, "Stay here," and raced out into the sunlight, twisting his slight body around to stare up at the cliff as he ran. I saw him cup his hands to his mouth and shout something to the man at the top of the bluff, and then he cupped his hand to his ear and listened, and then the machine gun started firing again and I took Karen's arm and said:

"Come on, I think we've got to get out of here, fast."

Her face was white and drawn, and we had hardly left the dark shadow of the cave when Marks was back again, out of breath and visibly agitated. He said:

"They're coming; let's go! Up to the top, and we'll have to hurry."

There was no time to argue, even if I'd wanted to; and I didn't. I knew that from up there they could see all of the battle going on to the west, and that they must have seen what had happened. And whatever the man up there had called out, from the expression on Marks's face it didn't look like very happy news.

We began to struggle up the steep side of the bluff, and I said, gasping for breath:

"You'd better tell us what happened."

Marks was moving like a mountain goat, an agile young man used to the rough life of the desert. He held out a hand to help Karen over a rocky projection as I pushed from below, and he said:

"It looks as though the counterattack didn't do much good. There are two groups of Egyptians on their way here, ten or twelve men in each. I hope to God that's all there are left of them."

I said between gasps for breath, "Can we hold them off up there?"

"In daylight, yes. Against anything but aircraft." Almost instinctively he looked up at the sky, wondering if the fighters were returning. But the wide blue sphere above us was empty; not even a wisp of cloud disturbed the hot air.

We scrambled up over loose shale and broken stones, and soon we came to the path the Jeep had taken. We crossed that too, and I knew that we were using a shortcut, getting to the safety of the top as fast as possible. For Karen's benefit I said:

"It's not us they're after, it's Martin and his friends."

She paused to look back, panting, the perspiration streaming down her face, and she brushed a strand of hair from her face and said, pointing:

"There, over there—"

I looked and saw eight or nine men running across the desert, not much more than a mile away, spread out in extended order, and as I watched, a few more came over a rise, moving fast through the sand, running lightly like animals with long, graceful strides. While we got our breath back we stood and watched, and Marks said:

"Bedouins, drilled into military machines. Look at the way they move."

They were in army uniforms and carried their rifles at their sides; some of them seemed to have heavier weapons slung across their shoulders, but at this distance it was hard to see what they were.

The top of the bluff was still five hundred feet above us, and the track could now be seen clearly, winding its way around and around over the gravel. We climbed the steep bank together, and then a soldier from the top was sliding down to meet us, an elderly, gray-haired corporal, moving with the ease of a young man. I was panting so hard I could hardly speak, and his gray hair shamed me, and he reached out a hand for Karen and said in heavily accented English:

"Just a few more feet, it's not far—"

We struggled up over the last bluff, and there, at the top, the whole world was spread out beneath us, yellow and red and burning bright, with not a tree or a shrub or a blade of grass in sight. As far as a man could see, and that was considerable, there were only dunes and flat plateaus of sandstone, and broken red gullies where the shadows were deep purple, and strange twisted shapes of rock that seemed like dying embers in a gigantic fire. The colors were unbelievable, bright reds and yellows and coppers, so startlingly bright that they hurt the eyes.

From up here, perched up in the sky, it seemed that the whole of the world was laid out at our feet, the Way of Shur and the Wilderness of the Philistines, and the great wastes where Ishmael the son of Abraham had found his miraculous well with his Egyptian mother Hagar. And the only thing that moved in that empty, sunburned space was the enemy.

We could see both groups of parachutists now, a mile or so away and a half-mile apart, and beyond them two of the Jeeps were smoldering, sending up tall columns of dark smoke. I could not see the others. When I got my breath back I said to the corporal:

"Do you have glasses?"

We were close by a reverted entrenchment, a circular pit about twenty feet across, dug into the sandstone and surrounded with sandbags. He handed the binoculars to me and I looked out at the little battlefield and saw that it was strewn with bodies; I could not see into the gully even from up here, but I counted eleven men lying on the ground; not one of them moved; one of them, I thought, was the colonel, but I could not be sure.

I swung the glasses around to the advancing men. They were Bedouins, all right, tall, lean men with swarthy faces and black mustaches, and they wore army keffiyehs on their heads, the big square of khaki cloth tasseled at the edges and held in place with black agals of twisted camel hair. As I watched, one of them stopped and aimed his rifle at me, and I instinctively ducked down before the shot went off. I did not hear the bullet and Marks said, squinting his eyes and watching:

"The legend of the Bedouin, the best shots, the best horsemen in the world, and there's not an atom of truth in it. They're lousy riders and worse riflemen, and that one's out of range anyway."

I said sourly, "It's an instinct I learned when you were still suckling."

I turned the glasses on the camp below. Everything was deserted. The door to the burning mess hall was open, and I could find no other building in sight, and Karen, reading my thoughts again, said:

"There must be some other buildings somewhere."

Marks nodded. "Yes, a little way beyond, under the bluff; it's supposed to be protection in case of an air strike. That was the first we've had, and they got the radio tower in the first pass. Beginners' luck, I'd call it."

He still wouldn't believe that they could be successful by anything other than luck. I said:

"I admire your spirit."

He laughed then, a little sourly, and said, "We like to kid ourselves that they're no good at anything, but I suppose we might be a little biased."

It was strange to be discussing them so objectively. The elevation gave us a massive feeling of security, because I knew that we were well dug in up here. I passed the binoculars over to Marks and he looked out at the battlefield and his face hardened. It was not nice to see so much bitterness in so young a face. I said gently:

"They didn't have much chance, did they?"

His voice was harsh. "No, they didn't. But they had to take it; there was nothing else they could do."

"If the radio's off the air—are you in constant contact?"

"Not constant, but if we don't come on the air when we should, they'll try and find out why."

"Before dark?"

He put aside the binoculars and gestured. "I think it's at six o'clock tomorrow morning, but I'm not sure. If they don't hear from us they'll send over a patrol."

"And that'll take how long to get here?"

"A couple of hours, a little more."

The corporal said, "*Bevakashah*—please," and gestured us into the sandbagged pit.

The other man there was a slight, very young man with a heavy black mustache, squatting over a Bren gun. He grinned broadly and said in Arabic, "*T'faddal*—you are welcome," and when I answered in Arabic and said, "*Ah'lan wa sah'lan*—you are welcome too," the corporal showed his surprise.

I said, "Thank God someone speaks a language I know."

"You speak Arabic?"

"Uh-huh."

"He doesn't know anything else. A Yemenite—his name is Osmani. A dozen words of Hebrew, and he's been here for nearly a year. Four Hebrew lessons a week, and still all he can say is what time do we eat."

The young Yemenite was enjoying the joke immensely, not understanding but knowing we were talking about him. He swung the machine gun around, and the corporal said in Arabic, "Give me that gun, you camelherd, they're not in range yet." He sat behind the Vickers and said, "As soon as I start firing, keep your heads down. Not one chance in a thousand they'll hit anybody or fire back even, because we are not a good target, but luck's on their side today."

He pulled out a pack of cigarettes and offered them to us— thin, loosely packed cigarettes that smelled strongly Turkish and burned away in a few minutes—and we sat there, smoking and waiting...

I could not place his accent, and I said, "Where are you from, corporal?"

It seemed he wanted to stress his affinity with the more-Arab-than-Jew Yemenite. He said with a half-smile:

"Once my home was half of Europe; now it's the State of Israel, and that's all that matters."

I took the glasses again, and when the corporal fired a quick burst, I saw two of the running men fall as the bullets spluttered in the sand around them. Another burst, and another man fell, and then they were running faster for cover, heading for the chasm itself. There was only one group in sight now; the others had disappeared behind a rise in the sands.

I said, "You got three of them," and there was another long burst, but they had dropped out of sight now. The corporal said with satisfaction:

"Well, at least it will discourage them from trying to get up here in the daylight." He looked at his watch, and when I said, "Three more hours," he nodded.

We could not guess what was going on down there. There was no more concentrated shooting, only sporadic single shots, and a great feeling of helplessness came over me. I said to the corporal:

"I think we ought to take the guns and get down there; we can't do a thing up here."

He said, "No." His voice was politely authoritative, and when I began to argue, he said, "The planes, the fighters, if they come back— and they will, mark my words. That's what we're here for. This time maybe we'll have better luck. And there just might be a couple of armored cars coming over the dunes any minute now."

"How many of your men down there?"

He said shortly, "Four, including the two medical orderlies. Two of them are wounded, but they can all use their weapons."

"And Nathan?"

I was trying to surprise him, but he paid no attention to the non sequitur. He said. "Nathan's in the mine with the prisoners, I suppose."

"By himself?" It didn't seem possible. The corporal grimaced.

He said, "You know more than I do about that, sir. I haven't left this emplacement for thirty-six hours."

Now the shooting started again. It was muffled, swollen to reverberating proportions by the echo effect in the canyon, a reboant clatter that seemed unbelievably close.

He said gravely, "All we can do is hope that the mines are as strong as we think they are. If they can get in there—"

"And we won't ever know the answer to that, up here, will we?"

He looked at me and said, "We'll know as soon as it gets dark. One way or another."

I put an arm around Karen's waist and when she looked at me I knew what she was thinking. At least twenty heavily armed men had fought their way into the compound, and the defense consisted of two wounded soldiers and two medical orderlies.

And Nathan.

And up here in the sky, as safe as an eagle brood in its nest, there was nothing we could do but wait for the outcome of the slaughter—nothing but wait for death to cut down a few more helpless men below us.

I said angrily, "But we can't just sit here and wait for them to be killed."

The corporal said firmly, "We wait."

He looked up at the sky, watching.

CHAPTER 10

The planes did not come.

For three hours we sat there, in growing anxiety, and all sound below us came to a stop and there was only silence. Our eagles' nest was cut off from the world about it, perched high on the top of a rock that was almost inaccessible.

From time to time I took the glasses and looked out at the distant, motionless marks on the ground that were all that was left of sixteen brave men; it was sickening to see them there, unattended by any of the sanctimonious pomp that is supposed to make death for the young a little easier to bear.

Karen said fiercely, "It's hard to be objective about this, but—I wish I had a telephoto lens with me."

I didn't believe for one minute that they'd let her get away with the photographs she had already taken—assuming that any of *them* were left who could stop her; after all, the raid was merely an overt answer to a series of covert machinations that had started in Rome. A blatant abduction on foreign soil, followed by a retributory raid into foreign territory—the fault was clearly on both sides, whatever the validity of the colonel's claim. But there was a partisan anger in her, and I kept silent.

When I had looked across at the killing ground for the tenth time, the corporal said gruffly, "It is no good to look. There is nothing we can do for them, even if any of them is still alive. And they will not be, not one of them."

"And where the hell did the Egyptians go? Are they still down there below us?"

"They are still there. They must have found their way into the mines."

"And so?"

He looked at me in surprise. "And so, they will stay there, safe from our bullets, until it is dark. Then they will cross ten miles to the border with the rescued prisoners, and—perhaps that will be the end of the operation."

"Perhaps? They can't miss."

"When we do not make our radio contact on time, our people will send a patrol out, perhaps even a fighter. If help comes while they are out there on the desert—" He said grimly, "They will be like—like ducks on the ground."

"If the relief party shows up in time. Tomorrow is a long way off, and you can't be sure they'll get here even then. So far, your competence hasn't impressed me."

I saw the corporal's lips tighten, and Karen put a hand on my arm, but I pulled away and said roughly:

"Some better shooting with your ack-ack would have brought those planes down, and it was lousy tactics to send the entire defense force out into the desert where they hadn't a hope in hell."

"There was nothing else they could do. If they had waited till dark—"

"Yes, I know all about that: they'd have broken in and rescued the prisoners. They're going to do that anyway, and like this—the cost has been—criminally high." It was building up into a first-class row. I said, "No one is going to question their courage, but courage is no substitute for strategy."

"They will not be the first, nor the last, to die for Israel. They will not grudge their lives."

I said angrily, "Well, I do! That kind of recklessness went out with the Thin Red Line. They knew damn well they weren't coming back, and all they could do was—sing! I don't feel like sitting here and doing nothing about it."

He was very angry, the corporal, but he contained his anger and said, "Yes, I know, we all feel like that. If it is true that you want to help—"

"Too bloody true." I could not write off the colonel's fortitude just because he didn't know his Clausewitz; his kind of quiet resolution is catching.

"Perhaps there is something we can do. Not now, but when it is dark."

The sun was brilliant on the horizon, a more startling red than I had ever seen, and the shadows of the distant dunes were long and crescent-shaped, making an eerie pattern on the sand below us. From this high vantage point I could see that the yellow dunes were all around us, massive, overwhelming, forbidding.

He said slowly, "I must guess what they will do, and if I am wrong—" He gestured helplessly—an old man, but still a corporal—and I said:

"Well, guess anyway."

He nodded. "I shot three of them with my machine gun as they went into the chasm. It is there that the entrance to the mines is, and they must come out the same way."

"A dead end?"

"Yes. It is not really a chasm, more like a long cave that has no roof, and they must pass me again when they come out. So they will wait until it is dark, knowing that the moon does not rise till after midnight. Then, perhaps, they will hurry to the border. Or perhaps only some of them will, with the prisoners, while the others climb up the track in the darkness and try to take us here by surprise."

I said, "Of course, we could just let them go, couldn't we, and hope they'll leave us alone up here?"

"You can. I cannot."

It was hard to sit on the sidelines and watch; with or against my better judgment I could see that I was getting drawn into all this whether I liked it or not. I noticed that Karen seemed to approve of what I was thinking, and that made it easier. I said:

"Let's assume that you're right so far. We'd better get down there and bottle them in till help comes—can we do that?"

"It will not be easy. They will not have left the mine entrance unguarded. But if we can kill the guards, then—you see? As you say, we can bottle them up in there."

"It makes sense to me and that's what we'd better do. There's only one thing."

He nodded and looked at Karen. He said slowly, "I can leave the Yemeni up here with her, but I do not like to because—if a party tries to get up here while we are down there—You see the difficulty?"

Karen said firmly, "I'm coming with you, wherever you go."

The corporal looked at her and said, "Can you handle a rifle? Or a pistol?"

She hesitated. "I never have, but—"

The corporal nodded and thought for a while, and Marks said gently:

"Our women have all been trained, and it's easy to forget that it's not normal for a good-looking woman to go around with a gun on her shoulder. A token of the place we live in."

Karen said, "Your women too?"

Marks nodded. "All of them, young or old; they all get their training."

Karen was looking down at her shoes, the smart high-heeled shoes I'd bought her in the Via Condotti; they hadn't lasted very well under the beating they'd taken over the last few hours, and the corporal said dreamily:

"We have our beautiful young ladies too; not all of them are very—soldierly. But they all know how to carry arms, and to use them, because we have not yet reached the state in which we can enjoy the— the little luxuries. I have a daughter younger than you"—he looked at Karen and smiled—"and she is even prettier, may I say that? At a time when most young ladies are thinking only of pretty things to wear— yes, when a father would like her to have them too—my daughter has just been decorated for bravery, in a border raid. By the Prime Minister himself. Her name is Yedida, and she is eighteen years old, and her hair is cropped short, not long like yours, and when she laughs—"

He broke off and stared up at the sky, and Karen said, "Eighteen years old..."

"Eighteen years old." He came out of his dream and said to me, "We cannot leave the lady up here, in case— She must stay with us."

I didn't like the idea too much, because the danger was obviously going to be acute, and there's nothing like the love of a woman close by to inhibit a man when he's fighting with every dirty trick he can think of. I said, "How long to get down there in the dark?"

"That's another problem. At least half an hour; it's not easy without a moon to help us."

"A moon—that's all we want and we wouldn't have a chance."

"I know." He sighed, a good man used to taking orders and not used to planning.

I was worried to hell about taking Karen down there where *anything* might be waiting for us. At one time it had seemed that we were as much prisoners as Martin and his men, and as the colonel had intimated, perhaps we could still hold that privileged position.

But then? Go over to the enemy? Let them "rescue" us from Marks, and the grizzled old corporal and the cheerful young Yemeni who could only speak Arabic? I found myself amazed at the rapidity with which I seemed to have been sweet-talked into partisanship in a war that had nothing whatsoever to do with me apart from its relation to Harry and his bloody story.

I said, "I'm a reporter, a journalist, I'm not supposed to take sides." It didn't impress anyone, and I asked the corporal if he had a spare rifle. He nodded and handed me an Enfield that was propped against the sandbags.

He took off his own revolver and showed it to Karen and said, "You think you could use this if I showed you how?"

There was a terribly gentle sadness in his voice, as though now that he had found a woman who didn't habitually carry a gun he was committing iconoclasm by breaking the image.

I said to Karen, "All you do is point it and pull the trigger; you've got six shots and I pray to God you won't need any of them."

I flicked the bolt out of the Enfield and squinted at the dying sun through the barrel and found it immaculately clean, as if it would be any other way, and Marks said cheerfully to Karen:

"It's really only for your own protection, miss; I'll be right behind you."

I had forgotten the colonel's instructions, but Marks hadn't. I added, "And so will I."

He said something like *"Bevakashah"* to the corporal, and while I packed spare rounds of ammunition into my trousers pockets and slung a cloth bandolier over my shoulder, he took the revolver from the corporal and showed Karen how to use it, how to aim and squeeze on the trigger, and how to get off a quick, unaimed shot by using the finger as an aimer. I watched him carefully, but he knew his stuff, and when Karen at last took it from him (her face was white and set), I said:

"Just don't point it at anyone you like."

Knowing I was trying to take her mind off the danger, she smiled and said, surprisingly, "You won't have to worry about me, Michael. If their women can do it, so can I." I knew she wasn't quite so tough and a hell of a lot more feminine, but I kept silent.

The corporal, also watching Marks's careful demonstration, watching for any mistakes, said, "My daughter is a very good shot with a revolver."

I grunted; it didn't seem much of an asset to me, but Karen said:

"Where is she, corporal?"

"In a colony, in one of the new *kibutzim* on the Jordanian border. We have trouble there too, sometimes. Trouble—all around us."

The redness went from the sun and it was dark so fast that I wondered where the twilight had gone. The corporal told the young Yemeni to move down the slope, fast, to a point halfway down, and to keep his eyes and ears open. Osmani showed his strong white teeth and said, *"Na'am ya sidi*—yes, sir," and he was gone in a moment, moving like a Bedouin, silently and with catlike speed, his rifle held easily in one hand with one up the spout and the safety catch off.

I said mildly to the corporal, "If he trips with his rifle like that—"

The corporal had seen it too. He smiled and said:

"He won't trip; he's like an animal, a mountain goat."

We gave him a few minutes, and I looked at the last red streaks in the sky and said:

"All right, let's get down there."

Patiently he said, "A few more minutes."

"Dammit, it's as black as pitch already!"

"Not from down there. We're silhouetted against the sky. A few more minutes." He was right, of course. He said, "They'll have to be sure that it's dark enough for them not to be seen too. My guess is they'll wait in the mines, if that's where they are, for half an hour or so, just to be sure."

"Just the time it takes us to get there."

He added, "And they will be expecting us, of course."

"I realize that. No trouble to find the mine entrance? In the dark?"

He shrugged. "Three hundred yards along the cliff, a big cave just the other side of it. The mine is—one sees that it is a mine, an entrance with heavy wooden beams."

"And how much underground?"

Again that helpless gesture. "I do not know, really. Very many passages."

"But, for God's sake, you know your way around them?"

"A little. We must look for the ammunition store; that's where the prisoners will have been taken when the shooting started, because that is the strongest place and the easiest to hold."

"But just four men, including the medical orderlies, to hold it."

Karen said, "And Nathan."

"Yes, and Nathan."

Maybe the ammo depot was the safest place, but I didn't like the idea of a fight going on inside it. A careless hand grenade... I said:

"Well, at least they haven't blown the place up; we'd have heard *that*, I hope. What about rifle fire—would the sound of it reach us up here?"

The corporal shook his head. "Perhaps; I think not."

"So we don't know what's happened while we've been waiting."

He said firmly, "*Adon* Nathan is holding some prisoners there with four men to help him. A party of Egyptians has gone in to try and rescue them, and we are going to their assistance. That is what we know."

I said, "So let's get down there; this waiting's getting me down."

He looked up at the black sky and nodded. He said calmly, "I think it is time now."

We climbed out of the emplacement and began to move over

the brink of the cliff.

I will never forget that terrifying climb down in the darkness. It seemed blacker than the soles of a mortician's socks, and only touch would tell that on one side of us there loomed the cliff; on the other was a great emptiness that seemed to tempt the feet into open space that hung over nearly a thousand feet of treacherous drop; the eagles coming down out of the sky had lost their wings and their feet were unsteady and fragile, and each pace had to be taken with infinite care to avoid starting a fall of loose shale and warning those below—and we did not know where they might be now—that we were coming.

The corporal saw us safely over the edge, and then went back for the Bren gun, which he slung around his shoulders. I needed both my hands and slung my rifle too, and together we lowered Karen bodily over the side of the high cliff. I was damned glad I couldn't see the desert below us; it was just too far down for comfort.

I wished we could use the track which the Jeep had taken; but it was a question of saving time by slipping fast down the quickest way instead of going around by the steep gravel path, and I knew too that if *they* were coming up to find us in the darkness, moving with the stealth of Bedouins, we'd be better off out of their line of ascent.

But the steep side of the cliff was dark and treacherous, and it was terrifying to move by touch alone; it had been hard enough coming up, in daylight. Now, in the black night, there was fear in the groping; sometimes, reaching out for the rock face, I found Karen's soft body instead, and sometimes it was the hard muscle of a powerful shoulder.

I reached back a hand for Karen once, over a particularly nasty outcrop, and felt instead the heavy boot of the corporal—or was it Marks? —finding its way onto my shoulder, and when I reached again there was another boot—and then panic, because Karen was not there, and I groped with my free hand and whispered anxiously, "Karen? Can you make it? Are you there?"

I heard her voice below me, very quiet and confident: "I'm here, Michael."

I slipped down after her and heard the corporal say angrily, "In silence, please." I knew that we were still too high to be heard, but he didn't want me to get into the habit of carelessness.

I found a soft waist in the darkness, and Karen was waiting for me, standing on a precarious perch and whispering:

"Can you see?"

I put out a hand to steady myself against the rocks, and found only air. I said:

"Not a goddam thing."

Her two hands were at my belt, fumbling, and I wondered where the gun was; I groped at her waist and felt that she had tucked it into the tight band of her skirt, and when my hand slid almost unknowingly to her breast she held it there for a moment and said:

"Don't worry, I can see, Michael, I can see well in the dark."

She could too. The way she moved down over the broken stones was unbelievable. I groped after her and then she was gone again, and I heard a heavy footstep on a rock above me and someone close to me touched my arm and said, "Mr. Benasque, is that you?" It was Marks.

I patted his hand twice, and then his face was close to mine and he was whispering, "I think there's someone up there, above us..."

We stood close together in absolute silence, and then I felt Karen's gentle touch on my ankle and I stooped down to find that she was clinging to the cliff a yard or so below me. And then the heavy footstep above us resolved itself into a slither of sound and a heavy body slid into me, nearly throwing me off balance; I wished to God I had a flashlight, and there was an instant of fright as I fancied I could smell an alien scent. I thought, *Are they up here already, above us, looking for us up there in the silent darkness?*

But it was the corporal. He was panting hard, and he muttered, "I slipped, I nearly fell..." and I said, "That noise, was that you?" He did not answer, and I could guess at the worry he was feeling; only the sound of his breath could be heard, and then he whispered, tugging at my sleeve, "To this side, it should be easier... Where is the lady?"

"Below us."

"Good. Watch your step here—"

"Watch it? I wish to hell I could see it."

He held my wrist in a firm grip as I dangled a foot over what seemed to be a ledge dropping down into eternity. I found a narrow shelf, tested it with my foot—it was no more than a few inches wide—and put my weight on it. The corporal let go before I had transferred my balance, but I landed on both feet, and then there was Karen's touch on my arm again and she whispered, insisting:

"Don't worry, Michael, I'm all right."

I whispered back, "I wish I could say the same thing for myself. Don't get ahead of me like that, stay behind, I want to be below you if you fall."

She whispered calmly, "I won't fall."

I could see the faint outline of her now, a lighter shape against the black of the rock and the sky; she looked so slim and fragile, and I knew that this was a lousy thing I was doing, dragging her into all this, but what else could I do? My eyes were slowly getting accustomed to the darkness, but not much. I have never known a night so dark.

We slid over a boulder and half fell onto a gentler incline, and for a few yards we moved along the old Jeep track. Then, with the corporal leading now, we went over the side again.

I looked at the luminous pallidity of my watch and saw that we had already been moving down for more than fifteen minutes, and I tried to remember the outline of the hill—was it steeper from now on? It was small comfort that now we had only four hundred feet or so to drop...

I stepped onto space and fell to my knees, and rolled over and down for thirty or forty feet and grabbed at a projection; was it the root of a bush? I could remember no bushes here. I dug my fingers into soil and pulled myself laboriously, painfully, back into a more or less upright state, and now I could no longer see Karen, nor the corporal, nor Marks.

I strained my ears and heard them moving to one side of me—I hoped it was them—and then a shadow brushed by me and made no sound, and I was sure that we were not alone on that damned mountain, that somebody, *something,* was moving along with us or past us. For all I could see or hear, it could have been a troop of cavalry. I stood panting against the sandstone wall for a moment or two, pressing my body tight to it and hugging the rough surface with my curled fingers. I explored carefully with one foot and could find nothing.

Nothing at all. *Space.*

It is hard to describe the fear. I was four hundred feet up on a tiny ledge that I could not even see; indeed, if I had been able to see it I would have been even more frightened, if that is humanly possible. There's no panic more terrifying than acrophobia. I could hear my own heart beating.

And then, somewhere ahead of me and a little way down, Karen screamed. The scream was cut off short and I heard her muffled outcry.

I did not stop to think. I did not care whether or not there was ground ahead of me or only a drop down to death, I knew only that the woman I loved had screamed and that only I could help her. Somewhere, a few yards off in the darkness, something terrible was happening to her and before I knew what I ought to do, I had done it.

I jumped forward with my arms and my legs spread-eagled, and I landed on two struggling bodies and one of them was soft and feminine and the other was wiry and tough and as slippery as an eel. I felt, rather than saw, that Karen had rolled clear, and the cloth that was rasping against my cheekbone was coarse, rough-to-the-touch military stuff, and I grabbed at it and swung myself and the other man up with the same gesture, dragging him toward me and throwing up a right-handed haymaker that would have felled an ox had it connected. My own rifle, slung over my shoulder and still there, fetched me a blow on the back of my own head and it was a second before I realized that it was not my adversary who had hit me. I still had that handful of military cloth, and I drew back my arm for another wild swing, and then he said urgently, "*Ya sidi, anna*—it's me, sir..."

The Arabic was strongly accented. Yemeni accent.

I said, "My God, you scared the daylights out of me." I spoke English and repeated it in Arabic, and then Karen was struggling to her feet and groping at me, and I said, "Its Osmani, the Yemeni soldier... Are you all right?"

She was too shocked to speak for a moment, but I knew what had happened. Osmani said haltingly:

"I had to stop her screaming, *ya sidi...*"

And then Karen said, "When I bumped into him—he put his hand over my mouth—it was so dark—"

I told her what he had said, and I felt her groping hands. When

I touched her, she was trembling. I put my arms around her and held her tight, and then the corporal was close beside us in the darkness. He whispered angrily:

"What went wrong?"

I said, "Nothing, it's all right."

He said grimly, "Now they know we are coming."

"They'd know that anyway."

I touched Karen's face and felt her tears, and she brushed them away and said:

"I'm all right, I'm—I'm sorry I screamed. I was—I was frightened."

The corporal began to whisper furiously to the Yemeni, and I said, in Arabic so they'd both understand:

"It's all right, it wasn't his fault, he did the only thing possible. Let's go on down."

My shinbone started giving me hell, and when I reached down to touch it I could feel the torn cloth of my trousers and the wet slime of blood; I wondered when and where I'd banged it. My eyes were slowly getting better, and I fancied I could make out the dim faintness of the light-colored sand down there below us; it still looked a hell of a long way off. Osmani was whispering to his corporal, saying:

"At the foot of the path, two men." His voice was almost inaudible.

I heard the corporal answer him, just as quietly, "Can you get them both?"

The only answer I heard was the faint sound of a knife being drawn out of a scabbard, and then the corporal put his mouth close to my ear and said, "We must wait here for a few moments."

I felt for Karen's hand, found it, and squatted on my heels, pulling her down with me.

And we waited.

The silence was so acute it almost hurt. It was so impossibly silent that it seemed we must be off the face of the earth altogether, somewhere detached in space with only a fragile footing below us that was, itself, detached from the hostile earth and hanging high in the sky, dreadfully high above a dangerous and empty desert where nothing moved at all, except our enemies.

* * *

I had known such silence only once before. Many years ago, a patrol of the Free French, coming up from Chad into Libya, had found me close to death in the middle of the Sahara, my solitary camel dead and silent beside me and my water gone—even the water I had drained out of its bloody body. For ten days I had lived in the silence there, drinking the water from its hump and eating its flesh raw because, although I could make fire with the lens I always carried in my pocket, there was nothing I could burn, nothing at all, not even a blade of coarse grass. The emptiness reflected itself in the silence then, because where there is even the sparsest scrub, even if it is only a single bush struggling for survival and nothing more within a hundred miles, then it seems that you can hear the insects and the lizards that will certainly be living around it; it seems you can hear the movement of its dry leaves in a breeze that does not exist; it seems that when an ant moves you are conscious of it, that the sound can be heard...

But when there is not even that one solitary bush, then there is *nothing*, and you cannot even hear the deadly, massive silence of the dunes, as they creep forward, a foot or two a year, moving under some mysterious power that you and I can only guess at.

The silence then is terrifying, because not even a bird wheels high above you in the sky and there is—*nothing*.

On the last few nights of that terrifying period, I had lain on my back in the sand when every drop of water in that camel had dried out and even the blood was powder, and there were no flies to torment it—and to catch for food—because we were just too far from—from *anything*. I had lain there, motionless, staring at the black sky and hearing nothing, feeling the draining of strength that comes with dehydration, not moving at first because of the desperate need to conserve even the weakest force, and then not moving because there was not enough fluid in my body to let my limbs move.

And then the coma had come, with patches of anguished coherence, and I knew the only reason I was not babbling was that there was no moisture in my mouth that would permit my tongue to move.

And then the tongue itself began to swell and choke me and I could not cough either, and still I could not bring myself to end the pain with my knife because there was not the strength in my arms to pull it from its sheath.

And then the coma came again, and there was a bearded man crouching above me and the hot sand of the morning was streaked with the long shadows of camel legs, and I heard a voice saying, "*Mais il vive encore...*"

They gave me a wet cloth to suck, and they put rags all over my body, and when I could speak they gave me a few drops of harsh red wine, the *pinard* of the Army which comes from the cheapest Algerian vineyards, and I said, "Château Margaux—nineteen thirty-four," and suddenly everyone, including me, was laughing and it was all over except for the shock that came afterward.

I knew I would never forget the silence of the desert as long as I lived.

And now, in the Negev night, the silence and the darkness were just as acute; only this time I knew that down below us was a deadly and ruthless enemy, hopelessly outnumbering our tiny force that was ridiculously coming to the help of men who might long have been dead.

The thoughts raced through my mind as I waited, and there was comfort in the closeness of Karen's body in the night; I let my fingers move over her shoulder.

A tiny pebble thrown to the patch of ground we were squatting on warned us, and then Osmani was there; I could see his white teeth in the darkness and was glad he was grinning again. He whispered, "*Ma'itein*—two dead bodies," and I said to the corporal, keeping my voice as low as his, "Surely we would have heard—at least something."

He said, "You don't know the Yemenis. Come on." He touched me on the arm and whispered, "A difficult piece here; go down ahead of me."

I slid over the edge and groped for a foothold, and when I grabbed at Osmani's ankle to steady myself, I felt that he had taken his boots off and was moving barefoot; the flesh of his foot was like hard leather that has dried out too long in the sun. I wedged myself into a tight crevice and patted his leg twice to let him know I had landed, and then Karen's body came sliding gently down; I could dimly see that he was lowering her to me.

I slid my hands along her legs, up to the thigh, the narrow waist, the breast and then the shoulders, and then she was beside me, still trembling and silent; and she still had her revolver wedged into her waistband. I'd long begun to wish that I could get rid of that damned rifle that kept impeding my progress, but I supposed if the others could manage I ought to be able to.

The last few yards now. We slithered down a gentle incline, and then, suddenly, we were at the bottom, on firm ground that spread out for a thousand miles in all directions, and I whispered, "Thank God for that; are we all here?"

The corporal was standing beside me, unslinging the Bren gun; I just could not believe he had managed to manhandle it so silently all the way down, and I said:

"You're a good man, corporal—"

"Ssshhh."

We stood for a few moments getting our breath. He whispered, "All right, now follow me. Marks first, then the lady and Mr. Benasque." He touched Osmani on the shoulder and said, "You bring up the rear." He switched back to English again. "Keep close behind me all the time, unless someone starts shooting. If that happens, we must scatter. Mr. Benasque and his lady will run east to get under the lee of the cliff, Marks and I will go to the west—is that understood?"

I said, "What about Osmani? I'd like to know where he'll be."

"Osmani will not run, and it's no good telling him to. He'll stand where he is and start firing, so make sure you move out fast. No one is to fire till I do, so wait till you hear the machine gun and then use your own discretion. Is that all clear?"

He may not have been a major strategist, but he knew how to make the best of a situation like this. He repeated the instructions in Arabic for Osmani's sake, and then said with satisfaction, "So far, so good. Now we will see what there is to see."

I said, "Won't it be nice if they're not there, after all this trouble?"

In the darkness, I saw him shake his gray head. "In the mine— the only place they can be. The noise we've been making—they'd have heard us."

We moved slowly along the edge of the overhang to whatever was in store for us.

CHAPTER 11

The entrance to the mine was unguarded.

We reached it just before the moon came up; there was a faint streak of saffron in the sky that told us it would not be long now, and we stood hesitantly by the timbered aperture, wondering why there was no one there.

I thought, *In this desperate game of tag in the darkness, nobody knows where anybody is.* We were playing it off the cuff, moving toward an unknown objective and not knowing what to do with what we found; but it was the only possible course open to us. If only they hadn't been so damned quiet! I cursed their Bedouin origins with relish.

A faint light was coming from down there somewhere, and I knew that whatever else there was under the ground in the old copper works, there was at least one generator of some sort that had not been damaged. I grew impatient with the waiting, but the corporal was a cautious man.

In a little while, the corporal posted Osmani on guard at the entrance, and the rest of us crept forward into the shaft, a long sloping passage that led down under the red rock, deep into the bowels of the cliff our eagles' nest had been perched on. The dust hung motionless in the air, and I wondered if it meant that someone had passed this way recently. I wanted to ask if there was another entrance, but I did not like to break the silence.

We crept on down, and soon we came to an underground chamber where a single bare electric bulb was burning, hanging from a wire that ran along the adze-cut roof. The room was roughly square, and had been hewn out of the solid rock, and there was an astonishing decoration on one of the walls, covered over with chicken wire for protection, as though one day someone with more leisure time to spare would come here and carefully carry it away. It was a prehistoric rock drawing, the outline of an animal sharply incised in the soft stone, with a bow-armed hunter close behind him. It gave me an odd feeling, as though I were an interloper in another age. As I stared at it I could dimly make out the form of a dog as well, close by the hunter's advancing foot.

There were still dark smudges of smoke on the walls, in one corner, and I wondered if this was one of King Senerefu's workings that had been put down more than fifty centuries ago.

The cave could have been carved out even earlier, when chalcolithic man was digging here for the native copper which he had not yet learned to smelt over his campfires, when all he could do was hammer the soft red metal into well-shaped knives and axes. It was in a deep, dark shaft like this, perhaps this very one, that metallurgy first began. The light bulb in the roof was an anachronism, and I felt we should be carrying flaming brands, or burning hanks of wool, tallow-soaked... And it was hard to bring my senses back to the present. I exchanged a glance with Karen, and she nodded, smiling, her eyes shining, all the tragedy and the death momentarily forgotten.

We stared around the empty chamber, wondering. It was a sort of anteroom, unfurnished, and there were three small openings leading off it, only one of which seemed to be lit. We were desperately vulnerable there in the faint light with darkness leading away from us in silent tunnels, and I edged nearer to the wall, pulling Karen with me. She was carrying her revolver now, holding it a little fearfully. Marks, I saw, had slipped the safety catch of his rifle, and I did the same, using the first finger of my trigger hand, then resting it quickly on the guard; the old drill was all coming back once more.

The corporal jerked his head at the lighted entrance, and I whispered, "What about the others?"

He shook his head. "Nothing; they lead nowhere."

We crept forward in single file, and soon we found some steps which led deep down into the earth, steps that in part were cut from the natural rock and in other places had been repaired with slabs of concrete.

The light was behind us now, and soon another bulb was visible up ahead. In its light we could see a massive timber door made of modern, plane-smoothed beams reinforced with expanded metal; beside it there was another of the prehistoric paintings, a spear-carrying warrior mounted on what looked like a camel.

But I could not allow myself the time nor the freedom to examine it very closely; the metal-framed door was ajar.

I looked at the corporal, and he nodded; his voice was so low I could hardly hear it: "The ammunition stores."

We approached it carefully, and in the dim light he signaled to all of us to stand well back while he flung the door open. It was like cops-and-robbers on TV, only here the walls about us were not the walls of a sleazy hotel, and neither was the enemy on the other side of the door merely a hopped-up punk with a gun in his hand... Here, the walls had been carved out by chisel God knows how many years ago, and beyond those heavy timbers there waited—what? A modern company of highly trained parachutists ready to shoot without warning? It seemed there could not be anything so out of place; I began to expect that a group of frightened hunters would be crouched there, shaggy-haired and draped in skins, their copper knives drawn and ready, with huge jaws and low foreheads and tiny black eyes that peered suspiciously out from under simian brows...

Again I felt desperately guilty about Karen, but when I looked at her I saw that there was no trace of fear on her set face; it is wonderful what a woman will face when she has to. Her revolver was leveled and steady, and its rigidity amazed me. I badly wanted to cough to free the tension in my throat.

And then the corporal flung open the door and stepped forward, his Bren gun ready. I followed him in, moving so fast that I had reached the far corner of the room before he even knew I had gone past him. But there was no sound or movement in that deathly room.

It was larger by far than the antechamber, with a tall curved roof of natural rock, a cave with the floor artificially leveled, and there were other doors leading off it, all closed, three of them in one straight line along the wall to my left.

There was a table there, and a few chairs, and a big filing

cabinet that had been turned over on its side, and eight or nine dead men lay on the floor in silence. One of them, staring sightlessly up at the light in the roof, was one of the Egyptian pilots whom we had seen in Rome; it was the one who had affectionately patted the aircraft he had never taken and said, "They don't make planes like this anymore." He'd flown his last aircraft, and there was a bullet hole in his throat, on the underside of his jaw.

I heard Karen shudder.

In one corner, the roof of the chamber had collapsed in a dangerous rock fall, and a dreadfully twisted leg was protruding from underneath it, a bare brown leg, well-muscled but now unmoving. A cloud of dust came down from the ceiling, and a little rubble followed it, and I knew that it would not take much more shooting to bring the whole lot down on us.

We looked over the bodies one by one. Both the Israeli medical orderlies were there, and one of them was doubled up as though still in pain, and the back of his head had been caved in. The others were all in Egyptian uniform, their parachute helmets gleaming queerly in the yellow light. I counted them carefully and said:

"How many men could have got in here?"

The corporal was looking at the line of closed doors. He took his eyes off them briefly and said:

"At most, eleven."

"There were nine in the first group—"

"No, ten."

"And it looked like six in the second, but they weren't in sight for very long... Could there have been any others?"

"We would have seen them. There were thirteen men left after my machine gun got three of them; they left two at the base of the path, perhaps two more on the other side?" He looked at me again and said, "No, I don't think so; they'd weaken themselves too much and those two men could keep a sufficient watch on the emplacement above them. So there are eleven of them in here, less—" He counted the bodies as I had done and said, "Less eight. The odds are getting better."

"Three soldiers, plus Martin, one of the airmen, and the civilian."

"We can discount Martin, a useless old man, useful for only one thing."

"Five men then. And there are five of us. What about Nathan?"

He shook his head. "I don't know. Perhaps he still has the prisoners somewhere. He would not surrender them easily."

"Easily? By the looks of the battle that went on down here—"

"Yes, I know. But he would do anything to hold on to them. He might have got them out in time."

The silence seemed all the heavier because of the reboant noise there must have been down here as the battle went on. I said hopelessly:

"If we only knew where the three soldiers are."

But the corporal said with satisfaction, "A major raid, and there are only three of them left."

"And look at the price. We're the only survivors."

"Yes. The price was high."

I could sense his partisan pride, but I could not so easily ignore the smell of death that was all around us. I knew that for the corporal it was part of a pattern, part of his daily life, from one short skirmish to another, from one secret raid to the next, all part of the struggle to keep his country alive in the middle of violent, ruthless enmity. I said, "I can't accept it as easily as you do, I don't even want to."

"You must." He looked at me again and said, "If you are part of us you *must* accept it."

"I've been spoiled by peace and luxury for too long. I can't."

He said quietly, "In Cairo, they have been boasting publicly, for many years now, that they would destroy us. Not an unspoken thought, but a published word, in the papers, on the radio, everywhere. They are sworn to destroy us, and what you see here is part of their attempt. It is failing, and it will always fail, and you must accept this because every one of us knows that until Nasser is stopped this is what we will always be doing—killing, and trying to save as many lives as we can." He said angrily, "This is *our* country; we did not ask them to come here."

The incongruity was too much to be supported by anything except the colstaff of his emotion. I said gently:

"You *did* invite them here. When you abducted them in Rome, you asked for them to come."

At least he was honest about it. He groped at the air and said:

"Of course, I cannot excuse it except—by the desperation of necessity. Even I know how needful it was to stop that man from reaching Cairo. Perhaps, to an outsider, it is not easy to explain, but—" He was so desperately anxious for me to believe with him.

I said, "I'm not really an outsider. Not anymore. Right or wrong, you can count me in."

The colonel had long ago convinced me. Does the end sometimes justify the means? Unless you're a pious idiot, of course it does.

But for the corporal it was as though his remarks had changed the whole course of his philosophy, and I echoed what I knew were his thoughts and smiled and said:

"All right, another goddam Gentile on your side, if that's the way you want it."

I looked at Karen and saw her smile, and I thought, *There's precious little to smile for, we're not out of the woods by any means; three dangerous men on the loose with machine pistols and grenades, and Malafir as well, who might be more dangerous than all the others combined; the odds are better, but it still takes only one bullet to kill a woman or, worse, shatter the beauty and leave it alive and wretched.*

During the war, in Benghazi, I once saw a looting Arab smash a marble statue just for the sheer joy of it, just because it was Italian; it did not matter to him that it was a marvelously beautiful piece of sculpture that had been dredged from the Ionian Sea two hundred years ago, still smooth and placid and full of the devotion the artist had given it when, in a civilization that was so far behind us that these works were its only memory, he had labored over it so lovingly... No, to the rampaging Arab it smelled of Italy and therefore had to be destroyed, and when I saw it lying there in broken pieces, a masterpiece that had survived a thousand wars but could not survive one man's reckless hatred, I swung my gun at him and beat the hell out of him, and left him lying there broken and bleeding among the wreckage...

I could not forget it; Karen's skin was as smooth as the marble of that statue, her breast as firm, her features as fine; and the thought of damage to her beauty was the thought of iconoclasm rather than of pain. There is so little beauty in the world we live in, and the way we're heading, it seems what has been left to us won't last much longer either.

I said, indicating the doors, "What's in there?"

There were inscriptions on them that I could not read, and Marks said:

"All it says is 'No Entrance,'"

"Well, that's useful."

The corporal jerked his head and said, "That one's the generating plant, the middle one is the pump for the water, and the other—"

I saw that the two doors he had indicated had padlocks on the outside, and if there were no other way in, that rather presupposed they'd be empty. Unless—

The corporal said, "We'd better try that one; the padlock's gone."

"Where does it lead to?"

He shook his head. "I don't know. I believe there are more tunnels, the old workings blocked off. They say they're not very safe."

"Lights?"

Again, "I don't know, I've never been down there. But there's no other way into those two, and they're locked on the outside."

"Unless Nathan had himself locked in there with the prisoners, before the fighting started."

He looked at me for a moment and thought about this, then his eyes went to the Egyptian pilot on the floor and he said:

"He wouldn't have left one of them behind."

"He could have lost him if there was a struggle. I don't think either Nathan or Malafir would give up very easily, and there must have been a bloody awful fight down here."

He thought about this some more and then went to the doors and banged on them, shouting out in Hebrew. The doors both sounded mighty solid, but I imagined that if anyone were in there we'd have been answered clearly enough. But only the echo of his knocking broke the silence. We moved over to the last door. I could sense an easing of the tension, and I knew it was dangerous.

I said, "We've been bloody lucky so far. All the fighting's

been done for us; let's not get careless."

I knew how easy it was, but it's the final bullet that wins the argument, not the first one that you don't even know has been fired. Three men with submachine guns and grenades and God knows what all else, somewhere in these tunnels—or perhaps up in the night above us, already heading for the border? Who could tell?

I was desperately tired of the scent of death, tired of seeing a battle I had known about but never really understood because I was not part of it. It had always been so easy to read the papers over the breakfast coffee and to shrug.

Four Israeli soldiers were killed in a border skirmish on the Egyptian frontier...

Two farmers were murdered by a group of Iraqi irregulars...

A Jewish settlement in the Negev was strafed this morning by unmarked planes coming in from the Syrian frontier...

Before, it had always been merely part of the news, and the news is easy to take because you get used to it, uncaring about it; it's too constant a pattern and too far from the breakfast table. *Pour me another cup of coffee, darling, and let's go to the theater tonight.*

Not anymore. I had not known, not really known, any of the young men who had died. But I could not help looking at Marks and wondering: A cheerful young Londoner who has remembered his heritage: will he be the next? Karen was my first care, but we were both the interlopers, the strangers—Marks was one of *them*. The fear of seeing his bloodless face staring up at the ceiling was intolerable, and he was suddenly my brother.

The corporal was standing by the closed door, the one without the padlock. I said nervously:

"For God's sake, don't throw it open like you did the last time; you're pushing the luck too far."

But he was a soldier. He said, "And don't follow me in; I told you where to stand."

I nodded. "I know you've had your orders, I know you feel a

responsibility, but I'm one of you now, another rifle, and I know how to use it."

It was no good arguing with him. He said:

"My responsibility is to all of you, not you alone. Stand where I tell you, wait till I call you in there."

I sighed, and he said more gently, "I know you want to help. Please, you must accept my orders."

"OK, you're the general."

There wasn't really very much humor in him. He said, "No, just a corporal, but I'm in command now, there's nobody else."

I stood aside as he had ordered, and he tried the lock. The door began to open slowly. He threw it wide open and jumped back and waited, and we waited with him. I fancied I could hear the ticking of my watch.

Suddenly he was in the room, moving fast for an old man, and there was a burst of gunfire and I saw him come out again, not stepping back but being thrown back, his arms grotesquely twisted and both his feet off the ground. The Bren gun was shooting up into the air, his hand curled tightly around it, the finger rigid on the trigger and the gun running away, and another burst from inside the room went over his head and splattered into the wall across the room, chipping pieces out of the sandstone, and as the corporal fell to the ground, with the gun still running off, I shoved Karen away and fell into the room, firing the rifle as I dropped...

There was just one man there, a wounded Egyptian parachutist who was propped up against a corner of the wall with a bloody bandage around his knee and his submachine gun trained on the door.

My first shot missed him, but the second hit him in the throat and he toppled over, and there was just time to see that there was no one else in the room before I scrambled to my feet and ran to Karen; she was bending over the elderly corporal, trying to help and knowing there was nothing she could do. His chest was torn open by the slugs, but he was still alive. He flailed his arms and clutched at her, and said something in Hebrew, gasping and spluttering and spitting out more blood than words, seeming to try desperately to make himself understood... And then he died.

I pulled her away from him and tried to comfort her, but she kept repeating over and over: "There's nothing I can do for him, nothing, nothing at all..." I knew she was close to hysteria and there were no words I could find that would help her either.

Marks was standing there, white-faced, staring at Karen. I looked at him, puzzled, and said:

"What was—the corporal—what was it he was trying to say?"

And Marks said, his voice hollow with pain:

"He thought—he thought she was his daughter. He said, 'Do not cry too much, Yedida, do not cry for me too much...'"

He turned on his heel and went into the other room and came back silently with the weapon that had killed the corporal and held it out to me. He said, "Do you know how to use it? I don't, but I suppose—" He looked at the corporal and said, "He put me on a charge last week, for a dirty rifle..." He was trying to find an easement, an alleviation of the pain in anything that was inconsequential. He looked at Karen and said, "A woman shouldn't even see such things."

It was not a pleasant sight, the terrible end of a man whose home was once half of Europe, and then the tiny state, and now—now it was no more than a bloodied patch of sandstone deep in the caves that his ancestors had carved for themselves untold centuries ago.

I said, "Two of the parachutists left. And the others?"

I wished the hell I knew if Nathan was still alive, but it was getting more and more obvious that he couldn't be. Somehow, in Nathan's easy confidence, in his taut assurance of authority, there was an intangible asset that I felt I needed now more than anything else in the world.

It was hard to reconcile the past image I'd had of him with what he seemed to be, now that I was, almost, one of them against the others. I could still feel the ache of the bruise he'd given me, but with so much that was hateful and sordid around us it was easy to remember that he could just as easily have killed me then; another life—it seemed so little when now we were in the middle of a pitched battle with no quarter on either side.

I took the submachine gun that Marks was holding out for me and checked the markings on it: it was a Skoda, made in Czechoslovakia, but the markings on it were Russian.

There was a time, in the bad old days between the wars, when every battlefield you came across was littered with the guns that came from Krupp in Germany, and it was fashionable to regard the armaments kings as the international villains. But today all the major markets have been taken over by the two giants, and wherever there's a war going on you'll find the abundance of weapons, in pious hands or evil, used well or badly, and they're either Russian or American. It's a sad thought.

We all went into the other room, and the only door out of it was locked. Not only locked; there was a damn great padlocked bar across the front of it, and it was made of steel. I looked at the inscription on it and asked Marks what it was.

He said briefly, "'Ammunition, keep out.'"

I checked the lock and the door itself and was reasonably sure that no one could get through it without leaving a trace of some sort, and we explored the rest of the room, and the two antechambers, and there was nothing. I checked my watch and found, to my surprise, that it was only half-past eight. In Rome, we'd just be starting dinner, maybe in the little gardened *trattoria* around the corner from Tasso's miraculous tree; it seemed an awfully long way off, both in time and distance.

Was it only yesterday? I wondered about Simona...

I said, "Not a goddam thing down here, just—dead men," and Marks said harshly:

"Let's get out of here, for Christ's sake." He looked at Karen and mumbled, "I beg your pardon, miss, but—"

She nodded. Her voice was terribly subdued, and I wished she would cry; but she could not. "There's nothing we can do for any of them," she said again.

I took her arm and gently guided her back the way we had come, and once we left the lighted rooms all the old childhood fears of the dark came back. We were three frightened people in a dark tunnel under the darker earth, and all around us were the spirits of evil waiting for a false step from any one of us, waiting to move in on us and crush us completely.

We climbed slowly up the slope to where the mine entrance was, and when we stepped out into the desert the moon had come up and everything was washed in a pale blue light that seemed unreal.

Osmani, the grinning young Yemeni soldier, was lying on the ground in the shadow of the cliff, and when I bent down and touched him, his head fell loosely to one side.

His neck had been broken.

CHAPTER 12

We stood there together, the three of us, the only three people on this planet left alive, all bunched up and asking for trouble.

It's no excuse, I suppose, that we had thought the battle was almost over, and that they'd all be well on the way to the frontier by now. It is no excuse that the fresh clean air after the terrible death trap of the mine seemed, stupidly enough, to be a token that the danger had all gone away; we'd forgotten that there can be just as much mayhem in the moonlight as there is in the bowels of the earth's secret places.

Somebody said, in English, and very clearly, "Don't turn around, and keep quite still." I froze, and I saw Marks begin to move. It was not a movement at all, just an instinctive arresting of motion, as though he were delicately balanced and might fall if he did not shift the support the tiniest bit. But it was enough. The voice said firmly—and I fancied that it was tinged with fright, which made it worse, "The gun is a machine gun; keep still."

The insistence was unnecessary. I don't know how long it takes to make a full turn, swing a heavy Skoda into action, get rid of the rifle I'd slung over my shoulder (what a hell of a surfeit of weapons!) and start shooting; I didn't even want to know; it's less time than it takes to pull a trigger, and bunched up as we were...

I said, "All right, take it easy, no one's moving." Karen was standing close to me, half-turned, and I could see the revolver back in her waistband; it seemed important that they shouldn't see her with it, for reasons that were not clear at all and probably were prompted by fright as much as by anything else. I took the ball with both hands and said loudly, "I'm dropping my Skoda, all right?" And as I let it fall I contrived to jerk the revolver away from Karen's waist too, and said, "Both of them, a rifle to come."

The voice said, "Slowly, please."

It was quite polite, and the fear seemed to have gone from it now that I'd shown mine; perhaps it was only nervousness, and that's important too, because when there's a gun pointed at me, and there hadn't been in a mighty long time, I like the finger on the trigger to be steady as a rock and to know what it's doing; it's much safer.

I unslung the rifle slowly and dropped it to the sand, and Marks, taking a leaf out of my book but not meeting my eye, did the same. I sensed the accusation in his manner, and I said to him sourly, "Among other things, there's a lady present and we don't take any risks."

The voice said, "That's right, Mr. Benasque; no risks and you won't get hurt."

Well, that was a pleasant thought. Not waiting for permission—arrogating to myself a limited assumption of action—I turned around slowly to see who it was; as if I didn't know.

It was Malafir, the man from the thing they called Special Military Projects, and both the remaining parachutists were with him; one of them held a light machine pistol trained on us, and the other was covering us very effectively with another of the Skodas, just like the one I'd uselessly taken from the room down below. The other pilot, young and nervous, obviously frightened even in the half-light, stood a little to one side, and he too was armed, with an automatic pistol which was wavering unhappily.

I said to Malafir, "That youngster with the pistol—it's going off any minute now, if he's not careful." He made no comment. He was unarmed himself, and I said, "Two bloody machine guns and a pistol—isn't that rather a lot, under the circumstances?" He still made no reply and so I asked, just to keep the ball rolling as long as I could: "How come you know my name? I don't know yours."

He shrugged. "I asked, in Rome, and there is no reason why you should know mine. But I would like you to account for your presence here."

I put on a surprised look and said, "Hell, you saw them kidnap us, all of us together." The scent of togetherness was pretty unpleasant, and I hoped Marks knew what I was trying, without much hope of success, to do.

Malafir said, "I mean here, on this spot, with a gun in your hand."

I said, "After the battle—"

He said quickly, "And where were you then?"

He might have known from the soldiers who had seen us, so I said frankly, "Up at the top there; they didn't want us to get killed."

"And so?"

"And so, when the shooting stopped, they wanted to come down and they brought us with them, that's all. I helped myself to a gun down there because I was afraid I might need it."

"Against us?"

Bless his foul heart, he still wasn't sure what side we were on. It looked hopeful. I said blandly:

"Against anyone who started shooting at us. I didn't intend to get hurt over someone else's political whims."

I did not dare look at Marks. I could not tell from his silence whether he believed all this baloney, or thought what I had been telling *him*, when my life seemed at stake from *them*, was the baloney... If you're going to lie to one man in the presence of another, you've got to be pretty sure that someone knows *when* you're telling the truth. And in less than eighteen hours I couldn't expect Marks to get to know me very well.

His quiet acceptance was a condemnation and I wanted to squirm.

But the immediate problem was going well. Malafir said:

"That is as may be, Mr. Benasque, but now, if you will all come with me..."

Safe in the knowledge of his bodyguard, he turned sharply away. A machine gun gestured us to follow, and I took Karen's arm and squeezed it, meaning something or other, and looked at Marks's tight-lipped face and winked quickly, hoping he might learn by so simple a gesture that something was going on even if I couldn't tell him what it was. But his look did not lose its tautness.

We followed Malafir over to what was left of the burned-out mess hall, and there, large as life and almost as uncertain, was Muller or Martin or whatever his bloody name was. He was sitting at a table with his head in his hands and an opened but untouched bottle of beer in front of him. I wanted to say to him, "You'd better not touch that, chum, it's Israeli beer and probably kosher," but I thought it wiser to keep quiet. I didn't even know if they knew we knew who he really was, if that's not too involved...

He looked up as we came in, and had the grace to appear startled, and Malafir said, in German, "Only the one left." He looked at me coolly and said, "You understand German, of course?"

I couldn't remember without hesitation whether or not I had spoken German in Rome to Muller, as he was then, so I played it safe. I said, "Badly, but enough to get by."

"And French and Italian, of course." He was trying to find out something else. He'd heard me talk Italian in Rome, and maybe French too, for all I could remember, but I knew what he was getting at.

I nodded. "French and Italian well; I spent most of my life in Europe."

Then he turned his back to me, and, switching to Arabic, said coldly to the young pilot—who, thank God, had put away his gun, "Kill him."

I swear that showing no alarm was the hardest thing I'd ever done in my life. I was looking at Marks and I saw that he had not understood and that was a point in our favor, and while the pilot (I dared not look to see what he was doing) was fumbling for his pistol I was aware that Malafir had turned again and was watching me closely.

I'd been expecting something like this, of course, though nothing quite as dramatic and frightening, so I looked down at my damaged shinbone and said as casually as I could, "I cut my bloody leg open," just as though I hadn't a care in the world.

It was a pretty good performance. The pilot's gun came out and he sort of began to aim it at me, and I sort of noticed for the first time and said, "What the hell's he up to?" without too much alarm on my face, and Malafir said, again in Arabic:

"Put it away."

Well, that was something at least. He was sure I didn't speak any Arabic.

I shudder to think what would have happened if I hadn't been ready for it. I would have leaped at the pilot and a lot of people, mostly us, would have been dead. I held out a chair for Karen, and Malafir said roughly:

"Sit down, both of you."

Marks pulled out a chair too, and Malafir, "Not you. You stand."

I could see that things weren't going to be very pleasant for Marks. I started making calculations about when an Israeli patrol might get here, and then Malafir, who was obviously thinking along the same lines, said to the pilot in Arabic, "We may not have much time."

I reached out and took Martin's beer bottle and said, affably enough, I hope, "May I? I'm desperately thirsty." Martin nodded miserably, and I held the bottle out to Karen, and when she shook her head I took a good long swig of it.

I waved the bottle at her and said quickly, *"Sempre soda,"* which was a pretty smart move, because to any ear other than pure Italian it would have sounded, accompanied by the gesture, like *sembre soda,* meaning "It tastes like soda water." But it actually meant something quite different and another attitude altogether...

In Roman slang, *sempre soda* means, robbed of its vulgarity: "still bedworthy, still capable, still working well"; or, at a pinch: "there's still a lot I can do and I'm doing it, so don't believe this nonsense I'm talking."

Karen got the message, because those eyes changed color at once. I wished Marks could get it too, but he couldn't, and he still looked sour as a glass of cheap wine; but Malafir capped it for me by saying:

"Jewish beer, Mr. Benasque, but soon we will give you some of our good Egyptian stuff. And please don't talk Italian; we all understand English better."

He still wasn't too sure of himself, wasn't sure which side I was on, but he didn't want to take any chances. He said:

"There's just one formality, and then we'll be on our way. Where is the man they call Nathan?"

I shook my head and said easily, "I'm afraid I don't know. Haven't seen him since we left the aircraft. He's probably as dead as the others."

I fancied that the hard lines around his mouth tightened a trace. Dammit, I knew he couldn't be sure if we knew anything at all.

I said, "We were still with Herr Muller when he left. They took us into the mess and we stayed there till the fighting started. Then this man showed us where the shelter was, and after the fighting stopped out there in the desert, we climbed to the top, where we thought it might be safer. As I said, I didn't want to get mixed up in it; I'm a peace-loving man."

"Ye-es." He looked at me for a while and then turned to the pilot. He said in Arabic, while I carefully paid no attention, "You know the desert well; can we make the border before the patrol gets here?"

The pilot looked at me anxiously and Malafir said with a trace of impatience, "He doesn't understand. How long will it take us?"

"Four hours."

Malafir made a gesture of impatience. He looked at me once more, to assure himself that I didn't know what was going on, and then I settled back, lit a cigarette from a pack on the table, and listened to a very interesting conversation. The pilot seemed to hold Malafir in a certain amount of respect, and he was nervous as hell, but he seemed to know what he was talking about.

The conversation, and I can remember it pretty accurately, went something like this:

Malafir: "It's ten miles; how can it take so long?"

Pilot: "In soft sand, dunes all the way, at least four hours, even more."

Malafir: "They'll send planes to look for us, day or night; it makes no difference."

Pilot: "They're sure to."

Malafir: "Any cover we can take?"

Pilot: "A patch here, a patch there. Open dune country, most of it, and you can't move fast in dune sand; it's up to your knees."

Malafir: "We've got to get them back! If these heathens catch us out there in the open... They should have sent a patrol in as well, with a troop carrier, to wait for us a mile or two out in the desert."

Pilot: "You can't move trucks over that stuff. And a chance air patrol might have spotted them. Besides, there wasn't time—"

Malafir: "All right, all right."

It was getting better by the minute. I kept my slightly worried look on, and said as though nothing else mattered, "Can I help myself to some more beer?"

Malafir nodded. "In the cupboard there." He looked at Marks, standing silently and stoically there, and added, "He doesn't get any."

It seemed very petty, but I said nonchalantly, "I should worry."

I got up to fetch the beer and contrived to let Marks see a gesture I made, a finger to my lips. I knew he wouldn't talk out of turn, but I desperately wanted him to realize we were still on his side. I thought I saw a gleam of interest in his eyes, and I searched the memories of London, where I'd lived for a while, to try and recall a phrase, a sentence, a word, in back slang that he would understand and the others wouldn't; but I could think of nothing, and his glumness was contagious. When I sat down again, the conversation went on, just as if we weren't there.

Malafir: "I wish I knew where—the other man is. Don't mention his name."

Pilot: "I know who you mean. He must be dead."

Malafir: "I'd be happier if we found his body."

Pilot: "I wonder if they'd know?"

Malafir: "How should they? They were prisoners too."

Pilot: "Yes, but not for long. And then they turn up carrying arms."

There was a long silence now. Malafir took a cigarette and lit it, and then went on with the friendly chat.

Malafir: "Once they landed here we didn't see them again. He's an American, and it's just possible he's on their side."

Pilot: "And he could have made a deal with them. He's the type."

Malafir: "Ye-es."

Pilot: "It shouldn't be hard to find out."

Malafir looked at me coolly and I said lightly, "Talking about me?"

He nodded. "Just wondering if you might be on their side."

I laughed shortly. "What civilized man is?" I wondered if that was laying it on too heavily; I thought perhaps not; there's nothing like the unsubtle shovel for laying on the prejudices.

Malafir looked back at the pilot and spoke slowly.

Malafir: "It's not hard to make a man talk, given time. That's the one thing we haven't got. Every minute counts now."

Pilot: "If I knew why it's so important to find—him."

Malafir: "I want to be sure he's dead. If we start to cross that desert with just one man behind us, a man with a rifle—"

Pilot: "Are we worried about pursuit by—that man, or by aircraft?"

Malafir: "Both."

Pilot: "Find out if he's alive from the man, through the woman. They're lovers, they must be. Give her to me, and he'll talk."

Malafir: "If I were sure he knows, I would."

Pilot: "Then take them with us, hostages; they won't dare attack."

Again that long pause. Malafir looked at Martin and turned back to the pilot.

Malafir: "You think we can cross to the border with all of them? The woman as well?"

Pilot: "She looks healthy enough. We've got to take the old man anyway."

Malafir: "I don't underestimate that man, even if he is a Jew, and I don't like it that we couldn't find his body. If he's still alive—he can put the planes onto us, and then where will we be? Planes wouldn't have time to see that we had hostages. Unless—"

Pilot: "Unless what?"

Malafir did not answer. He stood up instead and came over to stand beside my chair. He looked down at me and said:

"I wish I could feel sure you don't know about Nathan."

I put on a surprised look and said, "Nathan? How the hell should I? I wish I did." I touched the scar on my face and said, "I still owe him for this."

He was torn between acceptance and uncertainty. "You realize we could force you to tell us?"

"How could you? I don't know and that's all there is to it."

"But we could try and find out. I realize that you were abducted just as violently as we were. But since then, there's an area of doubt. We found you armed."

"Doesn't mean a thing." I snorted with what I hoped was disdain, and said, "Oh, I realize that my weapons could be misinterpreted; I'm in a spot, I know that. If I knew anything at all, I'd tell you like a shot; why should I worry on their behalf?" I touched my bruised face again, hoping the scar was still visible; it probably wasn't. "That bastard pistol-whipped me; why should I care what happens to him?"

Malafir looked at Marks, and I was as sure as I could be sure of anything that he was going to say again to the pilot or one of the parachutists, "Kill him"; and that this time he was going to mean it.

I could see it in his expression of utter contempt. I knew that to him, Marks was just a simple soldier who would know nothing of such secret matters, an armed and simple man who would do as he was told and ask no questions; a Jew who would be an unwanted passenger on the long trek across the desert, along the ten miles that took four hours because you could only labor forward an inch at a time.

I said quickly, showing myself to be friendly (and taking a desperate gamble on time), "This man here, he's not as simple as he looks. He's one of their intelligence men."

I saw Marks's look of surprise and it turned to horror; he knew just what they would do to him, but since he spoke no Arabic he didn't know what I had heard them say: "Time is the one thing we haven't got. Every minute counts now."

Malafir said, "Oh? That's very interesting." He spoke to the pilot in Arabic. "We'll take him with us; an intelligence man, they'll want to examine him in Cairo."

The pilot said, "Good."

Malafir looked at his watch and frowned. He turned to me and said, still with that suave politeness:

"We will all walk across the desert to the frontier; there's a post there. Only—I'm afraid we have to leave you behind."

Now, in almost any other language but English, you is either singular or plural but not both. In German he would have said *du* or *Sie*, and in Italian it would have been *lei* or *voi*, and I would have known at once what he was saying. But he spoke English, and I didn't know.

I touched Karen on the arm and said, smiling, "Good, that's

fine. I suppose they'll pick us up here in the course of time and send us back—"

Malafir smiled and said, "Just you. The lady comes with us."

Now it was all quite clear. The hostages and still someone left behind when the ground patrol turned up, someone to plead: "Don't attack them, they've got my girl; radio the planes, for God's sake."

Now I was really scared. I said angrily, "We stay together. If she goes, so do I."

"No. She goes, you stay."

I looked at Karen and saw that she was white with fear. She had not leaned on me for long, not more than a few months, but I had brought her something she was looking for even if I wasn't sure what it was. She knew she could trust me to look out for her, and I was standing there and letting them take her away from me merely because some goddam punk was holding a machine gun on me.

I knew they wanted me to stay there—alive. I put an arm around Karen and pulled her closer to me and said again:

"She stays. With me."

Malafir merely jerked his head at one of the silent parachutists who stood by the door; he raised his gun and Malafir said sharply, "Alive."

I stood and faced them for a moment, moving clear of Karen and standing there like an idiot waiting to do battle, with my hands hanging loose at my sides and not knowing what the hell to do next.

Malafir said calmly, making sure I knew what was going on:

"When the Jews come, you will tell them that we have hostages. Perhaps they won't care, but I leave it to you, Mr. Benasque, to convince them. I'm quite sure you can do that."

His tone of voice changed, and he said angrily in Arabic, "Hurry, we haven't got all day."

One of the parachutists grunted at the pilot and handed him his gun, and when he advanced on me I threw a right hook at him that came up from the ground; it didn't even connect, but my second one did, and when he went down I hurled myself at the second man and grabbed for his gun; it came up and the stock hit me under the jaw and I just had time to see his dark, impassive Bedouin face when all the lights in the world went out and then came on again in bright red flashes of pain.

I do not know how long I was out, but when I tried to finger my jaw to see if it was broken, I was already tied fast to the chair by the arms and ankles, and Marks, deathly white, was standing with his arms raised and a pistol held by the nervous pilot at his head, half moving and half not daring to; and Karen, the source of his worry, was struggling with the parachutist who had hit me. I saw Malafir put out a lazy arm and swing her around toward him, and then hit her hard across the face. She fell to the ground, her skirt incongruously up around her waist, and it was the sight of her long white thighs, I think, that worried me more than anything else.

I struggled against the tight ropes and shouted to her, "Don't fight! Go with them; it's going to be all right."

I could only hope that the almost pathetic trust she had in me would be justified. And I knew that now there was nothing I could do to help her. She climbed slowly to her feet and straightened her dress, and came over and crouched on the floor beside me and she was crying softly. I said quietly, "Go with them, my darling, it's the best thing." The sight of her worried and angry face was almost more than I could bear. I risked a word of Italian: "*Non è finito*—it's not over yet."

At that moment I didn't care a damn whether or not they thought I was up to something; it was a conscious reflex of hopeless desperation and they knew it. And so did I.

Karen brushed at her eyes with the tips of her fingers and then leaned down and kissed me, and when Malafir put out a hand again to touch her, I said angrily:

"She's going with you; leave her alone."

His hand dropped. He said shortly, "We must hurry. Come."

Before I could stop trembling with the fear of what was going to happen to her, they were gone. They tied Marks's hands cruelly to his thighs before they left, and then they left me with my thoughts.

I was trussed, and helpless, and alone; and God alone knew what they would do to my girl.

CHAPTER 13

Now, there's a drill all laid down for the predicament I was in, quite obvious to anyone who has ever seen Pearl White or read Edgar Wallace.

All you have to do, it says in the book, is find a piece of broken glass and cut yourself free; that's what the books says. And all I say is, just try it.

There was no glass in the windows, but there was a beer bottle and a tumbler on the table, so that was the direction I had to take. I jiggled the chair I was tied to over to the table without much difficulty, and that's where the trouble started.

I tried, with my back to it, to reach the glass and couldn't, so I sort of threw myself sideways against the table and upset it, and there was the glass and the bottle on the floor—unbroken, of course—and I couldn't reach them down there either; so I worked the chair into the proper position and rocked it sideways till I fell on them both, and the bottle, which did not break, caught me on the funny bone and gave me hell, and the glass, which did, cut a great gash in my arm that bled uncomfortably freely.

I thought, *Well, if it will cut me up it will cut the ropes too, just like the book says.* I very carefully wiggled myself around to take a good look at it, found the only piece I could use, which was the broken bottom part, because the rest was in tiny fragments, and then wiggled around again until my wrists were over it, more or less.

Seemed it was rather less than more. I cut myself badly again, twice, and I still couldn't find the sharp edge I wanted, which was everywhere except on the ropes, and I kept on wiggling until I got absolutely nowhere. Then a piece of glass broke off and stuck in my rear end, and altogether it was a pretty miserable effort.

I squirmed around again to take another look and tried once more the same as before, and again I got nowhere. A good large piece of window glass was what I wanted, something big enough to hold in position on the floor with my own weight so that I could gently saw at the ropes with the edge. I tried with a jagged piece of asbestos paneling from the bombed-out wall, but it was too soft.

It suddenly occurred to me that there were mirrors on the shelf in the bathroom, and if I remembered rightly they were not fastened to the wall but merely standing free. It couldn't have taken me much more than half an hour to get as far as the bathroom door, and then it was shut, and though I tried to turn the knob with my teeth—just like Rin-Tin-Tin—that was a failure too, even after it had taken me ten minutes to get my head high enough.

But I was getting good at maneuvering that damned chair around, if nothing else, and I went back into the hall and hurled myself at the sideboard repeatedly until it toppled over, and then it missed my head by half an inch and crashed to the floor with a wallop that would have brained me. And now the whole floor was covered with broken glass and there were at least a dozen pieces that ought to have done the trick, but—well, it just isn't easy, is all I can say.

I tried for another hour at least, and only succeeded in ripping great gashes in my arms and hands and legs, and that bloody glass was everywhere except where I wanted it. I was ready to weep with sheer frustration.

I gave it up at last and rested, almost exhausted, and then I began to think about Karen with those bastards out there in the desert, and of the desert itself, knowing that if that nervous little pilot didn't really know his way around on the ground, and most of them don't, they were going to miss the frontier post they were aiming at. It only wants a fraction of a degree off course in a ten-mile straight line to throw a wandering man hopelessly out. And in dune country they'd have to hit it right on the nose or they'd walk right past it, if they were still capable of walking at all.

The more I thought about it the less I liked it. You can walk past one side of a dune without seeing what is on the other side of it even if it's only a hundred yards away, and after their ten-mile hike there were another hundred and fifty miles of nothing, even if they weren't already walking around in circles, slowly drying out.

It's easy to discard the thoughts of desert danger when you talk only in terms of mileage. I lost a man once in the Sahara who died of thirst less than half a mile from his own camp; he just couldn't see it; the other side of a dune...

There's no stronger word than "arid," and it will have to do. When the sand is fine dry powder, dry as a bleached bone, and the heat of the sun is reflected back at you like the blast of an open oven, and you begin to gasp for moisture—and the thought of Karen out there...

I went back, bleeding all over the place, to the glass, and when it started to get light and there was still nothing but silence around me, no sign of a plane or a patrol, I was sick with desperation.

And then a rope gave. Whether it was cut or just worn out with my struggling I neither know nor care. One rope went, and a thumb was free, and then two fingers and then a whole hand, and in ten more minutes I was standing up and heading for the bathroom to wash away some of the blood and to find something to stanch its flow.

I found a first-aid kit, and a haversack, and a rifle, and a lot of other things I needed, among them some binoculars, and including some eggs in a kerosene refrigerator.

It may seem callous, but I forced aside the thought of Karen and the desperation to get there fast and broke open six eggs and swallowed them, and drank a lot of water to get my belly full of it, because I knew I might have to go farther than I reckoned; and I packed some bread and goat's cheese into the haversack and found room for a bottle of Carmel brandy as well; I drank another half-bottle of it there and then, and though it wasn't exactly Courvoisier 1909, it wasn't too bad really. In the kitchen there was a biggish aluminum tank that was made to hold about ten gallons of water and be strapped to the side of a truck, and I found some rope and put a half-hitch on it.

I could easily have carried seven or eight water bottles if I'd wanted them, and there were plenty lying around. But ten gallons is more than fifty bottles and, if you're in a hurry, it's easier to drag a hundred pounds along the sand than to carry it—a trick I'd learned a long time ago. Dragging my tank behind me, I was desert-equipped for one hell of a long time.

I found pencil and paper and wrote a note:

The Egyptians are heading for a frontier post ten miles west and they have Miss d'Arno and Private Marks as hostages; they'll kill them both if they have to. I am following. If you send planes, for God's sake tell them about the hostages.

I signed it and stuck it in what was left of the mess-hall door with a couple of nails, and then I went back to the kitchen, forcing myself to take time out for one last look around, to see if there might be anything else there that would come in handy. I settled for a long butcher's knife and put it into my belt, at the back where it was out of the way.

And then I took a twist of the rope over my shoulder and set off, dragging my water behind me; like a Bedouin's prayer carpet, it was the anchor for my whole existence.

The tracks I was following were the only signs of life in the flat stretch of sand that was limited only by the horizon, once I had passed the battlefield; and there, the only sign of life was the tragic abnegation of it. I did not stop there except to look briefly for the body of the colonel. His horribly mutilated body was upended in the wadi which the parachutists had held against the tiny force that had gone so foolishly out to attack it. I climbed down into the wadi and up the other side, heaving on my rope, and then the true dune country began.

These were the real dunes, eighty or ninety feet high, crescent shaped and moving at the rate of twenty or thirty feet a year, alternately covering and uncovering everything in their path, though here there was nothing to be covered except a few stretches of hard red rock and, once in a while, a ruined piece of Nabataean or Roman or Kenite wall.

The sand was so soft that I sank in all the time up to my ankles, and sometimes, with the weight of the tank behind me, as far as my knees. It was easier going down the other side of the dunes; I simply slid and kept tugging at that rope to bring the tank down after me, and then the long haul up the next dune would begin again. With the heat already blasting up on me from the hot-to-the-touch sand and mercilessly beating down out of a scorching sky, I wondered what it was going to be like at midday.

I went over the tops of seventeen or eighteen dunes before all the water I'd drunk had come out in sweat, and then the sudden cessation of perspiration gave me adequate warning that it was time to drink. I unscrewed the cap of the tank, soaked my handkerchief and sucked it dry, then moved on. A few more dunes, and then the tracks just disappeared. I'd covered, I supposed, five or six miles, but it was hard to tell.

I'd come to a break in the pattern, a wide flat ledge of burning rock, too hard to hold footsteps, and at the slope of the dune facing me I could not see any signs of them. I cast around for a precious fifteen minutes until at last I found tracks a hundred yards or so to one side; they were going around the dune.

It was a particularly high one, and I knew what it meant; someone, the old man perhaps, was getting too tired to climb. It was a good sign, though I only hoped they were using a compass. It was easy enough to take a true course on the sun if you kept in a straight line, as I was doing, but if you went wandering around and around the tips of the sandy crescents, it was the quickest way to get lost altogether.

I climbed to the top, used the glasses, and found the tracks again well ahead of me. They were still going more or less west; I checked my watch and the sun and made a mental note of the precise direction, in case I lost them again.

It was already ten o'clock and I must have covered more than half the allotted distance. Whether or not they were heading accurately for the frontier post I could only guess. But their footsteps were beginning to wander, erratic enough to make me certain I must be close behind them. I began to hope fervently that they were way off course. I used to be a pretty good sniper once, and I wasn't worried about the odds—perhaps the colonel had left me some of his nerve—but I didn't want to run into a heavily fortified army post.

And, two hours and about three miles later, I found them.

They were still walking around the dunes, staggering abominably and going over the crescent tips in a winding path rather than taking the straighter but harder route over the top. And when I lay down on a ridge and used the glasses I could see them moving very slowly, very slowly indeed, less than a mile ahead of me. They were moving southish, heading for the low tip again.

I hurried down the slope of the dune, fought my way as fast as I could to the top of the next one, peeked cautiously over the edge, and there they were, just disappearing around the gentle slope. Karen was a little ahead, God bless her, still moving fairly easily, and the two parachutists were out on the flanks but not far enough out.

The pilot was helping Martin, who was struggling along with a hesitance that not long ago I would have thought of as pathetic. Malafir, who had discarded his jacket and seemed pretty worn out himself, was bringing up the rear with Marks. Marks's hands were still tied, and I wondered how the hell he managed to negotiate the dunes like that.

Altogether it was an untidy party of weary stragglers, badly dispersed and moving with infinite weariness; even the parachutists seemed tired. I wasn't surprised; I've had a lot of experience in the desert, and I was urged on by the desperation of my love for Karen, but even I was close to exhaustion.

I knew now exactly what I had to do.

I gave them a couple of minutes to make sure they were out of sight—and out of hearing too; the faint scuffling sound of feet dragging through sand is not much, but in a silence like that... Then I took off my pack and piled all my possessions by the water tank, keeping only the rifle, and left them there while I raced down the dune and up the other side to the crest. I was not worried about losing sight of the water; it's easy enough to follow your own footsteps back.

I was there well ahead of them, moving much more easily without that load, and I lay down on the sharp ridge of sand at the top and I waited, with my rifle loaded and the safety catch off. And in a few minutes they came into my sight, not more than fifty yards below and ahead of me. It seemed I had caught up just in time.

It was the end of the dunes, or the first ridge of them, and they were heading for a flat pancake of hard ground, pitted with gullies and dotted with giant boulders among which I could easily have lost all track of them. The dunes began again a few hundred yards on, and I saw Malafir gesture at them hopelessly and turn to say something to Martin, who was so close to collapse that the pilot was having a job keeping him on his feet.

Karen was a little ahead, and I pulled back, in case she should look around to the others and see me. Then I eased myself gently into position again and they were all there, Marks, the Egyptians and the German and the lovely Italian girl, struggling slowly forward, heading for God knows what, moving so slowly that it would be a good five minutes before they were out of my sight among the red and jagged rocks.

I took a bead on the first parachutist, holding the V6 the sight easily on the small of his back, and then for a moment or two I practiced swinging around to the other one, to make sure I could get them both without any nonsense. It's supposed to be naughty to shoot a man in the back; at least, that's what they tell me. But the people who thought that one up had never been in this sort of fix.

"No heroics," Colonel Matley used to say. "You bust open a door and see the whole Gestapo there at dinner, looking surprised down the barrel of your gun, you don't say calmly, 'Good evening, gentlemen,' and then shoot; that's for the Boy Scouts. You go in there with your gun firing, and it doesn't stop firing till you're out again, is that clear?"

It was clear enough, and I'd never forgotten what he said.

My first bullet knocked the first man headlong into the sand, and the second shot took his companion under the armpit as he swung around and tried, with slowed-down muscles (I wondered how much water they'd had), to get his machine gun pointing in roughly the right direction.

I saw Karen run a few steps (she couldn't have realized how impossible it is to run in soft sand!) and then fall on her face, and down went Martin and Marks—the one from fear; the other from training—and the pilot looked back and pulled out his pistol. And although I'd reckoned on my third shot for Malafir, I didn't know how good or how bad the pilot was at fifty yards—it's a nice range for a marksman—so I shot him instead, right through the chest, and then Malafir was on his knees, not praying but reaching out for Karen, and a revolver was in his hand and held steadily at her head. It was a stubby, snub-nosed gun with a range of no more than fifty feet or so, a thing we used to call a belly gun; but close up against her head that was all he needed.

He was nobody's fool, Malafir. I heard him say to Martin, in German, "Don't move, stay just where you are." Not even to me; he was speaking to Muller-Martin, and that was enough to tell me that he knew he was safe as long as Karen was under his gun. Martin had fallen over on his back, his legs spread-eagled, his arms waving in terror or exhaustion, or both, and there was only Malafir left.

It was a duel between the two of us, and he had the upper hand because he knew that I could easily take the top of his head right off, and that if I did that, his own gun would fire and Karen...

I lowered my rifle and stood up. It was time for talk.

He was dark, and wiry, and strong, and he moved like a cat, even in the sand. He looked back at me once, and I was close enough to see that his expression did not change. Then he reached down and grabbed at Karen's shirt and yanked her to her feet in one smooth motion, still holding that toy gun with the big bullets six inches from her head; I heard the sharp rip of cotton as it tore, and I could see the expression in her eyes. There was no fear there, just a kind of triumph as though she had been expecting something like this all along.

I said with as much calm as I could manage, "All right, we'll talk."

I started to slither down the dune toward him and he said sharply, "Stay where you are. Not one foot closer." I stopped, and waited.

I knew it wasn't easy for him either. It was as close to stalemate as anything like this could be, and only a miracle out of the blue could help either one of us.

I said, "You've had it, Malafir. If you touch her, I'll kill you and you know it."

For the first time I saw an expression on his face. It was a sort of smile, and I wondered if it meant he was nervous. He said:

"And if you touch me, she will be killed too."

"And then what do you think I will do to you?"

"You will kill me, of course. But she will be dead, so how will that help you? You think it's worth it?"

"Of course not. But you can't move either. Once you try to move her away, the hell with it—I'll take the risk of a quick shot."

"A risk? The word 'risk,' Mr. Benasque, implies uncertainty. You think my gun might not go off if you shoot me?"

"It might not."

"I wonder. It's an interesting possibility, isn't it? Reflex actions, even in death. The muscles are supposed to tighten, but I've often wondered if they really do."

When I did not answer, because it wasn't a risk I was prepared to take, not yet, he began to jeer. He said, "Why don't you put it to the test, solve the riddle once and for all? You might easily find it's all a mistake, and all those stories we read are lies."

I said, "You're only safe while she's—unhurt." I could not bring myself to say, "while she's *alive*." I saw him shrug.

He said, "Somewhere ahead of us, not too far away, there's an Egyptian Army post. I'm going to walk there now, with her. And you can't stop me."

He waited a long time for me to answer, and I knew that he was still not sure. But all the cards were in his favor, and even if he did know that, I was the only man who could give him the assurance, by inaction. And yet, what action was there I could take?

There was a theory there too: *Get ahead of him and catch him unawares, let him get out of sight, move on ahead, wait for a meticulously careful shot at his gun hand, and then take him.* But the risk—it was awful.

And he knew it. And he wasn't taking any chances. While I was thinking desperately about it, he said, knowing he'd turned the stalemate into check:

"I'm moving off, and I want you with me. Just move over to the side and come down here, don't get too close. I'm not leaving you behind, out of my sight, for any high-grade marksmanship. So drop your gun and move down here."

So he'd thought of that too. But it was my turn to move my king out of danger.

I said, "No."

There was an instant's hesitation. Then his face tightened and he said:

"Believe me, I mean what I say. Move down here or I kill her, now, in front of you."

It was my turn to jeer. I said, "Do I have to remind you? She's only good to you—alive."

We stood there, like angry children, shouting at each other across a forty-yard space of no-man's-land.

There was the longest pause in history. Stalemate again. We stood there, the three of us, with Martin and Marks lying on the ground and the three servicemen still forever, because they were only the pawns. Nobody spoke, and the silence was intolerable.

At last I said, "Well?"

He said the same thing. "Well?"

"Are we going to stand here forever?"

He shook his head with a degree of certainty I didn't like. "No. Sooner or later the Egyptian Army will come out to investigate the shooting."

"Or an Israeli patrol will happen by."

"We are closest to my people."

"If they did hear the shooting, they'll all be hiding under their beds."

"No. They will be coming out to see what it was. In force."

"So we stand here."

"Until my people arrive."

"Or the Israelis."

I hated the smile on his face. I didn't believe for one minute he could be sure about the frontier post. For all I knew we'd missed it by a couple of miles, or gone on quite the wrong bearing. But how could I be *certain*?

I wasn't even sure we weren't already three or four miles inside Egyptian territory. Or, if the lie of the land wasn't as we'd all imagined it, we could still be ten miles from—anybody.

Stalemate again.

He said, "Is it any good ordering you once more to come down here? I hold her life in my hand."

"No. I hold yours in my hand. And I'm getting just impatient enough to wonder if it's worth a try. I'm a very impatient man, I might get reckless."

"I am a very *patient* man, Benasque. And it will not be the first time I have staked my life on my judgment."

"It might be the last."

"Yes, I suppose it might. I suppose you have a point there. But it's merely academic."

Stalemate.

I said, "How's your water supply?"

"Adequate. Like a camel, I carry my water inside me. But I think the lady is thirsty."

I wished she would say *something*—a word of reproach, of pleasure, of fear even, anything to break the impasse between us. But she stood there waiting, silent and full of confidence in my ability. I thought, *There's nothing like misplaced faith.*

I said, "I can stand here forever."

"Just until—somebody comes along to swing the pendulum in—somebody's favor."

I said, "Or I can force your hand and trust to your good sense that you won't dare shoot her. I know just how strong the urge for self-preservation is."

He did not answer immediately, and I thought I had an advantage. I said:

"I'll come down there and we'll go back, just the three of us. You can take your bloody scientist with you and go to Egypt; that ought to be a pretty attractive deal."

He said, "Except that I know you would wait for us to get out of my pistol range and then use your rifle on us. You are one of *them*, Benasque. No better than a Jew."

I was sickened by the way he spat the word out, and my anger made me reckless. I said, "I'm going to take that risk. I don't believe you'll sign your own death warrant by shooting her. I'm going to force myself to believe you won't."

I was too. I knew it was the only possible course to take, however hot-bloodedly reckless it was.

Malafir turned his gun away from Karen's head, his hand still gripping the front of her shirt, and aimed it at Marks. He said calmly:

"Must I shoot this Jew first?"

I stopped a movement toward him which had hardly begun. Stalemate again.

We stood there in a terribly long silence, with no life around us, nothing but emptiness and heat and silence. My throat was parched and only the palms of my hands were moist. And then, somewhere behind us, there was a single shot.

I heard no ricochet, no sound of a passing bullet, no echo—just a single shot? I saw Malafir yank at Karen's shirt again, heard him shout, "With me!" and he was moving toward the rocks behind him, struggling in knee-deep sand with her, half-pulling, half-dragging her along with one powerful hand, the other still holding the revolver close to her head; for the first time I saw that it was cocked.

I yelled, "Let her go, Malafir, let her go!" and tried to race down after them. I slithered in the sand and fell into Martin's prostrate body and stumbled over him, and then Malafir had reached the hard sandstone and was running across it, pulling at Karen. I was so livid with rage that I half-raised the rifle to fire, and I heard Marks, lying in the sand, yell:

"No, don't."

He was right, of course. I struggled to my feet and saw Malafir and Karen disappear among the boulders, falling to the ground as they went. I yelled out, "You stay there, Malafir. God help you if you move away an inch!" And I heard him yell back, "And if you come here, I'll kill her, I swear it!"

There was a frightening edge of excitement in his voice. I knew that he meant it.

I rolled over and climbed unsteadily to my feet, and I took the butcher's knife and cut Marks free, and he rubbed his wrists and said:

"And now what? How do we get her out of there?"

I stared at the cluster of rocks. Beyond them, the yellow sand was empty. I turned back to Marks.

"I wish I knew. Are you all right?"

He rubbed a hand over his mouth and said, "They didn't give me any water, not a drop." His voice was thick with pain, and his face was flushed.

I said, "Can you still handle a gun?"

"Yes. Yes, I can."

"Take the rifle. I've got water on top of the dune, plenty of water. And I want to see what that shot was. Take the rifle and—make sure they don't move out from behind those rocks."

He shook his head. "If they did, I wouldn't know what to do, I wouldn't even dare to guess what to do. Just tell me—tell me where the water is. I'll go for it."

I walked over to the nearest dead parachutist and unstrapped his water bottle; it was still half full. *Bedouin*, I thought. *A hundred miles on a mouthful of water*. I said:

"You can start on this, but take it easy, slowly."

"I know."

He did too. He wet his swollen lips first, then swilled his mouth and spat it out, and then he waited, breathing hard, and asked:

"You said *plenty*?"

"A ten-gallon tank up there, a couple of pints gone from it is all."

He grinned and said, "Then it's all right if—" Not waiting for my answer, he poured some water into his hand and splashed it over his forehead. He groaned and said, "My God, I didn't know what thirst could do to a man in so short a time."

"It's the dunes. They soak it out of your body, every drop of moisture."

"Seems like it. It's the first time—"

He took a long drink now, and handed me the bottle, I took a long swig and said:

"One of us had better get up to the top and see what there is out there. I'd like to know who fired that shot."

He nodded. "I'll go; you'll want to stay here." He gestured at the boulders and said, "What are we going to do about them?" He looked back at Martin and said, "And about him?"

I was too weary to go and drag Martin over to where we were. I said:

"On the way up, kick his arse and send him down here. Tell him if he doesn't come down right away I'll put a shot in his backside and the hell with him."

Marks said, "Right in the *rochus*, that's what he needs."

He was a good fellow, Marks. He took one of the submachine

guns the parachutists had been carrying, checked the mechanism, found it strange and looked at me with raised eyebrows.

I said, "Now you've got a round up the spout. Just point it and pull the trigger. That's the safety catch by your index finger and it's off, so it's all yours. Take it easy."

"At least the shot came from our side."

"Don't kid yourself. There just might be an Egyptian patrol around here too."

I wasn't trying to scare him, and he wasn't about to be scared either. He gestured at the gun and said:

"How many rounds in this thing?"

"Fifty."

He said, "Well, then."

I watched him stagger slowly toward the top of the dune. When he got to where Martin was lying in the sand he unceremoniously yanked him to his feet and pushed him in my direction, then went on up to the top and disappeared over the crest.

Martin came stumbling in and fell to the ground at my feet. He said, "Please don't hurt me; I don't mean—anyone any harm, any harm at all."

The silence around us was acute, with the stillness that no other place in the world can have. Only the desert can be so still, and empty, and parched, and sad.

I lay on my belly on the sand and looked at the great red boulders where Karen was held prisoner by a maniac with a gun.

And, not knowing what else I could do, I waited.

CHAPTER 14

I said to Martin, "You and your bloody rockets."

He looked up at the sky and fingered the collar of his shirt. He said:

"If only I weren't so *hot*."

"So take your bloody coat off, for Christ's sake."

"Yes, yes, I think I will."

He sat on the boiling sand with his legs thrust out in front of him and wriggled out of his jacket; it was solid German tweed, and the temperature was around a hundred and twenty, without a breath of air and the sun blasting down on us and up from the sand as well.

I said, "You realize that you're the cause of all this bloody trouble? And I tell you this, if anything happens to that girl, I just will not hesitate." I gestured at the rifle and said, "This. From me personally."

He had the nerve to be indignant. He said severely:

"Young man, I am a scientist, like any other scientists, doing the work that God put me here on earth to do, the only work I know how to do well. I am a pure scientist, with no political, no social, no other thoughts than my work."

"Which you have to do for Egypt."

"Like anyone else, I must go where I am needed. Whether it be Germany, or America—or Egypt."

"Making your damned cobalt bomb."

He shook his head. He said scornfully, "You are grossly misinformed. The cobalt bomb is a long way off; it needs a great deal of hard work and an enormous amount of money before it becomes anything more than a dream."

"A nightmare."

"No. An eventual source of overwhelming power."

"And whoever chooses to pay for your evil gets it."

He click-clicked his tongue at me and said irritably, "You talk like a shopkeeper. What does it matter who pays for it? It's the end result that is important. Compared with this, Hiroshima was a—a primitive hand grenade."

I said, "What a hell of an aim in life, one hell of an aim."

He spoke to me as though I were a child. He said didactically:

"Yes, I know, you are an American and all the Americans think that Hiroshima was a mistake, a—a sort of moral mistake—"

I interrupted him. "Well, I don't. It was necessary because thousands of our men were dying every day and the quicker the killing was brought to an end the better, and I don't care by what means. A nation at war must kill the enemy as efficiently and as speedily as possible; and that's what we did."

He said patiently, "Yes, I know, that is the logical view, and if you think well of Hiroshima, why can you not apply the same logic to the work I am doing? Tell me why?"

He just couldn't see the difference, and who was I to explain it to him, even if I could? But I tried. I said:

"I don't think well of Hiroshima in the first place, I hate everything about it, but it was necessary. I hate everything about what you're doing too, only that is *not* necessary."

He snorted, an impatient professor with an unlearned student.

"But of course it's necessary! Without our work on the rockets, there would never have been the slightest hope of—of any exploration of outer space, of the gigantic steps forward we've taken. This is science in its purest form, and science cannot ever stand still, it must always go on, searching for knowledge, searching for fulfillment."

I said sourly, "You talk like a professor I once had, only he was studying detergents."

"Yes, yes, detergents too, every step forward—the acquisition and the application of pure knowledge, the most important asset in man's complicated mind."

I said, "You never heard of good will? Is it any good talking to you about—about love? Or even about peace?"

He shrugged. "Peace is a word the soldiers use. I do not really like soldiers, as a rule. They seem always to be so—so limited."

I thought of the colonel and of his slim fingers caressing the rock when he struck it with his cane to get water. "When Moses did that," he'd said, "they called it a miracle... The growth of knowledge, from faith to the logic of understanding..." If the colonel was representative of one side of the fence, Martin was surely the other.

I said, "And so, in the search for pure science, you build your bombs and rockets."

He said eagerly, "Yes, the broadening of man's capacity, from the savage, sitting in his cave and terrified of fire, to the conquest of every other living thing on the earth and perhaps in the heavens too. Can't you see what a laudable aim that is? Surely you can understand that." He didn't say "even you," but that's what he meant.

I said, "And if London gets blown off the map in the process—"

He could not contain himself. He said explosively, "But that was a long time ago; we were enemies then and you yourself said— must I use your own words to confound your arguments? You said that a nation at war—"

"I know what I said."

"And that was just a by-product of our progress, a soldier's by-product of the progress of our science."

I took another tack. I knew it was hopeless, but I said, "Why don't you peddle your goddam bombs in Europe, at least? What's wrong with your own people—aren't they warlike enough for you?"

There was a worried little pause. He said at last, "Oh, but I tried, I assure you I tried very hard. I wanted to continue my cobalt research in Bonn, but they turned me down. Something to do with NATO, I believe. And in America too, but—" He looked down at the sand and said, "I wasn't very happy in America; they didn't quite trust me there."

"I'll bet."

"And in France—" He looked at me with pride and said, "I am a German, sir, a good German. The immorality of working for the French was very quickly brought home to me, so I did the proper thing:

I left them."

"And came to Egypt."

"The Egyptians trust me. They have been very good to me."

"I can't believe you don't know what they're planning to do with your bloody rockets."

He looked a bit awkward and would not meet my eyes. He said hesitantly, "Yes, I've heard that. But, really, I cannot allow these political arguments to distract the train of my thoughts. I have no time for them, no understanding of them; I don't *want* to understand them. This is a matter for the statesmen and is no concern of mine at all; I won't allow it to become a concern of mine."

I said, "It's been made pretty public, for God's sake; you know the threats Nasser has made, he hasn't tried to hide his intentions from anybody. He has promised the Arab world the destruction of Israel, with the missiles and warheads you people are making for him. You make me sick, the whole damn lot of you."

He said sharply, "And if you think your unlearned opinion is of any consequence to me... I am a highly respected man in my profession. In my chosen field there is nobody—no one, you understand—whose ability is more highly respected."

"The chosen field of carnage."

"Of science! And I shall continue to carry on with my work whether the grossly uninformed approve of it or not."

I made one last try. I said, "You're building a tool for genocide, and you know it. Or perhaps I should say: to continue the genocide your people started."

He said angrily, "We were building a better world, a world fit for men of learning to live in, and to make still better. And men like you should be on our side. Not—*theirs*."

I said, "I don't know why I don't bash your bloody head in, here and now."

For a moment the anger went, and he looked genuinely terrified. Then he swallowed hard and said, putting a brave face on it:

"I don't see—why you should—why you should want to do that. After all, you're not—not one of them, are you?" He looked carefully at my face and said, "No, of course you're not." He even looked relieved.

Overcome with disgust, I got up and left him, and wandered a little closer to the boulders.

I wondered how close I dared approach, and when I had moved a step or two nearer to them I could see Malafir peering out. Karen screamed shortly, a sharp cry of pain, and he shouted:

"No closer! Keep back!"

Helplessly, I went back to the hollow of the dunes and sat down to do some steady thinking. There seemed nothing to do but wait for darkness again, and I didn't think I could last that long.

The whole thing seemed so—so ridiculous. My girl was less than a hundred feet away, half hidden behind a few sheltering boulders. I had a good gun and I knew how to use it, and I was a better man in every way than that bastard Malafir, and yet... The odds had started out so heavily against us, and now they were evened out, and it was just the last step, the final movement; and the solution to the problem was beyond me.

I knew, I was *sure* that I could force his hand. There was not the slightest doubt in my mind that if I walked slowly up to Malafir and belted him under the jaw he would never dare to fire that gun, because Karen, alive, was his only hope of ever saving his miserable skin. He knew that, and he knew that I knew it.

And yet he had found the edge of my uncertainty and was clinging to it, knowing that if the risk was even infinitesimal, I still would not take it.

And damn him, he was right.

I had almost reached the point of making up my mind to do the only possible thing, to call his bluff; I got so near to doing that so many times, and then—always the fear confronted me and I held back.

And then, looking up at the dune above me, I saw Marks standing against the sky, the rope of my tank slung over his shoulder. I watched him stumble down to the hollow; on that map in the mess hall it might have been called The Place of Indecision. He dragged the water in and flopped to his knees in the sand beside me and said:

"It's hot, the water; too hot to put your hand in."

I said, "A metal tank, in this heat—"

"Are they still there?"

I nodded. He carefully coiled the rope and laid it in a neat bundle beside the tank, looked at me and jerked his head to one side. Puzzled, I got up and went a little way off with him, and he carefully turned his back to Martin and said in a very low voice:

"Nathan is here."

The pendulum, Malafir had said. It was swinging back in somebody's favor.

Marks wiped at the sweat on his forehead and said very quietly:

"He's alive, and only just, by God. You know that pile of rubble where the roof caved in? He was under it. It caved in before they broke down the door and nearly killed him, but—you don't know that man like I do. He fought his way out and he's here, just around the point of the dune there, waiting. He wants to talk to you."

I was worried about leaving Karen, and so was Marks. He said doubtfully, "I'll stand guard, of course, but—what do I do if—" He didn't know how to put it, and I said:

"I'll be as quick as I can. I don't think he'll move out. If he does, just yell. And let's take care of Doctor bloody Martin first; we don't want any diversions at this point, do we?"

We went back and made Martin take off his shoes and socks, and he squealed when he found out how hot the sand was to his bare feet, and I said:

"Just in case you get any stupid ideas."

He began to protest, and there was a pompous authoritative air about him which made me want to punch him on the nose there and then, and I would have done so if he'd been thirty years younger. I don't suppose he'd been treated roughly for a good long time, but I felt he ought to get used to it; there are people you can get tough with, and there are people you can't, and Martin thought he was in the favored category, but I soon disillusioned him. I took his tie off too, and tied it tightly around his wrists, behind his back, and he said, spluttering:

"I've never been treated like this in my life, never."

I said, "Just what I figured. But you'll get precious little sympathy from me. I don't want you fooling around on your own in a situation that might turn out to be tricky."

He said wrathfully, "What do you think I might do, attack you physically? I'm an old man, and I'm tired, and I'm hot and—and disgusted with—with you and—"

"Oh, shut up!"

He did. His lined old face was tight-lipped with brooding anger, and it was strange to see that under the strain of the bad time he was having, he was recovering a certain Germanic fortitude; I knew I was doing the right thing, old man or not, in keeping him out of mischief. He sat there, glowering at me, and I said:

"I've told Marks, here, to kick your teeth in if you so much as move a muscle. And he will too. He's one of *them*."

I looked at the boulders for a while, and saw that Malafir was peering out, watching me and wondering what was going on. When I turned away and started moving off, he shouted after me (and there was a note of anxiety in his voice):

"Stay where you are, I warn you! Stay there!"

I knew he wasn't going to throw away his only trump card for anything except the ultimate trick; even so, my heart was beating fast as I walked away. He didn't shout anymore, and I went on moving up to the top of the dune, as though there were other stores to be brought in; it seemed desperately necessary to keep from him the fact that the pendulum was moving again.

And when I reached the top, I walked down the other side until I was sure I was out of sight and sound, and then swung to the right and stumbled through the soft sand of the dune toward its lowest point.

A wind was getting up, and the fine dust drifted up from under my feet now, and the crests were feathered with wisps of sand. Soon the wind would be screaming and a full-scale khamsin would be blowing, covering everything with a heavy pall of clinging sand that would find its way into the mouth, the ears, the nostrils, choking out life and silencing protest as though the desert were pulling this terrible weapon out of its scabbard slowly because men were learning not to be frightened of it. Out on the horizon to the east, the sky was already hazily brown, and the sandstorm was moving toward us.

Well, I knew it couldn't do us any harm. And it just might make things a great deal easier.

I staggered through the last few yards of sand, and there was Nathan waiting for me.

Since I'd last seen him, he'd changed into a khaki shirt and dark-blue shorts, and he was wearing desert sandals. His long legs were bronzed and his strong arms were tight with knotted muscles; it somehow seemed incongruous, because in his neat Roman clothes he had always looked a little effeminate. There was a bandage around his head, his face was cut and scarred, and two narrow boards were tightly strapped around his left calf; his left foot was peculiarly out of shape, as though it had been twisted around the wrong way and would not go back again, and when I looked into his eyes I saw that they were clouded with pain. He was sitting on the sand with his legs thrust out in front of him, and his hands flat on the earth at his side. He wore a revolver in his belt.

I said, "My God, I don't believe you walked here on a broken leg?"

He took a deep breath and said, "I crawled."

"Ten miles? For God's sake—"

"Twelve. You were all miles off your course; they were heading for the middle of the Sinai Desert and they didn't have a hope in hell of getting anywhere. You'd all have been dead in three or four days, the whole lot of you."

You could hear the pain in the way he spoke. I said:

"Whoever fixed that leg made a hell of a mess of it."

"I did it myself; it wasn't easy."

My haversack was beside him on the ground, and he looked at it and said:

"Marks gave me some of the brandy. It helps a lot."

"Did he tell you about the others?"

He looked at me and grinned suddenly. "Yes, he told me, he told me a lot of things." He was suddenly serious again. "How do you propose to winkle Malafir out of the hole he's found?"

"I can't winkle him out, he's got Miss d'Arno, a gun at her head."

"I know. So you're going to sit tight until he falls asleep? It might take him a week. Sure, a patrol will be here long before that, but if we take him alive... He knows what will happen to him and he might decide not to be taken alive. What chance do you think she'll have if he does that?"

I said irritably, "She's got no damn chance now unless we do something about it. But, as a point of academic interest, can he be so sure that he won't get a fair trial and— Hell, I don't know why he should throw away his only chance for survival. As long as she's alive he's safe, and—"

He was listening to me politely, waiting for me to finish. I broke off and said:

"Well?"

He crossed his arms about his chest and I saw the muscles tensing; his leg was giving him a terrible time, and for a moment his eyes closed. Then he opened them and said slowly:

"Malafir is a member of the Special Military Projects Branch, and his particular job is not merely holding the hands of visiting German professors. His job is to protect them, and in the course of that duty he has personally killed three of our men. My three predecessors, to be precise. He is wanted on a murder charge in Switzerland, and also in Israel, since his last—killing was done on board an Israeli ship plying between Athens and Taranto. We nearly got him, that time, but—he's a slippery customer, as you may have found out."

"His last murder."

I had wondered about the hesitation. Nathan said calmly:

"I prefer to call it a killing. Merely because, as you probably already guessed, I am engaged in the same unhappy profession, but on the other side of the fence. Malafir is my counterpart in this rather nasty business of clandestine war. He kills off our agents, and I kill off theirs. He is good at his job, and I am good at mine. And now that you have seen him so closely, you will know what kind of a man I am too."

The bitterness in his voice was surprising. When I said nothing, thinking about his loneliness, he said:

"My only justification is that every time I kill one of them, it is not just an interested spectator, but a highly qualified man whose very existence threatens ours. Each time I kill, I am saving many of our own people's lives, and that, no doubt, is the justification Malafir uses too. We are both of the same breed, a dangerous and—unhappy breed. Sometimes"—the pain was there again, and his voice was a whisper— "sometimes I wish to God I could give it all up and live the life of a decent human being. But long ago, in times that were worse even than these, I learned, I had to learn, that if one man will permit himself to become a savage, his people can live better because they can feel safe. I am the man who wields a sword to keep the king's enemies at bay; and my king is this country which I love and will serve till I die."

Well, that was quite a speech for a man who could only whisper because of the pain that was racing through him. Twelve miles on his hands and knees...

I said, "Take some more of the brandy, lots of it. I'm going to reset that leg."

"I wish you would, it's quite painful."

I handed him the bottle, but he shook his head. I said, "Go on, it's not as bad as all that. Good Israeli brandy, guaranteed six weeks old."

He said, "As a matter of fact, it's quite excellent and you know it. But in a few moments—we are both going to need all our wits."

I said, "You don't mind if I do?" I took a quick swig and said, "It's going to hurt like hell."

"Just be as quick as you can. Please—don't fumble."

"I know."

I cut away the crude splints and sat down, facing him, and when I put my foot in his crotch he closed his eyes and lay back on the sand, and I was glad that I could not see his face. I took a firm grip on his foot, and pulled hard and twisted quickly and let go again, and by the grace of God it went right the first time, and he sat up and said quietly:

"Well, that wasn't so bad, was it?"

I said, "You tell me."

He watched while I put back the splints, and I said firmly, "But you can't possibly move on it."

"No? I have to, don't I, if we're going to get your girl away before it's too late. Tell me precisely where they are."

I said, "The other side of this dune, there's a group of boulders, a patch about, oh, fifty feet across..."

I explained the lie of the land in the most careful detail, told him how far it was from one stone to the next, the height of the dunes, the shape of each and every rock. I went over every detail that could possibly help him, and when I'd finished he sketched an outline on the sand with his finger and said:

"And we are—here, right?"

"Exactly here."

He looked up at the sky and at the blown sand and said, "A khamsin blowing up; in a few hours no one will be able to see a thing."

"I don't think we can wait that long. God knows what fresh idea he might have tucked up his sleeve. A sandstorm would help us, though."

"Yes. But you're right, we can't wait. There's a patrol on its way, and the moment he hears those motors he's going to know what they mean. That's a moment we can't afford to wait for. You realize there's only one way to do it?"

I nodded. "One of us holds his attention, the other creeps up on him from behind. There's only one snag. I'll have to do the distracting myself because I'm the one he knows is here. That leaves you the job of jumping him, and in your condition—"

"I don't jump him. I shoot him. If necessary, I will shoot the gun out of his hand. How are you going to account for your absence? He'll be wondering, you know. I'm sorry I fired that shot, but—"

I knew why he'd done it. He just couldn't go any farther. I said curiously:

"Did you know it was my track you were following?"

"I read your note."

"Oh."

"I'm sorry I messed it up."

"If you hadn't fired, I'd still be standing there, wondering what the hell to do."

"And he'll be wondering what it was too. Let's not forget he'll assume it was nothing that bodes good for him."

I didn't like the idea of his crawling around to outflank Malafir. I wasn't even sure that he could make it, but that was one of the things I was going to have to take on trust.

And there were other things as well. I said anxiously:

"What kind of a shot are you?"

"Good. On that score at least you need not worry."

"Tell me."

He knew I was looking for comfort, and he smiled and pulled the revolver out of his holster. It was a Bayard .38 with an eight-inch barrel and a very small butt. He weighed it in his hand thoughtfully and said, "A lot of people don't think much of these, but it's the most accurate long-range revolver you can find."

I said, "You'll be shooting at more than fifty feet, maybe a great deal more. His gun might be a couple of inches from her head, you realize that? You've got to be right on target. I still think I'd better do it."

"It needs the dispassion that you don't have, so forget about it." He stuck a finger into the sand of his sketch map and said, "I'll be here, right behind this rock. If he faces you, I'll be at a hundred and twenty degrees or so to his line of sight. And if I can't get a clear shot at the gun from there, I'll move around again to this point—here, right behind him." His finger dabbed at the sand again and he said, "The first one, probably. Just keep him talking, keep him occupied."

"If I keep that up for long, he'll guess something like this is happening."

"Yes, you may need Marks as well. Use him."

"I wish you could make a signal of some sort when you're in position."

He shook his head. "That's out of the question."

"Sure you can move around?"

"I don't need my legs. And you'd better get back; he's already worried enough."

I picked up the haversack and looked at my watch and said:

"Worked out just right, about the same time Marks was gone for the water. I'll take the haversack and he'll assume that it was farther off than it really was."

"Fill it with sand first."

"Sand?"

"If you don't have to drag it, he'll wonder why Marks didn't just slip it over his shoulder."

I scooped a lot of sand into it and said, "Good luck. I hope to God you don't need it."

"Just keep his mind off what's behind him. Fifteen minutes should see me in position."

He turned over onto his belly, dug his elbows into the sand, and started to drag himself forward. It was the best way to move with a broken leg, and the best way to keep his profile good and tight to the ground. It reminded me of the bad old days when we used to crawl around the German lines like that.

When I reached the top of the dune he was already out of my sight.

I could almost hear my watch ticking.

We sat huddled together, Marks and I, watching the glowering Dr. Martin. I took a swig out of the brandy bottle and hoped Malafir was watching.

Twice I got up and walked a few paces toward his shelter, and each time he called out, just as he had done before, "Get back! Keep your distance, Benasque, I'm warning you!" Each time I turned back and sat down sullenly, trying to get him used to the idea; and the third time I went a little closer and when he ordered me back I held my ground and started arguing.

The fifteen minutes were up.

He was standing close behind an angular tock, only his head and shoulders visible, and I could see from his upper arm that he still had the gun held ready. I could not see Karen at all, and I guessed that she was on the sand at his feet. I thought, *My God, Nathan won't be able to see the gun that he's got to hit.* I held my ground and hoped.

I said, "What the hell do you think the good of all this is, Malafir? You can't possibly win and you know it."

He said smoothly, and now there was a note of confidence in his voice:

"But I can. Sooner or later, someone is going to worry about all the shooting. Our frontier post is within easy reach of us."

"Unless you walked right past it."

He did not hesitate. He said firmly, "I hardly think that's likely. The young pilot you murdered knew this desert very well. Another mile or two ahead—my people, Benasque."

I said, "I'll bet there's an Israeli patrol looking for us right now."

This time the hesitation was there. He said, "That is a risk I am quite prepared to take. Now get back to your chosen friend. And did you find it necessary to tie Dr. Martin's hands like a common criminal?"

"Yes, I did."

"I think you'd better untie them."

"Go to hell."

He said coldly, "I have done the same with your woman." His voice was suddenly filled with fury, and I knew he was close to the breaking point. He shouted, "Untie him!" and before I could move he leaned away for a moment and there was a harsh ripping sound, repeated twice, and when he stood up again he was holding out Karen's torn khaki shirt in his left hand; she had not made a sound. While I Stared at him furiously, he shouted again, "Untie his hands!"

He threw the ripped pieces of the shirt toward me and said, "Do you want the rest of her clothes too?" He was taunting me again, deliberately trying to make me angry, finding out just how reckless I was prepared to be.

I looked back at Marks and shouted, "Cut him free, Marks."

I saw Marks go to work with the knife, and then Malafir, knowing he was onto a good thing now, said:

"And send him over here!"

I knew that I could not refuse, but even before I had a chance to say anything, Malafir jeered:

"It never occurred to me that a woman's body was such an effective weapon. I should have used it before, shouldn't I?"

I shouted to Marks quickly, knowing that at this time I must keep my wits about me and not be sidetracked by what looked like was turning out to be a nasty business.

"Send him over here!"

Malafir said, "It's an interesting speculation, isn't it? For your lady's modesty you will give me your prisoner—and what else? Will you give me your life too? No, I suppose not. If you approach within range of my revolver, I will kill you, as you must know. And if you try to shoot me with your rifle, I will kill her, as you must know too. The area in between, then—what do we have there?"

He leaned out of my sight for a moment again, and pulled Karen to her feet beside him. As he had said, her hands were tied behind her back, and even at this range I could see the angry flush to her face. He took her by the hair and shoved her out in front of him, his gun still close to the back of her head. The white of her torn brassiere was bright still against the amber of her skin, and I fancied that even at this distance I could see a livid weal across her throat.

I was trembling with helpless fury, and the strain was showing on him too. He let go of Karen's hair and swung an arm around her body, his hand on her breast, crushing it, pulling her tight to him. He shouted:

"And give me the Jew too, send him here, send him closer."

I shouted back, "You're going too far, Malafir!"

"How far is too far? Give him to me! Or you want to see what I can do to her?"

There was a livid fury in his voice now, and I trembled for Karen. I saw his hand move over her body, and I began to step forward, forgetting our plans, not caring anymore, knowing only that I had to do—*something*.

Marks said quietly, "Take it easy, sir. I'll go to him."

I said, "You stay where you are." I spoke quietly, but Malafir heard me. He shouted furiously:

"Send him to me! You want me to tear her body apart?"

She did not even struggle. I do not know whether it was the fear of the dreadful proximity of a loaded revolver at her head, or the urgent need she must have felt to show no fear that might make me lose control and rush to help her. She was a silent puppet, manhandled in silence, and I stood close by and unable to help her, waiting.

Marks threw down his gun and began to move forward. I did not dare say a word to him. But he was moving off at a tangent, and I could see that Malafir was watching him closely. I could see the hard smile on his face as he clutched at Karen and watched.

And then the single shot sounded.

I had not seen Nathan, nor heard a sound from him, and the shot came out from the side and Malafir spun around and his clumsy little snub-nosed revolver went flying out of his hand and Karen fell to the ground, and I was racing across the hard sandstone rocks, falling over my own feet in my haste to get there, and as I came in close she struggled to her feet, and I got her hands free, and we fell into each other's embrace and the tears were streaming out of her eyes and down her cheeks unheeded, and as I clutched at her I saw Malafir reach out with his left hand for the gun and I did not move to stop him.

But Marks was there. He bent down, took hold of him by the hair at the top of his head, and chopped him hard under the ear with the flat of his hand.

He said, "A present from Blighty, chum."

CHAPTER 15

As Nathan had said it would be, the sound of the motors was the first sign that came to us of the patrol, and we held the tableau for them when they arrived.

Nathan was stretched out on the sand on his back, half-drunk with the brandy I had poured down his throat. Martin and his buddy Malafir sat face to face propped up against the rocks, with their legs tied together; it was a neat trick which Nathan had showed me how to do, a left leg to a right thigh and a right ankle to a left knee. It didn't look very comfortable, and Nathan had said, "If they should try and get out of that, you might watch, it's quite interesting." Martin's hands were roped behind his back again, and Malafir was nursing his shattered wrist, around which Marks had silently put a tourniquet.

There was not one of us, Nathan, nor Marks, nor myself, who could trust himself to fight off the exhaustion very much longer. The long battle had come to an end and the strain was telling. Strangely enough, it was only Karen who seemed to have any physical strength left, but she was silent, detached, and only keeping out of the dark well of shock by sheer will power.

Marks was back on top of the dune now, watching for the patrol and holding his weapon ready, trained on the late opposition which had been giving us such a bad time; but they weren't even trying to move now.

Malafir's eyes were glazed, and he was back to that tightlipped silence he had affected when I had first seen him.

Karen and I sat close together, my arm around her waist, and it was good to feel the proximity of her warm body once again.

The sound of distant gunfire had told us that something was in the wind, and we saw first, in the sky to the north, some small dark puffs of antiaircraft fire; it was quite harmless and merely told us where the frontier post was—a hell of a long way away. And then a small plane came roaring in, flying low enough to scare the daylights out of me, swooping low over the dunes and seeming to brush the sand of their crests as it went over. He did a roll and waggled his wings and then he was gone again, and a few minutes later we heard the sound of the approaching patrol.

Marks stood up and waved to us and shouted:

"Troop carriers, three of them."

He erred there, but on the nice side for a change. The three half-tracks lumbered up the side of the dune and came unsteadily over the top, and then two more came in from each side, and I said to Nathan, "How the hell do they get those things up the side of a goddam sand dune?"

He shook his head, and I wasn't sure whether he didn't know or wasn't in a fit state to answer. And then he said drunkenly, "Half— half-tracks—special—they have special tires—it's not—not too hard, really."

The patrol wheeled in, and there were men in uniform running toward us, moving fast and easily, well-schooled in their desert abilities, setting up their guns all around us while a small dark man with a captain's badges of rank came hurrying over to us, an elderly man with a haversack on his back coming with him. I went over to meet them, and the captain held out his hand and said:

"Captain Shlomo Abbas, how do you do?"

He was bright and cheerful and affable, and we might have been meeting in the bar of the Eden. He introduced the elderly man.

"This is Dr. Fleischman." The doctor looked quickly around and saw that Nathan's eyes were closed. He said quickly:

"Is he all right?"

I said, "A couple of amateur leg-settings you'd better look at. He set it himself, crawled a million miles, and I reset it for him, and I don't suppose either of us made a very good job of it."

"Is he unconscious?" He was staring at the motionless form almost in surprise, as though he knew him well and knew that Nathan was not the kind of man ever to fall from absolute alertness, as though a man like Nathan was not expected ever to be found even asleep.

I said, "He's drunk as a lord, thoroughly sewn up."

"Drunk? Good God!" He was quite genuinely shocked.

I said, "He got here dried out, dried out like a bleached bone, and I poured half a bottle of brandy down his throat."

The doctor nodded and went over to him with his haversack, and the captain busied himself placing his men against any surprise attack with a smooth efficiency that gave me a lot of comfort; it was almost as if the desert were no longer part of that empty, other-planet world, but once again host to a vigorous and energetic people. He stood looking down at the two bound men, ignoring their sullen glares.

He said, "Martin and Malafir; are there any others?"

"Just the two of them. A few dead bodies, if you're interested."

"No, not particularly. We'd better get back as fast as we can, I think, don't you?"

"There's not much left of the camp back there. Have you seen it?"

"Oh, yes, yes indeed. They're rebuilding it."

"Already?"

He said gently, "We have a lot to do in a very short time; a man's life is not very long if he wants to see the result of his labors."

I introduced him to Karen. She was quiet and unemotional, and she gave him her hand in silence. He glanced at me rather worriedly, and smiled at her and said:

"The doctor will take a look at you before we move back. You must have had a very bad time."

She shook her head. "Not as bad as—as some of them." I took her arm and led her over toward the half-track we were to ride in, and when I helped her aboard and said anxiously, "Are you all right?" she merely nodded. She saw my worried look and smiled quickly, and put out a hand to touch me and said, "It's all right, Michael, I've not been hurt."

I had found her little Tessina camera in Malafir's pocket, and when I offered it to her she did not seem to hear; I slipped it into the haversack and began to worry about her some more.

And then the captain came over and told us we were moving

off, and she looked at him and said slowly:

"There was—there was a corporal at the camp, an elderly man who was on the gun emplacement; you know who I mean?"

The captain nodded. "Yes, that was Corporal Bronislawski."

"Where was he from?"

The captain glanced at me and frowned, not knowing why it was so important. I looked at him helplessly, and he turned to her and said:

"From Poland. Warsaw, I think—"

"No, I mean here, in Israel."

"Oh. From one of the colonies in the Negev. He was a farmer once, but a professional soldier during the war." He waited and said gently, "Why do you ask?"

She shook her head. "Nothing. Just—just curious."

It took us two hours to lumber our way back to the camp, and all that time she did not speak. I sat beside her very conscious of her sadness, and knew that Corporal Bronislawski had somehow, quite inconsequentially, become the emblem for her of something she had discovered, that she had not known existed before; as though she had never known, in the quiet and comfortable world she lived in, that the things she had suffered as a child were still going on all over the world once you stepped outside that favored circle of safety and prerogative which is the normal confine of our everyday life.

The shock of what she had been through, personally, was less than the shock of finding out that the filthy animal that is Death still prowled around outside that circle inside which it had been comfortably forgotten.

I remembered the sight of Malafir's hands clutching at her young breast, hurting her, shaming her; and I knew that it just didn't matter to her because she had been brought shockingly close to far worse things than any outrage of her purity.

Nathan was in the half-track with us, slung out on a stretcher, and when he opened his eyes and looked at me, I said, "What happens now?"

The drunkenness was still there, but he was visibly thrusting it away from him. He said, "Now, now you can give me a cigarette."

I lit one for him and he said, "In my business, we don't deal much in apology. But I feel I owe you one."

I said, "It's not very important, not anymore."

"Oh, but it is. It's important to me because it's the first sign of—of what?' He inhaled the smoke deep into his lungs and said, "Perhaps it's the first sign of a weakening, of a return to normalcy. If it is, I must say I welcome it."

"Weakness isn't the word I'd have thought of, not in your case."

He sighed. "I've been doing this—this filthy job for a long time now, hating it and knowing that it's necessary, and it took—" He looked at Karen and said, "I never really doubted the sure knowledge I had that when someone—outside my specialized little war got hurt, it was all right as long as it was *unavoidable*, that was the key word. It took a woman in that—line of fire to make me re-examine the question." He shrugged and said, "It's absurd, isn't it, to find excuses for writing off a man and to draw the line when it's a woman?"

"It makes us men, instead of machines."

"I suppose so. I wonder if, as a man, I could go back to a more normal sort of life? You think I could?"

"You? A farmer? Or what?"

He shrugged. "Who knows. I must have other talents, if I look for them hard enough."

Making a joke of it, I said, "You're backing out because I still owe you a punch on the nose. Like the guy who puts his glasses on when someone's going to belt him."

He looked at the bruise on my cheek and said, "That's the least of your hurts. You look a mess."

I did indeed. There were bloodstained rags around my wrists, a thirty-six-hour stubble on my chin, my clothes were in tatters...

He snorted and said, "The end of a battle, and it shows, on all of us." He looked at Karen and fell silent.

I said, "What happens to us? Now?"

"We can only send you back and hope that—I suppose it's too much to ask for your complete discretion?"

I said, "I'm a journalist, and this is the story I'm being paid to write."

"Objectively?"

"It's one of those stories that you start to write objectively and finish up as biased as all hell. My editor will probably throw it in the trash bucket."

I wondered how Harry was feeling, what he was doing, how he was salving his conscience. I knew damn well that he had been aware of the trouble I was heading for. That night in Rome he hadn't really tried very hard to hide it from me. He was paying me handsomely for nearly getting my throat cut, but I was still alive and in one piece and I was beginning to worry about my responsibility to him; I knew I couldn't really write the story in the way he expected me to. And then I remembered something he once said to me:

"Just remember," he had said, "that the top of the fence is not the only place that gives you a good view." We were talking about journalistic objectivity, and he had said, "You can wallow in the mud at the foot of the fence too, because that's where the truth usually lies. Provided, of course, someone else is wallowing just as searchingly on the other side..."

I wondered if one of Harry's boys was across the border there now, writing *his* story—or living it as I had lived it.

We got back to the interrogation center without incident, and the Army had taken over in force. There were Jeeps and half-tracks and armored cars by the dozen, and as the captain had said, a group of ten or fifteen workmen were already clambering over the ruins of the mess hall, setting new wooden beams into position, pouring concrete, laying down power lines. An Israeli flag was flying, at half-mast, over a long line of white-draped coffins that had been laid out on the sand, and as we walked past them I tried to pull Karen away; but she stopped and looked at them for a while, and all she said was, very quietly:

"I'm glad we were here, Michael. I'm glad."

A young girl in uniform came over to us and saluted smartly and waited, looking at Karen and saying nothing. She was a pretty little thing, saucy rather than beautiful, with a quick, easy manner. When Karen turned to her, she said:

"I was told to take care of you, Miss d'Arno. If there's anything you want, anything at all... Whatever I can do..."

Karen nodded and went off with her and left me standing there alone and wondering, and then the captain approached and introduced me to a short, stocky man with a bald head, who wore civilian clothes but who seemed to carry quite a lot of influence. His name was Israel Breck, and he didn't tell me what his position was, so I didn't bother to ask. He was treated with a great deal of respect by everyone, so I did the same thing.

I said, "I'd be glad to know, sir, what plans you have for Miss d'Arno and myself?"

He must have been seventy years old, and his skin was heavily wrinkled and sunburned, but he looked fit and as hard as nails. In spite of his shorts and open-necked shirt, his attitude was one of solidified authority. He spoke in short, jerky words, biting off the ends of them as though there wasn't time to complete them. His eyes were sharp, alert, very controlled, and he sounded a little impatient. But he was courteous enough. He said:

"We will send you both back to Rome, Mr. Benasque, at once, if that is satisfactory to you?"

"Yes, of course. Are you going to ask me to hold my tongue too?"

There was just the trace of a smile on his face. "No, I am not. I have been informed that it would be a waste of time, and I prefer to put every moment I have to some useful purpose. I also understand that whatever you chose to write about what you have seen might not be— too prejudicial to us?"

"I plan to be as objective as possible."

"I see."

"You don't think it's a secret, do you, what your people are doing? We may have forgotten about Eichmann, but anyone who reads the papers knows your boys are still at it, all over the world."

He said dryly, "Someone has to search out the war criminals, and we happen to be rather more proficient at it than most others are. And if our methods do not fit into the accepted pattern of international morality, then that is something which we will deplore, but about which we will do nothing."

"In other words, the hell with everybody."

"Er—I would not have put it quite like that, but perhaps that puts our philosophy in a nutshell." He reached into his hip pocket and brought out a folded newspaper. He said, "There's something here you might like to see."

It was the front page of a Swiss newspaper, and there in the middle was the photograph Karen had taken and which I had sent to Harry. Underneath it was the caption, in German: "This surprising photograph of Dr. Walter Martin, the eminent German missile expert, was taken by our special correspondent in Rome, Michael Benasque, whose detailed report on its significance is eagerly awaited."

Struggling a little with the *Schwyzer-Deutsch*, I read the beginnings of the story:

> We are informed that three attempts have already been made on the life of Dr. Martin, whose work in General Nasser's missile factories has aroused a great deal of resentment, and has led to the strongest representations to the West German Government. Bonn's official position is that constitutionally it has no control over the free choice of its citizens to work where they please. But that position is already weakening...

I handed it back to Mr. Breck, and he smiled and said:

"Good journalistic sense would dictate, surely, that a picture like that ought to await a more detailed explanation, wouldn't you say?"

"Uh-huh. Normally, it would."

"I see." He looked as though he were thoroughly enjoying some sort of joke at his own expense. He said, "It did occur to me that whoever released that photograph was making quite sure that your assignment was publicly known. A sort of—insurance, shall we say?"

"My boss is a very careful man. And thank God for that. If it hadn't been published, would you still have sent me back so easily?"

"No comment."

I shrugged, and he said quickly, "No, perhaps that isn't fair, under the circumstances. I will say this: there was a time when your personal position, through no fault of ours, was—a little tenuous. There was a time when we were very worried about you. But that time, I am happy to say, is now past." He spread his hands wide and said, "It is very easy to be glib and say that you are either for us or against us, but I know that this is never quite true. It is possible that had we asked you yesterday which side you were on, you would have said truthfully that you were on neither. And though I will not ask you that question now, I will take your attitude as implying an answer which, under the circumstances, will have to satisfy us."

Well, that was neatly put.

I said, "What about Martin, now?"

He hesitated, and I thought he was going to tell me to mind my own business; but he didn't. He said mildly, "You're a very stubborn man, Mr. Benasque. Frankly, I do not know. Because of your activities and those of your editor, we are no longer able to hide the fact that our concern for the niceties of international relationships has not been, in this case, immaculate. But, on the other hand, there are certain ministers both in Rome and in Bonn who have knowingly encouraged Dr. Martin and his fellow scientists in what can only be regarded as an extended warlike act. I do not believe the outcry against us will be more than we can bear."

"That's very interesting, sir. But it's not a very definitive answer, is it?"

"No? Then I can only say instead: no comment." He shot his hand out and said, "I am very glad to have met you. Perhaps, one day, we will meet again. And now, if you will excuse me—"

He turned and began to move away, but then he turned back and said slowly, "We do not always know, Mr. Benasque, how other people see us. If we must sometimes be—zealous in what we do, all we ask is that they understand why. Good day, sir."

There is only one thing more to tell, really. I did not see Karen for a very long time, and I was beginning to worry about her. I found the doctor and spoke to him, and he told me there was nothing to worry about.

He said pedantically, "Shock, the things it can do are never fully understood. Nor is it a sudden condition; sometimes it takes a little time to come, and a little time to go. But she's all right, there's no cause for you to worry. She's with some of the women, some of the Army girls, and she'll be all right."

They had fitted me out with some clothes and I had cleaned

myself up, and when the small plane came in to land, Karen came out of the mess by herself and waved to me, and I went over to talk to her.

She was wearing a khaki drill skirt and blouse, and neat white ankle socks and flat-heeled shoes; she looked like no one I had ever known. But she was smiling, and she put an arm around me and said:

"The doctor told me you were worried about me, darling. There's nothing to worry about."

I said, "You look a little different in that rig. How do you feel?"

"Fine."

"Sure?"

"Sure, my darling. Just fine."

There was still something I could not get to; the eyes were just the same as ever, but there was a mystery in them, as though there were something at the back of her mind, something she was keeping even from me. But I did not press her; it was just a matter of time.

We were the only passengers on the plane, and it was dark when we landed in Rome.

A car was waiting to meet us, and the driver took us, without instructions from us, straight to the apartment in Trastevere, and there was Simona, unsurprised to see us (except that she raised her eyebrows at Karen's clothes), and ready, as always, to pour the drinks and make the coffee. We told her briefly what had happened, and I said wearily:

"I'll tell you all about it in the morning. If I don't get some sleep—"

Simona, understanding as always, merely nodded. She turned down the bedclothes, and then came to the bathroom, where I was getting out some bandages, and she watched me for a while as I started to fix my wrists, and then said:

"Let me do that."

She wrapped them carefully around my wrists, and asked no questions, and looked at me and half smiled, and I said again:

"In the morning, Simona. I can hardly keep my eyes open."

She reached up and kissed me quickly on the cheek and said, "Get a good night's sleep, both of you; you'll both feel better for it."

Karen and I went to bed, and she loved me as she had never loved me before, and I woke once in the night to find her awake and staring at the ceiling, the moonlight that came in through the windows falling across her naked body and lending it an ethereal glory. I fell asleep again, and when I next woke it was already nearly midday and she was not beside me anymore. I sat up with a start, vaguely and unaccountably troubled.

I put on a dressing gown and wandered around the empty apartment, wondering where the girls were, and then they came in together, with fresh rolls from the bakery around the corner, and we sat down to breakfast.

Karen was bright and cheerful and smiling, and Simona was quiet and subdued and—a little fearful. I waited a long time for them to tell me what it was all about, and at last I realized that Karen was waiting for help. There was something she had to say which she could not put into words, not without my help.

When I passed her a cigarette I saw that her hand was trembling slightly, and when Simona looked at me there was an unaccustomed sadness on her face, as though under the placid surface of her innocence there were disturbing thoughts. I guessed the girls had spent the morning talking quietly, and I waited.

After a while, I said gently, "What is it, Karen?"

She smiled quickly. "What's what?"

"You never could hide anything from me, you know that."

The smile went and came and went, and she stubbed out her cigarette and took another, and looked at Simona for help, and I thought, *Well, that's a new thing, if she wants help from Simona.*

I said, "There's only one way to say it, darling. Just—say it and—whatever it is you have to tell me."

She put out the cigarette as soon as she had lit it and said, groping for the words, "The corporal—what was his name, Bronislawski—"

I waited.

She said, hesitantly, "I can't—forget him."

"I know. But it's not that, is it? There's something else."

I had never seen Karen so disturbed, not even in the heavy hours we had just come through. She said, "It's—it's going to hurt you, Michael." She looked at Simona again, desperately, and Simona stood up and took a deep breath and said:

"She's leaving us, Michael."

I said, "What?"

Simona took away the coffee cups and went with them to the kitchen, and Karen said to her, pleading:

"Come here, Simona, please, I need you."

Simona came back and sat down again, and said quietly:

"She's going away, Michael, and there's nothing I can do to stop her. I don't think you can either."

"But—going where, for God's sake?"

Karen said, "To Israel."

"But—what on earth for?"

She sighed. Now the damage was done and it was a lot easier. She put a hand on mine and said:

"How could I tell you before? Even now it's—it's almost impossible. I'm going back to one of their colonies, in the Negev."

"But why, Karen, for God's sake why?"

"It's something—I just have to do."

"The corporal?"

"Partly. I can't forget him. I don't want to forget him. And the women I spoke to, they told me—I'll be welcome there, Michael. They need women, they need anyone who will go there and—and help them."

"And so you're breaking this up, just like that."

"Yes. I'm breaking it up. I'm sorry, Michael. If you only knew how sorry—"

She was calm and quiet and no longer afraid. I wished she would cry, because then I would know that sooner or later she would change her mind. But this was more than just an emotional fling; it was something deep inside her, something so important that nothing in the world would prevent its fulfillment. I felt as though my world had suddenly stopped moving. Searching for comfort, I could find only one thing; the shock had gone from her and she was her competent, strong-willed self again, and that was at least something...

I looked at Simona. "And you? What about you, Simona?"

She shrugged. "It's time I stood on my own two feet, Michael."

I went over to the window and looked out across the rooftops, listening to the midday noises; soon everything would be still and empty down there too, as the siesta time approached. Karen came and stood beside me and put her arm around me and said:

"Will you be able to forgive me, Michael?"

"Of course. If it's what you want—"

She said fiercely, "It's what I must do."

"A time like this—it always comes, to all lovers, doesn't it?"

"I suppose so."

"But it doesn't make it any easier. When will you leave?"

"This afternoon. I bought my ticket this morning—"

Dismayed, I said, "This afternoon! It seems so—so soon—"

"I know."

I could feel the gentle pressure of her body against me. It was hard to let go.

Simona stayed home when I went with her over to the airport, and we kissed and said good-bye, and when the plane took off the world was suddenly empty and useless and no longer valid.

I went in the cab back to the center of town and sat around in a pavement bar, drinking more than I should have done, and then I walked from there over the bridge to the Isola Tiberina, where in the days of the Empire the prisoners were left to die of starvation, and I wandered for a while around the ruins of the old palace of the Tarquins; and then when it was night I walked along the Lungotevere to the tiny piazza where Tasso's oak was still sprouting to show that life was still going on.

I waited there a long time, trying to bring back the good days by finding the things we had known together. The bricks, the stones, the fountains, the trees, they were all still there; but the good days I could not find.

I went slowly up to the apartment, and there Simona had the table laid for dinner, and there was a frosted bottle of wine on the white cloth, and there was a rich, homely smell coming from the kitchen.

We ate together in silence, and when Simona went to pour the brandy, I said:

"Not for me, Simona."

She came and sat down again and poured some more coffee from the machine. She said:

"What will you do, Michael?"

I said, "I have some writing to do, a lot of writing."

"Here? In the apartment?"

"No, not in the apartment."

The delicate tinkle of the eggshell coffee cups was the only sound to break the silence. Simona brushed a crumb from the tablecloth and looked at her long, pearl-polished fingernails. She said at last:

"In Florence? The most beautiful city in the world, Michael?"

"All right."

"We could get a car and drive up there, if you like."

I looked at her to see what she was thinking. But she was learning, like her sister, to veil her eyes.

I said, "First thing in the morning, I'll go out and get a car. If we leave about noon, we'll be there in good time for dinner."

She nodded, saying nothing, and started to clear away the dishes. I watched her slim body through the open door as she worked in the kitchen for a while, and then I dragged chair out onto the veranda and sat down to take the cool evening air.

Soon the kitchen noises stopped, and Simona came out silently and stood beside me, and then she leaned on the iron railing and lit a cigarette and looked out over the piazza, saying nothing, just staring out into the darkness, watching the moon shadows on the tiled roofs and castellated towers and creeper-covered walls.

The doleful bell in the church began to chime.

Nobody spoke. The sounds below us were all that was left in the world; and soon, the dark of the Roman night descended on the ancient, indestructible city.

THE END

ABOUT THE AUTHOR

Alan Lyle-Smythe was born in Surrey, England. Prior to World War II, he served with the Palestine Police from 1936 to 1939 and learned the Arabic language. He was awarded an MBE in June 1938. He married Aliza Sverdova in 1939, then studied acting from 1939 to 1941.

In January 1940, Lyle-Smythe was commissioned in the Royal Army Service Corps. Due to his linguistic skills, he transferred to the Intelligence Corps and served in the Western Desert, in which he used the surname "Caillou" (the French word for 'pebble') as an alias.

He was captured in North Africa, imprisoned and threatened with execution in Italy, then escaped to join the British forces at Salerno. He was then posted to serve with the partisans in Yugoslavia. He wrote about his experiences in the book *The World is Six Feet Square* (1954). He was promoted to captain and awarded the Military Cross in 1944.

Following the war, he returned to the Palestine Police from 1946 to 1947, then served as a Police Commissioner in British-occupied Italian Somaliland from 1947 to 1952, where he was recommissioned a captain.

After work as a District Officer in Somalia and professional hunter, Lyle-Smythe travelled to Canada, where he worked as a hunter and then became an actor on Canadian television.

He wrote his first novel, *Rogue's Gambit*, in 1955, first using the name Caillou, one of his aliases from the war. Moving from Vancouver to Hollywood, he made an appearance as a contestant on the January 23 1958 edition of *You Bet Your Life*.

He appeared as an actor and/or worked as a screenwriter in such shows as *Daktari*, *The Man From U.N.C.L.E.* (including the screenwriting for "*The Bow-Wow Affair*" from 1965), *Thriller*, *Daniel Boone*, *Quark*, *Centennial*, and *How the West Was Won*. In 1966-67, he had a recurring role (as Jason Flood) in NBC's "*Tarzan*" TV series starring Ron Ely. Caillou appeared in such television movies as *Sole Survivor* (1970), *The Hound of the Baskervilles* (1972, as Inspector Lestrade), and *Goliath Awaits* (1981). His cinema film credits included roles in *Five Weeks in a Balloon* (1962), *Clarence, the Cross-Eyed Lion* (1965), *The Rare Breed* (1966), *The Devil's Brigade* (1968), *Hellfighters* (1968), *Everything You Always Wanted to Know About Sex* (*But Were Afraid to Ask)* (1972), *Herbie Goes to Monte Carlo* (1977), *Beyond Evil* (1980), *The Sword and the Sorcerer* (1982) and *The Ice Pirates* (1984).

Caillou wrote 52 paperback thrillers under his own name and the nom de plume of Alex Webb, with such heroes as Cabot Cain, Colonel Matthew Tobin, Mike Benasque, Ian Quayle and Josh Dekker, as well as writing many magazine stories.

Several of Caillou's novels were made into films, such as *Rampage* with Robert Mitchum in 1963, based on his big game hunting knowledge; *Assault on Agathon*, for which Caillou did the screenplay as well; and *The Cheetahs*, filmed in 1989.

He was married to Aliza Sverdova from 1939 until his death. Their daughter Nadia Caillou was the screenwriter for the film *Skeleton Coast*.

Alan Caillou died in Sedona, Arizona in 2006.

LOOKING FOR ACTION AND ADVENTURE
AUTHOR ALAN CAILLOU
NOVELS DELIVER!

WWW.CALIBERCOMICS.COM

AVAILABLE IN PAPERBACK OR EBOOK

FROM FANTASY AND SCIENCE FICTION AUTHOR ROLAND J. GREEN

TWO EPIC SERIES

FROM CALIBER BOOKS IN PAPERBACK AND EBOOK

DON'T MISS ANY OF NEIL HUNTER'S NOVELS FROM CALIBER BOOKS

Reporter Les Mason is completing an expose on the Long Point Nuclear Plant. But before he can finish he dies an agonizing death. The doctors are baffled—and there are similar cases to follow...Chris Lane, his girlfriend, and organizer of the Long Point Protestors, discovers Mason's notes, and decides to find out for herself what the plant has to hide.

2 BOOK SERIES

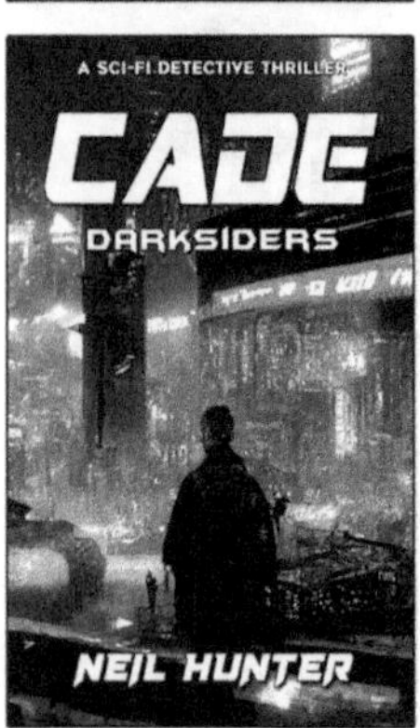

In middle of the 21st century America – over-populated decaying cities are ruled by hi-tech gangs pushing every vice and wastelands are controlled by bands of mutants. Ordinary citizens are oppressed and face a hopeless future. But Marshal T.J. Cade is a new breed of law enforcer. Teamed with his cyborg partner, Janek, Cade takes on these criminals and works in the gray areas of the law to get the job done.

3 BOOK SERIES

The village of Shepthorne England wasn't being gripped, but strangled by a winter's blanket of heavy snow and Arctic temperatures. The trouble began innocently enough with a massive pile-up of autos on frozen roads leading to and from the village. Then, from the sky, a military transport plane with its top secret cargo of devastation crashed down towards the center of the village. Hell was just beginning to touch Shepthorne and its unsuspecting citizens...

FROM CALIBER BOOKS

www.calibercomics.com

CALIBER COMICS GOES TO THE EDGE!
Science Fiction and Horror themed graphic novels

DEADWORLD
ISBN: 9781942351245

RENFIELD
ISBN: 9781942351825

NOSFERATU
ISBN: 9781942351931

**LOVECRAFT:
THE EARLY STORIES**
ISBN: 9781942351634

**THE WAR OF THE WORLDS:
INFESTATION**
ISBN: 9781942351962

TIME GRUNTS
ISBN: 9781635299472

DRACULA
ISBN: 9780996030649

**DRACULA:
THE SUICIDE CLUB**
ISBN: 9781635299571

**JACK THE RIPPER
ILLUSTRATED**
ISBN: 9781942351917

THE SEARCHERS
ISBN: 9781942351979

A.A.I. WARS
ISBN: 9781635299168

**AUTUMN: TERROR IN THE
LONDON UNDERGROUND**
ISBN: 9781544624020

www.calibercomics.com

www.ingramcontent.com/pod-product-compliance
Lightning Source LLC
Chambersburg PA
CBHW070535100726
47907CB00004B/1130